In This Block There Lives A Slag . . .

and other Yorkshire Fables

Bill Broady

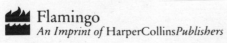

Flamingo
An Imprint of HarperCollins*Publishers*

Flamingo
An imprint of HarperCollins*Publishers*
77–85 Fulham Palace Road,
Hammersmith, London w6 8jb

Flamingo is a registered trade mark
of HarperCollins*Publishers* Ltd

The HarperCollins website address is:
www.fireandwater.com

Published by Flamingo 2001
1 3 5 7 9 8 6 4 2

Grateful acknowledgement is made to the following publications in
which these stories first appeared: *The Devil*: 'Wrestling Jacob'; *The
London Magazine*: 'My Hard Friend'; *Southfields*: 'Songs that Won the
War', 'Coddock' and 'The Kingfishers ... The Distances'; *Stand*:
'Mr Personality in the Fields of Poses'.

A catalogue record for this book
is available from the British Library

ISBN 0 00 225947 8

Set in Monotype Centaur by
Rowland Phototypesetting Ltd, Bury St Edmunds, Suffolk

Printed and bound in Great Britain by Clays Ltd, St Ives plc

Contents

Wrestling Jacob

'. . . For we wrestle not against flesh and blood,' St Paul wrote, 'but against principalities, against powers, against the rulers of the darkness of this world, against spiritual wickedness in high places.' I don't know whether the Ephesians paid any attention to such exhortations but the only thing I ever wrestled with was Jacob.

I remember the pains and pleasures of our strivings . . . How the ground seemed to buck like a ship's deck beneath my planted feet, while a pressure built in my chest as if a second, internal adversary was trying to force his way out through my sternum . . . How I tried to stifle my gasps for fear of having to acknowledge some repressed sexual imperative . . . How my head reeled from my opponent's mephitic breath, with his flaring nostrils suggesting that he found mine equally repulsive . . . I remember the soft rustling and sudden stench as he chose, mid-combat, to void his bladder and bowels, and the dead clack of horn against bone, as if there was no mediation of flesh or fleece . . .

To wrestle spiritual wickedness, principalities and powers would, I imagine, seem a breeze after freestyle grappling with a Swaledale ram.

✳   ✳   ✳

When I first met Jacob he was about nine months old – a wether hogg, running with the yard-dogs. A wall-eyed liver-and-white collie, a fulminating black hellhound and a grey-masked sheep: they looked so frightening that you knew they just had to be safe. He'd copy their leaps and bounds, trampolining on his front legs with an Elvis-style snarl, simulating a tail-wag by withershins rotation of his white stub and even managing a feeble bark – like my college tutor clearing his throat before demolishing my drug-addled thesis on 'Beauty and The Sublime'.

His mother had died nameless in a snowdrift: his sister, Jessica, nannygoat-fostered, had long since slipped meekly back into the flock. It had been unusual to house-rear and bottle-feed a ram – 'But there was always something special about him,' said the farmer's wife, vigorously scratching Jacob – his eyes shuttering in ecstasy – behind the ears. 'Do you believe in reincarnation?' she asked. 'He sometimes reminds me of my granddad.' She struck me as unusually sentimental for a farmer's wife. Her tabby cats had evidently taught Jacob to bury his own shit and to spittle his inner forelegs to wipe-wash his face. He could climb, too – regularly breaking his kennel chain and scrambling back through the pantry window. 'He misses the telly,' she told me, 'But you can't house-train a sheep. Mind you, we can't even house-train the kids.' With a pitted slab of toad-grey tongue Jacob licked her hand. 'He's unusually loving,' she said, giving me a sharp, sideways look. 'Especially for a male.'

On those late summer evenings I'd leave work sick with shame – as if this latest Exclusive Estate was something we'd half-demolished, rather than half-built – and I'd drive like the devil up the valley towards the fells. How I hated those silent, roofless houses, like emptied cereal packets, each supposedly 'individuated by their unique window shapes and dispositions' – insane shufflings of portholes, dormers and bays. I didn't like to think of the lives people were going to have in them: I lived – unindividuated – in one myself. Exclusive, like Auschwitz: I was having those silly concentration camp dreams again. Only when I'd climbed to the heather line could I breathe properly: my mind stopped racing and I accepted that my dad was dead and Pam would never come back, that my novel was rubbish and that all my aches and ailments were psychosomatic and all my railings against the world mere self-pity.

Beyond the farm, up the beckside, along the crinkled ridges then, in the gloom, back down the steepest of the disused smelters' tracks: I never tired of this habitual walk. The light, the wind, the shadows were always different: angles and distances seemed to change – landmarks shifted position so that one day I'd be unable to locate a familiar cup-marked rock but the next would go straight to it. The dogs soon stopped barking and ignored me but Jacob always greeted me with obvious delight. He'd launch himself, legs extending sideways to control and accelerate his progress down the shifting scree, like double sculls over water . . . then my hand would cup his chilly muzzle – he'd picked up purring from the cats but was able to simultaneously sound up to four discrete trills and rattles. I'd given up on even the possibility of affection from any source, so this enthusiasm meant a lot to me. I'd long suspected that while we only ever see in other people that which we desire or fear, animals can calmly scan and judge – from aura to essence – the whole of us.

That winter they moved Jacob to the big field, building him a stone-flagged log shelter, wired and tarpaulined to keep out the rain: I wondered if there was a television in there. He'd sit on his threshold, as if fronting the essentials of life, like Thoreau at Walden. His co-tenants – three doomed, embittered geese – periodically assaulted him: he'd just stand still, unblinking, lost in the transcendental, while they pecked themselves out, to finally collapse, exhausted and choking, their beaks wadded with fluff. Sometimes he'd jump the wall and, unhefted, move about the hirsels, wrecking the grazing systems, even reaching the Herdwicks beyond the hause. Mandibles clicking like a power loom, he passed over the grass like a blight, leaving not so much as a green stain. No one seemed to mind, although the other sheep avoided him – more out of respect than aversion, slipping away if he dowsed towards them. The farmer and his wife bore oblations: Waldorf salad seemed to be Jacob's staple diet. Where would it end? Suppose they were to anthropomorphize their entire stock?

Jacob would roll his eyes sarcastically if I joined the weekend procession of red and yellow hooded figures trudging into the mist but then follow to share my sandwiches and crop around me when I stopped to read. Sometimes the farmer joined us: once he told me that the only book he remembered reading was *Papillon*. He said it was wonderful but that he'd only got seventy pages in: what with the weather, the seasons, the animals and their births and deaths, his world must have seemed already fully-stocked with wonders. Jacob would always walk me back to the car park, often even trotting a few hundred yards down the lane in pursuit . . . In the driving mirror I'd see him gradually slow, stop, then turn away in apparent desolation.

The wrestling began one afternoon as we sat by the side of the summit tarn. I was lost in the epicene, exquisite world of Firbank's *Vainglory*, absently patting Jacob whenever he nudged my arm. At last, with a hurt and derisory snort, he moved away. Then there was a pause — 'just long enough,' as Firbank puts it, 'for an angel to pass, flying slowly.' What happened next I had to piece together later: at the time it felt as if I'd been struck by lightning. He must have retreated for a considerable distance, like a fast bowler pacing out his run-up, then turned and charged into my back, tumbling me, legs still crossed, for what seemed a full half-dozen revolutions. As I struggled to my feet he was dancing around like a boxer, head jerking back with an evil, equine grin of triumph. I grabbed his horns like bicycle handlebars and twisted as if I was trying to unscrew his head. Then he reared up on his back legs and pushed — I pushed back. Then he pulled and I pulled and we fell on to all fours, then rose up again. And so we proceeded, in a stately to-and-fro waltz, to circle the water, until the ridiculousness, the sheer delight of it hit me and I collapsed, helpless with laughter. Jacob was trying to laugh too but a series of explosive sneezes was the best he could do. My copy of *Vainglory* had been trampled, well-pulped in the process: I wondered how aesthetic Ronald would have got on against Jacob — OK, probably, better than the Hemingways and Mailers.

The next morning my face and neck were scarlet-rashed from friction with that coarse fleece, more kemp than wool. In the following months my body was mapped with bruises, their colours shifting through the spectrum, as if I was turning into a chameleon. My shins were the worst: Jacob's pipe cleaner legs kicked like steel-capped Docs. These welts didn't hurt – they seemed, strangely, to have taken my previous pains away. Every Sunday morning we'd wrestle. Sometimes he'd stop fighting and suddenly become dead weight, sheer mass, toppling on to me like an oak wardrobe . . . At others he'd abruptly break my hold, as if my fingers had been cobwebs, then amble off, cropping . . . But usually I'd force him down and press one horn to the ground for a three-count. I was under no illusions, though: he was letting me win – he could have decked me any time he liked. Once, as we were locked in close combat, I lost my balance and rolled him over in an inadvertent Kamikaze Krash, stunning him. I saw something like respect in his glazed, refocusing eyes before he laid me low with a butt to the breadbasket. He'd imparted an extra twist to his horns that left my spleen twanging – for the next two days I was pissing blood. I realized that all these animals bred to slaughter for our covering and food could turn and crush us in an instant. The terrible goose-strikes absorbed by Jacob's coat would have broken my arm or leg: a well-organized herd of Friesians could devastate a town – I liked to imagine them, rampaging through the Vista View Estate.

Whenever Jacob rushed towards me – like a fist-shaped, fast-blown cloud – I felt a residual flicker of fear. Suppose this was a different sheep, an evil cousin on a family visit? Or suppose he'd forgotten me? When I dive into water I always wonder if I'll still be able to swim and when I get into my car I fear that I won't remember how to drive – or, rather, I fear that the water or the machinery will have forgotten that I'm supposed to be – however notionally – in charge. I didn't drown, I didn't crash and Jacob kept letting me win. Sometimes the farmer and his wife would watch – he'd offer tips as an ex-Cumberland wrestler, she'd suggest that we do a novelty act at Grasmere Sports – or passing tourists took photographs, leaving lines of small denomination coins on top of the field gate; but mostly we fought unobserved, under the shadows of the domed, silent mountains, like decrepit titans who'd long ago fallen asleep or died.

Our wrestling reminded me of something I'd read or heard about – maybe archetypal, out of anima mundi? – but I could find no sources in the legends of Greece or Rome, *The Golden Bough* or Joseph Campbell. Maybe I was a new god, making my own mythology from scratch? There was only the British Museum's beautiful sandstone relief of Khnum of Elephantine, the ram-headed god who created first the sun, then the pantheon of other divinities, then at last, out of Nilotic silt, formed Man on a potter's wheel. Perhaps the dust in me was raging at its creator, all my constituent atoms striving to return to their previous carefree existence as motes? Or were they embracing him in thanks, celebrating by mock contention his gift of life? Khnum: Lord Of The Two Lands, Weaver Of Light, Governor Of The House Of Sweet Life, Guide And Director Of All Men – I tried these titles out on Jacob but he either didn't or pretended not to recognize them.

Not only had I entered a second, blissful childhood – with a best friend who was always ready to play out – but the next three years were also my golden time of bewildering sexual success and potency. Although Jacob was gelded, maybe I'd picked up some residual pheromones in our rollings? Younger girls wanted to learn about life, while older women wanted help to forget what they already knew. To teach or divert, to reveal or conceal, to disturb or console? — luckily, these two contrary roles involved my saying and doing the same things, in roughly the same order. For that second, crucial assignation I'd always suggest a nice country stroll: taking them to meet Jacob was like a rite of passage. I'd put on my paint-stained jeans, well-holed sweater and ancient Barbour jacket, crusted with lanolin and suint, impacted with boluses of mud. One girl asked me if we were going potholing, another — sniffing — if I was a fan of Charles Bukowski.

They never seemed to wonder why I'd begin shouting when we got out of the car. Jacob, on hearing my voice, would run towards us. We could feel the earth shake, hear his hooves thudding like tymps: the air seemed to shimmer, and there was a malevolent hissing sound like expelling steam — I suspected that he'd been taking lessons from the stud bulls in the next valley. Eyes bugging, swollen to twice his normal size — awful personification of rapacious nature and patriarchal lust — he'd arrow towards his victim, the maiden sacrifice . . . but then, with a great wordless cry, I'd throw myself upon him and we'd grapple. Curiously, none of my companions ever screamed after his initial appearance, never ran for safety or assistance, never even tried to help me with so much as a prod of a dainty foot. They'd just drape themselves, Andromeda-style, over the badger-shaped boulder to watch the show. Maybe mine was a common ploy and they were thinking oh no, here comes that old tame sheep routine again? Whatever, they obviously soon realized that the monster was harmless . . . When I finally turned towards them — with the dragon slain, or at least pin-falled — I'd always see laughter transfiguring their features and glimpse for an instant, behind all their masks, the same woman's face.

No one I recognized . . . it certainly wasn't Pam or Mum. Then she'd chuck the parchment-like folds under Jacob's chin as he, nuzzling, gave out his full polyphonal hum. Then she'd kiss me – long and deep – and I'd tell her my secret lover's name: nothing occult or sentimental, just what was on my birth certificate, but unshortened, undiminished.

Jacob's particular favourite was Marianne: hair sun-bleached to white, I think he took her for some goddess or perhaps just another sheep. He let her ride him round the field: I wanted so much to, there and then, couple with her, like the incestuous Phrixus and Helle on the back of their magic golden ram . . . There was Jan the artist who put in her contact lenses to study him: she said that his fleece reminded her of some Manzoni achromes in the Herning Kunstmuseum. She clapped her hands with joy to see nature so sedulously imitating art: that night, the same transformative enthusiasm was able to perceive my scanty, rufous pubic hair as Titianesque . . . And there was Janine, who took the best photo of Jacob – just-sheared to designer stubble, in my homburg and shades: she said he looked like Bruce Willis and that she fancied him more than me . . . The only one who wouldn't touch him was Helen, who walked the winter mountains bare-midriffed, with lacy halter-top, leopard-print stretch leggings and open-toed silver sandals: but who still beat me to the summit . . . Jane fed him mangetout peas, posing like Louise De Kerouaille – décolleté, her raw nipples burning white-hot . . . Caro spent hours plaiting his wool into dreadlocks and epigonic hippie Sara decked him in fantastical garlands, like Bottom . . . 'It's like in Genesis,' said Bernie, lapsed Catholic and mild masochist. 'If you're wrestling with Jacob then you must be an angel.' Which was the exact opposite of what she was calling me a mere seventeen days later.

Within a month they all lost their various illusions: no longer wanting to explore or hide, seek or find, make love or fuck – at least not with me – they went their separate ways. They tired of me at about the same moment that I tired of them, but the farewell messages left on my answerphone or scrawled in Alma-Tadema greetings cards were oddly bitter. In what way had I been using them? – I'd never once mentioned the future or, indeed, the past ... Whenever I turned up alone Jacob didn't want to wrestle. He'd shake his head, wobbling his overshot jaw: 'I can get you women OK,' that look said, 'But you just can't keep them'. I told him how I only wanted to keep that first smile, first kiss, first night ... how I wanted someone I'd never get used to, that intimacy would render yet more and more unfathomable and who would, finally, make me a stranger – ever stranger – to myself. Jacob just sighed and returned to his cropping. He didn't get it, but then in certain matters he was still very much a sheep.

That final winter was the best time of all. Everything thrilled me: I'd sleep three hours a night but arise full of energy. I had life taped: I felt as if, after thirty-four years, I'd at last got up the courage to be young. Being on the fells was like an acid trip: I was really *seeing* things – not just the sweeps of peak and scarp but also every insect, every tiny blade of grass and flower beneath my feet ... all the details, but God, not The Devil, seemed to be in them. Everything kept going pointilliste, as if my gaze was penetrating through to that dust from which Khnum had created the world. I wondered if I'd somehow learnt this from Jacob: was it a mystical vision or just a sheep's-eye view? I was worried about him: some days he wouldn't come out at all – from the shadows of his cabin I could sense a baleful stare. Perhaps while I'd contracted his blitheness he'd been taking on my fears and guilts?

I no longer endured work but actively enjoyed it. The houses seemed to vanish into their components – a whirl of bricks and mortar, of glass, scaffolding and rances gleaming in the January sun. Vista View and the Parthenon were both ultimately just piles of stones. As Sally the macrobioticist told me: 'Everything is edible if you chop it up small enough.' My relationships were getting shorter and shorter, as if my lovers were also perfectly content with intensity and evanescence: although I was slightly perturbed when the two I liked best both sat down the instant they got home – after the first, unforgettable night – to write that they never wanted to see me again. Both ended with the same phrase: 'I'm sorry I can't share your feelings'. I didn't understand what this meant: maybe there were husbands or other lovers in the picture? I hoped that I hadn't somehow made them afraid of me.

One Sunday the traffic was heavier than usual. We crawled up the valley: Easter. A charity fun run was assembling. Every car was full of nuns and spacemen, ballerinas and demons. The sheep fled in panic from pantomime cows and horses. My companion was annoying me. She said her name was Miki – 'Short for what?' I asked – 'Short for nothing,' she replied. Thirteen years younger than me – a third-year music student at York – she didn't seem to realize that *I* was supposed to be telling *her* things. I'd never heard of her favourite writer – Broch – or her favourite composer – Barraqué. She talked about performing the latter's setting of the former's *Death Of Virgil*, in which, apparently, the dying Nolan, embittered, contemplates destroying 'The Aeneid'. I suspected a trap: perhaps she'd made them both up so that I'd either feel ignorant or – if I did claim some distant familiarity – run the risk of revealing myself to be a fake? She started singing: 'Il sera possible de traverser la porte corne de la terreur pour atteindre a l'existence' . . . To enter being through the horned gates of terror: I thought of the waiting Jacob's baroque crown and smiled . . .

As we passed the farm he still hadn't appeared: I could only see, at the bottom of the field, a motionless human figure. It appeared to be contemplating, in the lee of the wall, a last remaining snowdrift. The summoning shout died in my throat: by the time its echoes had finished rolling round the cliffs I had almost reached him. The farmer, looking up, scissored his dangling arms across his thighs, like a cricket umpire signalling dead ball. He'd taken off his cap, holding it folded and crushed in his fist: his scarlet scalp was dappled with greenish patches of hair, like moss. Two long creases had appeared in his face, conduiting the tears past his pillar box mouth to drop off his chin and on to the still mound of Jacob, lying collapsed on his stomach. The legs seemed to have disappeared, as if the dust had already begun to consume the god that had moulded it. I knelt and touched him: he was stiff, immovably heavy – harder and colder than the Badger Stone, as if he'd never been alive. A chill wind had begun stripping his fleece like a dandelion clock. I looked up and met Miki's eyes – uncomprehending, hard, young . . . as she watched two middle-aged men sobbing inexplicably over a pile of dirty wool. And I knew that now Jacob – metasheep, laughing wrestler,

Lord Of The House Of Sweet Life – was gone, no one – not for a few days or hours, not even for a second – was ever going to love me again.

In This Block There Lives A Slag . . .

In those days I could really sleep. I'd never have woken up at all if it hadn't been for the clocks. It was bad sleep though – I never remembered my dreams but I knew that they must have been nightmares. I had these three clocks set at thirty second intervals: first the bedside radio alarm that I'd tuned to a frequency of ghostly static, then, on the floor, the second, hooting like a robot owl, and finally, on the window ledge behind the curtain, the biggest – a great copper thing bearing a face with long-lashed eyes and a lipsticked mouth that smiled while, with twin hammers, it tried to beat its own brains out. I had to get over to it before, in detonating, it destroyed the world.

That morning, as usual, I wrenched the curtain off the end of the rail and down on top of me. For weeks I'd been chanting 'baulk screws, baulk screws' under my breath like a mantra but I never remembered to buy them. I even wrote the words on my hand but either they rubbed off or I forgot to look. The sunlight was dazzling me, reflecting off a fourth-floor window of the adjacent block: it looked as if The Yellow Man was hiding out in a Bradford Council flat. I was out of bread and milk so I breakfasted on a leftover half samosa and the dregs of six cans of Skol, crushing them as if to squeeze out any last drops. I knew that my depression wouldn't lift until lunchtime, about halfway through the third pint.

To wake up fully, I threw myself down the stairs, Starsky and Hutch-style. I never used the lift: it smelled of burning and felt to be going not up or down but sideways or even somehow *inwards*, like a time machine. Outside, I could feel the glass from broken milk bottles even through my Air-Wear soles: although it had been there a year no one had cleared it up. The lad who cut the verges wouldn't do it: 'It's not my job,' he'd said, 'I'm the gardener.' So I'd kicked it onto his grass but he'd merely mowed around it. Still, it was useful for finding my way back when I was out of it: I knew to turn left when I heard the glass crunch under my feet, then to kick each stair riser until I recognized my floor by the sound of some liquid steadily dripping from somewhere. When I first moved in I was always getting lost, finding myself fumbling with a key that suddenly didn't fit a mysteriously repainted door.

My lock-up didn't lock — but it would only open if you banged the jammed shutter top left while simultaneously booting it bottom right, then, while it was still vibrating, pulled and twisted its handle so sharply as to nearly dislocate your wrist. It was thief-proof, but then who on earth would have wanted to nick my van?

This morning only the dogs were about, sweeping back and forth in splitting and recombining packs: they weren't like ordinary mongrels — it was as if a transplant surgeon had crazily jumbled up a dozen pedigree breeds. Now as they mobbed together it seemed that the legs and heads were frenziedly trying to match themselves up with the right bodies and tails. The Health Department had been baffled by the speed at which our local typhoid epidemic was spreading until they'd established that it was through all those dirty nappies the young mums kept throwing out of the blocks' windows: The dogs would lick them, then lick their owners' faces.

I set out for a roofing job in Bradford 13. The van jerked and roared and pumped out black smoke. Even through the city centre they gave me ten yards clearance, front and back. I hated driving up Thornton Road. First its mills had closed, then its light industry, then the butchers and the bakers, until all that was left was dereliction and decay. I'd liked that fine but then bright new frontages had appeared with bewilderingly kaleidoscopic window displays: Waggy's Fancy Dress Hire, Ken's Kendo Accessories, The Moonchild Magick Shop, Pets and Patios . . . I was glad I'd had the sense to drink away my own redundancy money.

The woman who'd rung greeted me as if I was a Boy Scout on a Bob-a-Job. At five feet nothing she still managed to give the impression that she was looking down on me. Her pipe cleaner legs bent under the weight of her sack-like body and the skin of her face, above three rolls of chin-fat, was stretched taut, as if she was suffocating inside a plastic bag. She was wearing tight flowered shorts with a cake fringe border and a black Lycra sports bra that was gradually disappearing between folds of flesh. She pointed up at the roof and clicked her fingers, then went into the house and made a cup of coffee, without offering me one. I told myself that she must have had a lot of pain in her life – although probably it had been nothing like enough. I could hear her sniggering when I couldn't get my ladders off the van rack. My usual granny knots had some-how mutated into a complex network of weird loops, hitches and twists. As I unpicked one, another three seemed to form: finally I took my Stanley knife and just slashed the ropes to pieces.

Most of the slates were missing on the roof's west-facing side; even on a still day, gusts of wind kept exploding out of the two hundred square-miles of nothing much between here and Lancashire, sneakily trying to pitch me off. I started to clean the dead leaves out of the guttering. The woman sun-bathed below: a thick book was propped open in front of her but she never turned its pages. Her tinny radio was tuned to Classic FM but I knew that she didn't really like the music, just had it on to impress. To 'The Dance of the Sugar Plum Fairy' she extricated her top and rolled over on to her front. I resisted the temptation to bombard her with the three slimy tennis balls I'd just uncovered. You came across some strange things in gutters: I once found a gold octagonal ladies' watch – maybe it had been dropped by a jackdaw or fallen from the wrist of a passing angel? Suspicious of good fortune, I'd just left it there.

I went to the pub for lunch: four pints of Landlord, to wash down a Brontë Booster – an enormous egg, bacon and sausage fry-up. I tried to imagine Emily, Charlotte and Anne, born just across the road, getting their teeth into that. I watched a coachload of Jap tourists videoing each other being blown up and down Main Street; why were they so obsessed with the Brontës? Whenever I was driving over Haworth Moor I'd stop and twist the new signposts of Japanese characters to point in the opposite direction.

When I got back, my employer had turned over, her poor little tits slopping on to the grille of her rib cage: the sun seemed to be not tanning but bleaching her. The beer had restored my courage or my balance: from the roof I looked down like a God into the bowl-shaped valley that contained Bradford. My block and the others were sticking out of the heat-haze like the clutching fingers of a drowning man. I began to replace the corroded section at the back with the grey plastic guttering I'd nicked from the site of the hospital extension: I still felt guilty about this, so I wedged two blackbirds' nests back in place. Sometimes they come back, year after year – what must it feel like, living in a nest?

A red Audi swung into the drive. Hubby was home: she didn't even twitch as the car door slammed. I watched him enter the house: the top of his head, like a tonsured monk's, looked familiar. He returned in matching floral shorts, carrying two cans of Heineken: he popped one and threw the other up to me. It was the manager of the Jobcentre where I signed on: I hoped that he hadn't recognized me, silhouetted against the sky. He lay down alongside his wife in the shrinking patch of sunlight, his bare yellow feet next to her head.

When I finished he was waiting ready with another beer. He knew me all right. 'Seventy for cash,' I said. He smiled and counted three tens into my hand, paused, added two fives and then tucked his wallet back down the front of his shorts. There was nothing to be done. I glanced over at his wife, then at him, then dropped my hand and checked my flies but he wasn't falling for it. His grin broadened and he shook his head slightly: he gave me credit for more taste.

After tearing my T-shirt into strips to tie the ladders back on, I let my van slide down into the city. At every red light I expected them to shoot off their rack and go through the windscreen of the car that crawled in front all the way, pulling out whenever I tried to pass, its driver's billiard-ball head bobbing on a long, easily-severable neck.

As I was readying myself to lay into the shutters of my lock-up, coppers suddenly came at me from north, south and west. Two of them pinioned my arms while Mark the Community Policeman strolled up. He'd never decided whether he wanted to be a hard cop or a soft cop: one day he was all smiles, the next slamming anyone he saw up against the nearest wall — he even *looked* different, alternately fat and jolly or thin and mean. His hands dropped gently on to my shoulders, as if in a blessing: 'So why did you do it, then?' he asked me with a sigh.

'Do what?'

The scrum broke up as they all skipped aside like chorus boys to point dramatically towards the windowless rear of my block.

In this	block
there lives	a slag . . .
she's hurt Him	and now
she has	to pay . . .

The enormous gloss letters were bisected by the leaking downpipe, their ultrawhite glare almost bringing tears to my eyes.

'I don't know anything about that,' I told Mark.

'You've got paint and ladders.'

'It's not my writing. You can check.'

'Clever bastard. No one has ten foot handwriting.' His hands returned to my shoulders, this time squeezing hard.

'Have you been hurt by any slags lately, sir?' asked a pale, earnest constable who looked to be about twelve.

'Dozens,' I said, 'but none in this block.'

Mark's grip tightened. 'Where were you last night?'

'The Puck, The Harp of Erin, The Castle, The Queen's, The Bedford, The Station, The Armstrong. Then the Karachi. I got back about one.'

'So you just walked past and didn't notice it?'

'You know how it is; you never see anything unless you're looking for it.' I put a slight quaver into my voice: 'I couldn't have done it, lads. I get vertigo. I can't go too high since they drained my sinuses.'

All I had to do was keep denying everything. Coppers these days have shorter attention spans. If you can keep them talking for longer than three minutes you're in the clear: a few at the fringes had already begun to slope off.

'Did you see or hear anything unusual?'

I thought it best not to mention my re-tied ladders: 'You know how it is: it's only unusual if there isn't something unusual round here.'

As I switched from laughter to a fake coughing fit they dropped me and returned to their vans, slamming the doors and gunning the engines to cover their embarrassment. They'd been overcome by the novelty of the situation: it was only unusually big graffiti, after all. What charges could they have brought? Trespass? Damage to Council property? Threatening behaviour? Nothing quite fitted the bill: they would have to make a new law. I turned to Mark. 'Whatever made you think it was me?'

'Well,' he said, 'you're supposed to be some kind of poet, aren't you?'

I unloaded the van and then checked my shelves. Someone had tidied the place up: the paint brushes were glossy and restored, still slightly wet, and a new tin of white one-coat gloss paint had been left on top of the emptied one. Whoever it was must have been local, to have watched and learnt my trick of freeing the shutter.

In this	block
there lives	a slag . . .
she's hurt Him	and now
she has	to pay . . .

I went back outside and looked up at it again: it seemed an awful lot of trouble to have gone to. Only an artist or a signwriter could have done that in the dark without a single drip or tremble, unless they'd clipped on an enormous pre-prepared stencil. Even the dots of the i's and the ellipses were perfect little circles.

In this	block
there lives	a slag . . .

It reminded me of the opening of a song that we used to sing at school. 'On Richmond Hill there lives a lass/ As bright as any morn.' I tried humming it but it came out like 'Old Mac-Donald': ee–i–ee–i–o.

she's hurt Him	and now
she has	to pay . . .

It's always a bad sign when you start thinking of yourself in the third person, especially when you give it a capital letter.

Doris, my next door neighbour, had been standing by the main entrance since my return, watching the whole thing. She knew everything about everybody: if there was even a new dog in the pack she wouldn't rest until she'd discovered its owner and, more importantly, its name. The unusual warmth of her greeting immediately confirmed my suspicion that it was she who had put the coppers on to me. 'I knew it wasn't you, love. It'll be those lads in the seven-fives: they're all on drugs. Nothing's sacred to them: they've even scratched that new paint off the lift doors. As for the slag' – she jerked her head towards a group of girls pushing prams up the ramp towards us – 'It'll be one of this lot.'

Having obviously decided that if it was to be open season on slags there was safety in numbers, they were advancing in a V-formation, like a motorcycle gang hitting a seaside town, flushed over their usual pallor, shouting at each other as if they were trying to drown something out. They wore tight calf-length denim sheaths that would have hobbled them if they hadn't extended the fraying slits all the way up the back, allowing clouds of grey slip to billow out behind them like ectoplasm. Their bare legs were scratched, blotched and bruised, red-dotted with fleabites around the ankles. They ignored Doris and just nodded or blinked at me. The prams were all expensive, grey steel and rainbow-canopied, three-braked and toggle-wheeled, but the babies were thin and silent, with frightened eyes.

They hated children, I'd noticed, but loved babies. They needed something weak and dependent to make them feel strong and in control, keeping kittens until they grew into cats, puppies until they were dogs. They wanted to be babies themselves, to start their own lives over again, or to create happy childhoods that would somehow erase the miseries of their own ... but after a while they started to feel even worse than before, under attack from unaccountable creatures that refused to chuckle and gurgle, just shat and ate, got sick and cried, cried, cried. And then the creatures would begin to speak, using words they'd never taught them, asking questions they couldn't answer. Only blows would shut them up and then not even blows would make them speak again. But after the social workers had taken them away the mothers would bring forth yet another wave of magical babies. A lot of the boys were called Damian: maybe they were trying for the Antichrist.

Doris took the lift: I was up the stairs and back safe in my castle long before she emerged. The sun still filled the bedroom with light, still strangely reflecting in via the same window opposite. Standing on the sill, struggling to hook the heavy curtain back on to its rail, I looked down and registered that every flagstone on the pavement far below was cracked. Stifling in the summer, freezing in winter: it suited me here. I loved to lie on my bed, feeling the block swaying with the winds, listening to the toilet cistern's whisperings as it took three hours to refill, watching as the ceiling seemed to slowly descend then recede, so that I felt deliciously claustrophobic or agoraphobic by turn.

It had driven my wife crazy, though: everything had been OK until we'd moved in here. 'I've always hated flying,' she said. Suddenly we were arguing about everything and nothing.

All the food she cooked was burnt black or raw. She tried to kill a dozy wasp crawling on the window by throwing the kitchen chair at it. Soon we'd stopped talking altogether: it was soothing for a while, as if we were members of some contemplative religious order, but after we stopped screwing it got bad again – there seemed to be a permanent hissing in the air, like a pan of water boiling dry. The plaster of the bedroom wall was studded with little knuckle rounds from all the times I'd smashed my fists into it – not instead of her or to mortify myself but because I knew that Doris' ear was pressed against the other side.

The explosion came one Sunday evening as I was singing along with *Songs of Praise* from Hereford Cathedral, feeling nauseated at the way the eyes of the congregation were opening and closing at the same intervals as their mouths. My wife came out of the kitchen, skidded across the carpet on her knees and turned off the TV. As she turned, straightening up, I hit her, for the first and last time, with closed fist in the face. I pulled the punch but too late, making it more of a twist than a pull. Leaving the ground, she seemed to float horizontally for ages as if weightless, until her head hit the far wall. She lay there motionless. Just as I was working out how to dispose of the body she abruptly returned to the vertical, like a round-bottomed bodhidharma doll.

'You hit me.'

'No I didn't.'

She dropped her hands from her mouth: her teeth were etched in scarlet. 'Oh yes you did.'

'It was lightning' – I gestured at the placid grey sky – 'A miracle: a ball of lightning rolled in, knocked you over, then left by the keyhole. Let that be a lesson to you: come not between man and his redeemer.'

She leaned forward and kissed me, hands fumbling for my zip. I tasted blood and gin: she'd been hiding the bottles again. It felt as if I'd knocked her upper front teeth out of alignment but she insisted that they'd always been like that. For the next few days it seemed as if that one blow had somehow broken the spell. We couldn't keep our hands off each other, we laughed and chattered as if we'd just met – but then she was gone without leaving a note, taking only her clothes. I hadn't heard from her in the two years since: Doris, I knew, was saying that I'd buried her somewhere.

I went into the living room and picked up my dad's old dictionary: it stood where the television used to be. SLAG: I looked up the word. It came from slagen, middle low German, meaning to slay. 'Has many senses or nuances, all pej'. Pej, I decided, could only be an affectionate diminutive for pejorative. It wasn't only a slattern or a prostitute, then: it could also mean rubbish or nonsense. It was a limp, a watch-chain, a bully or a coward; flux, scoria, gangue, pyrites – whatever they might be – silicates or pigs. It was soft moist weather, a quagmire or a slough. It was to pain with severe criticism: to lag, to idle, to spend recklessly or eat voraciously. It was a dottle: dottle! What a wonderful word! It meant the unburnt remnant of tobacco at the bottom of a pipe bowl. I'd kept my dad's old black bone briar: if I put it to my ear I'd seem to hear the distant echoes of his coughing, if I stuck my finger into its bowl I could feel something rough at the bottom – the last dottle, his soul. Language is power, he used to tell me: if you know a word it can't hurt you – which was strange because I was pretty sure that he'd known the word cancer.

A slag was carny slang for a punter who looks at the free attractions but avoids the paying shows. In Australia it meant to spit. A slagger was a brothel-keeper; a slaggering was a row – but was that a great commotion, a trip on a lake, or a line? It meant unwashed, useless, a petty criminal, a third-rate grifter. It was a slack-mettled fellow, one not ready to resist an affront . . . the word seemed to encompass everything. I myself was a slag, living in a city of slags – in a country, a world, a universe of slags, in an infinity of pej.

On the way down to Park Road for milk and bread I decided to stop for a quick pint which meant of course that I never made it: beer was a food anyway. Having been gutted to create one huge circular bar, the place had recently reopened, now designated a Fun Pub, renamed The Puck after its randomly-chosen ice-hockey theme, with netting and sticks depending from the frosted ceiling and rows of goalminders' masks staring down like Jason Vorhees in *Friday the Thirteenth*. But now the regulars were gradually drifting back like wraiths, smothering any Fun in its cradle. The new green-on-red carpet was meta-morphosing into its predecessor – ash-grey and polka-dotted with brown and black burns – and the gleaming bar already had a layer of dust that wouldn't brush off. I wondered if the extirpated partitioned snugs and games-rooms would just grow back, like branches of a lopped tree.

Without my even asking, Eleanor the barmaid slammed a plateful of clingfilm-wrapped egg sandwiches in front of me. 'Leftovers from yesterday,' she said, but they tasted far too fresh for that, with fine-chopped onions and home-made lemon-based mayonnaise. Her eyes, perhaps distorted by the thick lenses of her glasses, always looked to be full of tears. Everybody seemed to think that I was starving but all I ever did was eat and drink.

All around me, people began to just materialize out of their chairs. The usual conversation began: football, always football. I tried to convince myself that I found this familiarity comfortable. They were still picking over the Barnet game: I'd been there and couldn't remember a thing about it. Only triumphs and disasters registered with me, which meant that the whole season had been a virtual blank. I couldn't bring to mind the names of any of the current City players: they were all the same, with no first touch, donkey haircuts and unfocused eyes. The old ones – Rackstraw, Corner, Swallow – I used to dream about them, even though they were crap.

'This club's got no ambition, taking that Tolson off Oldham in part-exchange for McCarthorse. They should have held out for Sharp, or Beckford, or Palmer.' Dave could tell you any football fact: his bed-sit was piled to the ceiling with red Silvine exercise books full of statistics. He knew more about the game than any player, manager or journalist ever could: they had distractions – wives, children, food, sleep – but with him it was his entire life.

Whenever a woman came in silence fell, followed by a hubbub of fevered speculation. Which one was the slag? Naturally, the three best-looking were the favourites. Was it the grey-haired one? There was something sinister about her: although she had four kids – two in the army – her face was still unlined and her body remained as tight as a sixteen year old's. Or the crop-haired one? She was never seen with a man so she could only be a lesbian, the wrong kind of slag. Or the little blonde? Her husband's legs had been shattered at Forgemasters' and she had to help him along like a third crutch while he cursed her: it was said that she took home three different men every night but no names were ever mentioned. Huddling together, even going to the ladies' in pairs, all the candidates looked too hesitant and frightened to me. The Slag should have remained unconcerned or, at least, defiant — peroxided, mad-eyed, mean-mouthed under a scarlet lipstick bow, with the names of her victims tattooed from shoulder to wrist . . . Finally Dave broke off his unheeded monologue on City's left backs of the last two decades. 'It could be any of 'em,' he growled. 'All women are slags.'

'What, every last woman in the world?'

He thought hard for a few moments: 'Nay, round here. I only know round here.'

I noticed that all the men were looking at each other with furtive, complicitous expressions that tried to say at once 'It was me' and 'I know it was you'. The women were doing the same. It was as if war had been declared but The Puck was still — just — a neutral Zone.

In this	block
there lives	a slag . . .
she's hurt Him	and now
she has	to pay . . .

If there was any way out of this entire mess I'd always felt that it must have been something to do with women — although in my life they'd invariably only made everything worse. I wondered if The Slag didn't even know she was The Slag and was getting on with her life unawares. Maybe she'd hurt Him by not noticing Him, by remaining entirely unaware of His existence?

If you really put your mind to it you could be hurt by anything. I'd spent all the previous summer watching from my window the arrivals and departures – at 8.10 and 5.05, Monday to Friday – of a girl who, to avoid the NCP toll, used to park her blue Volvo on the slip road below the garages. Tall and dark with a long pony tail, she was always dressed the same: black soft leather jacket zipped right up with tight moleskin trousers tucked into high-heeled green half-boots – I always liked people who settled on a look and then stayed with it. When it rained she held an umbrella with her arm fully extended and a dead straight line of neck and back, like Mary Poppins. Her car gave no clues as to which district she came from or where she worked: no dealer's flash in the window, no clothes or books on the back seat, no cigarettes or sweets in the dashboard, no mascots or fuzzy dice, not even a radio so I could see what station she listened to. Its windows and body-work, though, were always scrupulously clean.

Although I must have been invisible to her as I stood far above in the darkness behind nearly closed curtains, she often paused and, shading her eyes, looked up in my direction. Although her figure far below was tiny I could discern the colour of her eyes – somewhere between blue and green – read 'AERO' on the catch of her jacket's zip and pick out on her back pockets the strainings of every single white stitch. I sometimes considered waiting around down there – to smile, strike up a conversation or follow her – but I never did: I liked things just the way they were.

Then, one lunchtime, as I lurched, refocusing, out of The

Ram's Revenge, I literally bumped into her. Laughing, she steadied herself with one hand on my shoulder. My mind raced, trying to adjust to how she'd suddenly blown herself up from half an inch high to – in those heels – slightly taller than me. Although she didn't need it, she was heavily made up. It couldn't conceal a cold sore at the side of her nose – my fingers automatically scratched the same place on my own face. Our eyes met and then her smile twisted into an expression of horror or disgust. She turned white, then beetroot-red, then ducked her head, clutched her boxy handbag as if it had been a threatened baby and went clattering and stumbling down the steep cobbles of Ivegate.

I stood there frozen. It was as if with that one look she'd taken in everything about me. How could she believe any more in her guardian angel on the seventh floor now that she knew that he was waiting for her every morning and evening, unzipped and ready, with a wad of Kleenex in his hand? On the way back to the block, without premeditation, I kicked-in her car's passenger door. At five past five she stood with hands on hips and stared straight up at my window for a full two minutes before getting in and driving away. She never parked there again. It felt far worse than when my wife went, as if I'd destroyed the most important relationship of my life – but I didn't think of her as a slag, just as I hadn't blamed my wife for liking or not liking being hit. Probably I was no kind of man at all.

As soon as the quiz started I left The Puck: The only question that interested me was 'What are you drinking?' The craze would soon pass – like striptease, karaoke or strip-karaoke. Even on a Friday evening the city centre was deserted and silent, except for the starlings screaming from the roof of the Town Hall – the pavements below them were whitened over like snow. Every attempt to get rid of them – birdlime, nets, ultrasonic sound, hawks, stuffed and real – had failed. I loved Bradford at night: I felt light-headed and freed, like one of those kings who would roam unrecognized among their subjects – I never bothered with a disguise, though . . . leaving off my crown sufficed.

The Royal Standard, The Gladstone, The Peckover, The Perseverance, The Junction – most of my favourite pubs had been closed down. I ended up in The Shoulder of Mutton, drinking sweet weak Sam Smith's, alone except for a muttering lunatic who Eleanor, good Catholic, had recently banned from The Puck for insisting that Mary Magdalene and the Blessed Virgin had been one and the same person.

In my teens I scoured Bradford for the perfect pub. I used to see it in my dreams. The interior somehow combined patches of blazing white light and impenetrably dark shadows; it had a fifties jukebox with 'Let there be Drums' and 'Endless Sleep' on it. The landlady resembled Eleanor – but without the religious fanaticism – and although the landlord was permanently drunk you never needed to count your change. It served Taylor's bitter, had Powers & Bushmills' optics and Ram Tam Winter Ale on all year round. It was always packed, with good company when you needed it that didn't need telling when you didn't. There was no gossiping or talk of football. Search as I might, I'd never found it, but even twenty years later if I stayed in one place for more than an hour I still started to get restless, to feel that I should be out searching, that maybe there was one street that I'd missed. That was how I'd come to be a regular everywhere.

I used to hear tales of a group who I suspected of being on the same quest as myself. There were three men — one fat, one medium, one thin, one fair, one dark, one shaven — who, so it was rumoured, ran a waste disposal business together. Drinking didn't fuddle them but inspired them: they'd argue brilliantly and interminably about everything under the sun. They weren't universally popular, though, as they had a curious habit of killing any animals that were in the pub. Beautiful women — always different ones — were said to attend them, ferrying the drinks from the bar while themselves nipping from garnered hip-flasks as they waited to be served. Sometimes I just missed them, entering a pub that was still rocking with laughter as a grinning landlord cleared up the broken glass and splintered wood. Once I found the body of a mynah bird, torn out of its cage and throttled, still quivering on the counter. I never did catch up with them. I'd wondered whether as I sought them they might also have been seeking me, so I'd forced myself to spend entire evenings in one likely place but they were probably sitting across the street doing the same thing.

When The Lord Clyde closed I walked back through the still empty city. Even the starlings were quiet now as I crossed Town Hall Square and climbed towards the Central Library's block of misted over glass. On alternate windows large red words had been placed to spell out the lines:

HE WHO BINDS TO HIMSELF A JOY
DOES THE WINGED LIFE DESTROY
BUT HE WHO KISSES THE JOY AS IT FLIES
LIVES IN ETERNITY'S SUNRISE.

It was OK but nowhere near as good as 'In this block . . .' On the ground floor slightly larger green capitals revealed the name of the author: BUTTERFIELD SIGNS. I passed the slate-grey statue of J. B. Priestley, depicted as part-golem, part-monkey, with his feet firmly planted against an eternal force nine that had ripped open his flasher's mac to reveal him to be frigging the slender stem of his trademark pipe. In Bradford we never forgive the ones that go . . . or the ones that stay.

I crossed the empty tarmac, walking the white lines that had been marked out as spaces for cars that never came, then negotiated the ghostly six-lane cross-town ramp that linked nowhere to nothing, to reach The Karachi. Everyone I knew seemed to hate the Asians but to me they were angels, sent like Elijah's ravens to sustain me. In fifteen minutes I had consumed a poppadum, meat samosa, onion bhaji and chicken karahi at a cost of £3.50. Who cared what they wanted to do to Rushdie? – after that meal, I'd have dragged him in there and helped them to bhuna him myself.

Around the blocks up ahead it seemed as if a lunar glow from the painted letters was outshining the streetlamps' yellow light.

In this	block
there lives	a slag . . .
she's hurt Him	and now
she has	to pay . . .

The writing on the wall: it was like Belshazzar's Feast. I pictured a disembodied hand crawling across the building like an enormous snail, sliming its white trail: MENE, MENE, TEKEL UPHARSIN – 'Thou art weighed in the balance and found wanting'. It had always seemed unfair to me: all the other miracles in the Book of Daniel had been to protect the Israelites or at least to keep their spirits up but this one was sheer cruelty. As poor old Belshazzar would be dead within a few hours, with no time to change his ways or even express contrition, what was the point of telling him, except to gloat?

I remembered a nursery rhyme that my gran had taught me:

> 'How many miles to Babylon?
> Three score miles and ten.
> Can I get there by candlelight?
> Yes, and back again.'

Babylon: the mother of harlots and abominations of the earth – I'd always wanted to go there. As a kid I used to check the departure boards at Forster Square Station but it appeared that there were no direct trains.

Babylon: last year I'd had a three-week plastering job down in London. My workmates were Cockneys who kept waving rolls of banknotes in my face and spitting to just miss my feet but I only smiled and called them all 'love' – it drove them crazy – while setting up a series of little industrial accidents for them. Otherwise I mostly slept in my van in the garage off Malet Street, except for Sundays which I always spent in the National Gallery. I liked those big fleshy Rubenses and the very old ones with dusty wooden doors but after a while I just walked straight past them to gaze at one painting, Rembrandt's 'Belshazzar's Feast'.

I could still recall its every detail: a bowl of nectarines and grapes with a little gold and silver fruit knife, Belshazzar's gut splitting open his waistcoat, his bitten fingernails, the crown perched absurdly on top of his outrageously tasselled turban. In turning to follow the progress of the glowing hand he upsets his goblet: The spilling wine is yellow, as if he's pissing himself with fear. His women aren't looking at the hand but at him, to see how they ought to be reacting. One girl, part-obscured by the others' plumes, remains oblivious, still playing her recorder, cross-eyed with concentration as she goes for that tricky low D.

The real attraction for me, though, was that Belshazzar looked exactly like Kenny Burns, the fearsome centre-half from Nottingham Forest's cup-winning team. As a veteran, dropping through the lower division, he'd played for Derby against City in our promotion season. Flabby and pale, with a crosshatched moustache and a layered haircut in need of darning, he cruised his ten square yards of pitch, dead-eyed as a shark. No one dared go near: even Crazy Bobby Campbell wouldn't take him on. At one-all, late in the game, we brought on our teenage substitute, Don Goodman. 'Oh God, here comes the headless chicken,' Dave said. Goodman was lightning-fast but wildly uncoordinated, usually falling over in his sheer excitement whenever the ball went near him. This time, though, receiving his first pass, he managed to stay on his feet – he turned smartly and headed straight towards Burns' sector. We cringed, awaiting the inevitable terrible impact . . . then, at full speed, Goodman feinted right and left then, having thus opened Burns' legs, slipped the ball clean through them and went by him like the wind. In Rembrandt's picture I relished again Burns' horror-struck expression as he'd turned to see Goodman, already twenty yards on, lobbing the keeper for the decisive goal. That win had put us top: we stayed there for the rest of the season.

I used to look at it for hours with the gallery attendants watching me like hawks. They knew that my presence – a man in stained overalls, his hair weirdly full of unmelting snow in mid-July, standing in front of a painting, laughing wildly – must be against all the regulations but – like the coppers with the big graffiti – they couldn't find anything that covered it. I became aware that I was laughing again now, standing alone in front of my block. Goodman and Burns: it hadn't been about football or even about how the old fall prey to the young, it had just been a perfect moment ... an utterly unexpected intrusion of pattern and grace that had set off simultaneous explosions of somehow sugary warmth in my head, heart and gut, like when I'd stood by my window watching the stitched chevron of those back pockets moving around on that tight white arse far below.

In this	block
there lives	a slag...
she's hurt Him	and now
she has	to pay...

Since the afternoon the words seemed to have slid down the wall as if to create space for further bulletins. I felt that there was something about all this that I wasn't quite getting, as if it was a code that I couldn't crack – as if, on some other level, it had nothing to do with blocks and slags at all. When I closed my eyes I found that the letters were still visible on the red field of my lids.

There was a roar of approaching engines and then a loud squealing of brakes from behind me. At first I thought it was the boys in blue returning for a second shot but these three grille-windowed vans were smaller, blue and gold with Graffiti Removal Unit painted on the sides. The dozen men who came spilling out were all wearing balaclava helmets and dark uniforms with epaulettes and what appeared to be cartridge belts. Some of them had thick droopy moustaches like seventies TV detectives. They jogged past in step, in two precise lines, bearing gleaming steel ladders above their heads. Within thirty seconds they were high above me, scrubbing away at the side of the building.

The Council didn't usually react so quickly – or at all. Most graffiti was just left well alone: my own favourite – WEBBO/ VICIOUS/JEDI – still remained on the railway bridge – in its proud but fading letters of dripping scarlet lake – after fifteen years. Someone powerful had obviously found ours – whether because of size or content – unacceptable. Perhaps there were hundreds of such notices all across the city that were being immediately erased, with all reports suppressed, like they do with UFO sightings.

The sprays and brushes couldn't shift the letters, so the men had to return to the van for their pressure hoses to blast them away. One of the moustaches ran so fast that he overshot and, in trying to turn, tripped and crashed to the ground. I gave him a mocking slow hand-clap and slurped my tongue round my lips. 'I just *love* watching *men* at work,' I said. He didn't reply or even react, just strapped on his hose and shot back up his ladder. I was looking for a chance to make off with a bucket or torch, but then realized that a thirteenth man had remained by the vans with a mobile phone, mumbling incomprehensibly to somebody. Aloft, they worked on in total silence, flat out. I couldn't stand these new model working men. No talking, no tea or toilet breaks, always running, never walking – if the Council had tried that on when I started on the bins twenty years ago we'd have had the whole city out on strike. We used to work at half the speed for half as long: did we think the world owed us a living? – No, we *knew* it did. For working on Friday, after midnight, this lot were probably getting only time-and-a-half, at best.

Some of them were working inwards:

n this	bl
ves	a s

– While the others worked outwards:

she's h	ow
she	ay . . .

Although I knew that they shared a shabby Canal Road hut with the dog-wardens and pest-controllers, it appeared that the GRU wasn't merely another council department but something sinister, even supernatural. As I watched, it seemed as if they were ruthlessly wiping the words from my memory, as if I'd awakened in the middle of the night to discover them standing around my bed, sandblasting away my dreams. I felt sick and giddy, as when I'd once rested against the electric fence at the edge of a field of cows and thought it had been God's hand that had struck me down. There was a strange ticking sound that I finally decided could have only been the knocking of my knees. Up until that moment I'd thought this to be merely a figure of speech: maybe my hair would have been standing on end as well, if my head hadn't been shaved – or rather, bald.

Even when they finished the men didn't relax, marching silently and expressionlessly back to their vans without looking at each other or at me. I didn't turn around to watch them go, just continued staring at the empty wall. I was pleased to see that, in their haste, they'd missed the final dot, bottom right. I hoped that the words might also begin to reconstitute themselves but nothing further appeared. I'd always thought that my block was grey but now there was a golden, star-shaped patch where the letters had been. At least our prison had been built of the finest Yorkshire Sandstone. I realized that I was able to recall the words in two halves, by concentrating on the rusting drainpipe and shutting first the left eye:

> In this
> there lives
> she's hurt Him
> she has

and then the right:

> block
> a slag . . .
> and now
> to pay . . .

– and then combining them.

I walked up close to look at that sole surviving dot. It hung about ten feet off the ground: I jumped up a few times but even with arms fully extended couldn't quite reach. It was a perfect circle, slightly larger than my own hand, like the porthole of a ship.

I leapt once more and this time my finger-ends slapped against the whitened stone. Nothing happened for a moment and then it was as if I'd touched the button that opened some cosmic portal, as the hungry hole rapidly hoovered up everyone and everything. They all went past in a blur: a daisy-chain of coppers, Cockneys and GRU, then Goodman and Burns laughing together, Eleanor and the apostate, Doris and my wife, the innocent slags with their prams, a perfect arse and a pony tail ... the pubs, The Karachi, the house in Thornton – despite its new slates and guttering ... the Town Hall, the library and all its books ... all the words in the world and all their meanings. Then there was no glass or grass under my feet anymore, no stars or moon, no light or darkness ... I was suspended in nothingness for an instant but then – just as I was beginning to fret over why I'd been excluded or spared – everything and everyone came spewing right back out again ...

Songs that Won the War

Radiation salvoes, for a while, had held the cancer at the left lung, but then supposedly arthritic side-effects were revealed to be an all-out offensive on the spine that hadn't – for some reason – shown up on the scans . . . Hopeless, so they moved my father from infirmary to hospice.

I was glad to see him out of there. When I'd heard talk of NHS demoralization I'd imagined longer queues in casualty, higher levels of sickness and staff turnover, more snapping and sighing, undusted window ledges, the odd mislaid corpse: I wasn't prepared for the hospital's descent – in the five years since my mother died – into an abyss of unfocused fear and hatred. Compassion and competence had been shut down along with the dark, echoing dermatology wing. A series of specialists – with half-moon glasses and gold pinky rings – sidled up to rubbish each other's prognoses: an endless Tom and Jerry dialectic, until the disease itself shut them up. Half the housemen were German, over on cheap short-term contracts: one of them had prodded my father's chest, where the blue-black shrapnel seemed to swim subcutaneously, like fish in a silted-up pool. 'Vere did you get zis?' he asked in best Gestapo fashion. 'Narvik

1940' – my father rolled his eyes – 'Your lot.' He didn't forgive: the last real animation he'd shown was in punching the air when Lechkov's bald head put Klinsmann and Co out of the World Cup.

The nurses were even worse. Vampire-pale, stony-eyed, at visiting times they moved from bed to bed, weirdly vibrating, avid for the drama and tears: the ICU was better than *East Enders* or *Corrie*. They hated my father for grimly recording each cracked window, jammed radiator and empty light socket, every little oversight and cruelty, everyone's names: after his red Silvine notebook had mysteriously vanished he hid its replacement inside his pillow. They hated me for my lack of obvious grief: my diffidence cracked just once – when they offered me pre-bereavement counselling and I burst out laughing. After that, eyes averted, they stumped past us, as if crushing hideous vermin under their thick soles. Whatever happened to the bow-tied doctors who used to work the wards like game show hosts, the ward sisters like opera divas, the Hattie Jacques matrons? Whatever happened to the student nurses of my youth – vivid, tender, blithe as spring throstles and self-parodically hot to trot . . . though seldom with me?

The hospice was high above Wharfedale, the last house before the moors. As I left the car I got, as always, a tang of ozone, although a hundred miles from the nearest coast. It was a wool baron's Italianate mansion, converted, ringed by immaculate parterres, pulsing and blaring with crude life and colour: where were the bosky, bowering cypress and yew? The residents were never seen outside, though today I glimpsed lemur-like flittings in the sunporch shadows.

*   *   *

The hall's darkness enveloped me like squid's ink and I groped towards the window lights' tiny lozenges at the top of the mock-baronial staircase, toe-kicking each invisible riser. Half-way up, the Pain Management Team — three grinning boys in luminous white, like a tumbling act — passed me in mid-air, breasting the front door with one more kangaroo bound. The oak bannister I'd cowered against was strangely warm and yielding: time rubs off hard edges, makes things kind — old buildings are the best to die in, or die into. 'It's bad luck to be the first to die in a house,' my grandfather had said, just before he was.

My favourite nurse was on station: the one who, by night-light, had rubbed my father's back with toothpaste instead of muscle relaxant and hadn't stopped giggling about it since. Above the ligature-tight chain of her St Christopher her soft, wet face beamed perpetually on her 'ressies' — as if, in dying, they were essaying some much-loved party piece. She winked and wagged her finger at me, knowing that I carried a whisky bottle in my poacher's pocket. She'd got my number: a dinosaur, whose pain took an age to reach heart or brain. It had been three months after my mother's funeral when, traversing the ridge away from Ingleborough, I looked back to recognize, in the mountain's beetle-browed profile, her dead face.

My father's grey hands lay in a plate of untouched food. On the white traycloth was a line of crimson splashes — lung blood — like a restaurant critic's five-star recommendation. His pills were laid out ready — the doomed fleet he was about to launch on his bloodstream. His eyes opened and his arms elongated to reach the t-bar above the bed, to give the illusion that he was raising himself in welcome, his fingers fluttering

on the metal like a flautist's. The more he wasted away the
heavier he got: it took two nurses to cross-lift him, tightening
a plastic sheet or straightening a pillow were major under-
takings. His head looked to be getting larger, doming, with a
strange metallic sheen: his arms seemed to retract into his sides,
his legs to fuse: it was as if impotence and anger were turning
him into a lethal projectile, a shell in the breech ready to be
fired into the infinite.

I gave him a slug of Chivas Regal and poured the rest into
his empty lemon barley bottle. 'Ah, Jeepers Creepers,' he said,
'Jesus Lethal!' – he always pretended to forget its name – 'Still,
you don't have to be able to say it to be able to drink it.' He
rested his bristled chin in the plastic drinking trough, as if
taking the liquor through his pores. I'd turned him on to Chivas
in those days when in every bad, bold photo of the Stones
Keith Richards seemed to be finishing a bottle.

I'd swapped my Red Army watch for the huge self-winding
Timex, dying on his motionless wrist, that now slid, its metal
strap ripping out hairs, along my arm. The fluorescent hammer
and sickle seemed to be affecting him – he spent the last of
his strength on raging against capitalism. Or maybe it was a
symptom of the cancer or his finally admitting the anger he'd
always felt. I remembered watching Tebbitt, white-plastered
like a pierrot, being lugged out of the bombed Grand Hotel
and, as his teeth bared in an equine grimace of agony, I had
seen my father respond with one of his rare smiles. It obsessed
him that it was the Navy – out in The Falklands, with inad-
equate air-support – that had saved Thatcher's bacon: that the
dead sailors of the *Sheffield* – 'Rejoice! Rejoice!' – had bought
her two more terms. He told me that after VJ Day, when

he was CPO on a carrier ferrying ex-POWs out East, the demob-happy crew had stopped saluting and taken to calling each other 'Comrade'. The Captain had asked him whether his life would be safe when they got back to England. After my father had reassured him they'd shaken hands and toasted the future with rum – but the ship's postal election votes were still mysteriously lost in transit. At the time they'd all laughed at their officers' ludicrous fears of mass purges and seizures of assets: 'But now,' he said, 'I wish we'd done just that.'

As my father had observed, his ward was like a convention of Delius impersonators, copying the James Gunn portrait of the dying composer – right down to the tartan blanket over the knees, the fleshless left hand gripping an arm-rest, the right pointing to the floor. Even Mr Siddiqui – wrapped in the pearly aura of death – somehow pulled it off. In the next bay was a kid of no more than twenty, spending his last days reading Coleridge. Impossibly attenuated, his extremities jumbly-green and blue, he lay among propped-open copies of *Biographia Literaria*, the poems, the letters, volume one of Holmes' *Life* – he would never read the second. He hadn't been amused by my father's rendition of *The Ancient Mariner* or my tale of chickening-out of following the mountain-mad poet's series of ledge-jumps down Broad Stand. With heavy emphasis he slowly dragged his bed curtains across, breath singing in his throat like an Aeolian harp.

I gave my father the latest bulletin on Halifax Town – kicked out of the league to the hospice of the Vauxhall Conference – and told him how the cheating kraut Klinsmann had signed for Spurs and, after a series of spectacular goals followed by ironic swallow-dive celebrations, become a national hero. He

47

looked reproachful, as if such jokes were out of order at this time. We sat in silence. There wasn't much I could do for him – just bring in whisky, swap watches, lend him my Walkman and Jelly Roll Morton tapes. I could give him no handy hints for the afterlife unless, God help us, 'The Divine Comedy', 'The Human Age' or 'Hellzapoppin' proved to be reliable guides. Stephen Crane wrote of 'the impulse of the living to try to read in dying eyes the answer to The Question,' but I didn't have any questions, not even lower-case ones.

He flapped his hand towards an unopened jiffy-bag on his table. I prised out the staples with his fish-knife. A video cassette fell out, followed by a postcard of the *Bismarck* on fire, with the message, 'Hope this cheers you up and reminds you of those good times – STAN.' They'd been boy sailors together on *HMS Ganges* – 'and he hasn't changed,' my father always said. Stan's spare time was spent at reunions, the Navy was all he ever talked about – my father pitied, despised him: 'The war's never ended for him, like those Japs they keep finding in the jungle.' Now he just rolled his eyes and sighed. I'd known little about his own war: as a child I'd found, worn and lost his medal ribbons ... once he'd casually mentioned that the shrapnel roaming his body had first passed through that of his best pal.

I held up the video. *Songs that Won the War*: on its cover searchlights over a blitzed London picked out the enormous grinning face of Vera Lynn about to snap up a passing Heinkel. He rolled his eyes again, spoke faintly. I put my ear to his mouth, then rocked back deafened as he near-shouted, 'Put it on!' I wheeled the TV over: static electricity crackled as I dusted the screen – like a cat, it knew I didn't like it. I'd dumped mine, though when I went to my ex-wife's to babysit I'd take along my Buster Keaton videos.

A perfect English sky was invaded by an anvil-headed storm-cloud, from which issued the voice of Neville Chamberlain: men and women broke off from pipe-tamping or knitting to present resolute profiles. Then Vera Lynn appeared, sitting in an empty theatre – 'the girl they left behind.' 'The girl we were running away from,' said my father. She smiled thinly: 'We are a nation of backbone and spirit, so that when we were forced into war in 1939 there was no fear in our hearts.' 'No, we just crapped ourselves,' said my father. It cut to her singing fifty years earlier – looking older, if anything – her awkward hands rinsing and stacking invisible washing-up, in what looked like the garden set of *L'Age D'Or*. 'Johnny will go to sleep in his own little room again . . . Tomorrow, just you wait and see.' 'Well I've waited,' said my father, 'and I've seen.'

A cruiser slid out of Pompey Harbour: most of the crew were waving to the crowd – parents, wives, children – but as the camera jerked away I glimpsed a sizeable number to starboard greeting the open sea. I think that's the side my father would have chosen: our family holidays were always littoral – he'd sneak out hours before breakfast, as if to meet a lover . . . Then the whale-like calls of signalling ships segued into the voice of Our Gracie. 'We're all together now . . .': she approached the audience, transfixed as by the lights of an oncoming lorry, like someone trying to coax out from under the sofa the last puppy to be drowned. 'Whadda we care?': she did a little dance, as if shooing chickens, reminding me of Mrs Thatcher.

Forgotten songs, forgotten singers. George Formby, his cod's head emerging from the best-cut suit I'd ever seen, strummed and gurned in front of a curtain seemingly painted with tantric demons. Flotsam and Jetsam sang how London Could Take It, a majolica vase perched on the piano presumably demonstrating the ineffectiveness of The Blitz. Churchill appeared among bombed ruins, in a romper suit, sucking at his cigar, a behemoth baby. 'We weren't fighting for *him*,' said my father, 'we remembered Tonypandy and the *British Gazette*. We were fighting for the peace – jobs, education' – he shrugged – 'a health service. A better society, before Thatcher told us there was no such thing.' The video had certainly livened him up, though not in the way Stan might have intended.

Flanagan and Allen sang 'Rabbit Run' over the celebrated film of a Spitfire tracking a German bomber, while below, on a Cotmanish field, a lurcher chased down a rabbit: for a few dizzying seconds animals and machines moved from left to right in perfect synchronization . . . Then the anaesthetic washes of 'String of Pearls': the Glenn Miller Orchestra was bombing Pearl Harbor. America's entry into the war involved a great improvement in musical quality – Dinah Shore languorously exploring 'The Last Time I Saw Paris' – and colour film – the Andrews Sisters exploding in their crimson dresses. 'I always fancied that middle one,' said my father, 'the double-jointed one that could scat.' In comparison with this released New World energy the Home Front looked drab and costive, the stock fading to saffron, the confused crowds at railway termini half-obscured by London particulars or dragon clouds of smoke from their perpetual Woodies and Cappies.

Then a ribald fanfare sounded: into a mob of sailors, milling about below decks, there descended an enormous chin – Tommy Trinder, in uniform, kitbag on shoulder, head cocked, was coming down the rope and chain ladder. Having surveyed the scene with a nod of satisfaction, he began to sing:

> Of all the lives a man can lead
> There's none that's like a sailor's
> It's very much more exciting
> Than a tinker's or a tailor's
> He leaves his home sweet home
> It seems he loves to roam . . .

He got lost in the bustle, kept approaching the wrong berth and being pushed away. His grin got wider. He approved someone's pin-up with a raised thumb, then attached himself to a passing close harmony trio, a cerberus of raffish cockney grifters:

> . . . All over the place
> Wherever the sea may happen to be
> A sailor is found knocking around
> He's all over the place!

Trinder moved in an absurd yet hieratic glide, like something obscurely sinister in a Kenneth Anger movie, his profile like the elongated eye of Horus gripped in the vice of brow and cheekbone:

> The North and the South
> The East and the West
> There's half of the world
> Tattooed on his chest
> And all over the place!

Then a scanty-haired dodderer began to intone the signal before Trafalgar – 'England expects that every man today will do his duty' – only to reel away from his shipmates' volleys of pillows, boots and brushes. His crew would have done that to Nelson too if they hadn't loved him – as my father always said – because he upped their grog ration, fought polar bears, chased beautiful women and was clearly, heroically, off his head.

> He's here for a day
> And then he's away
> He's all over the place!

The music burst into a hornpipe and the sailors danced, wildly stamping on the decks. I imagined the officers up top getting nervous, hearing in that satyr rout their approaching nemesis, the revenge of the subhumans, revolution ... only to be confronted at the last not by bloody Jack Cade but by Clem Attlee in his MCC tie.

> He's here, he's there, he's everywhere
> He's all over the place!

Tommy waved a huge baton over the swell of sound but kept delaying the climax: 'He's all over the – wait for it! wait for it! – place!!!' After the last chord someone crashed a folded deckchair over his head but his ecstatic smile didn't waver.

I pressed the freeze frame. My heart was pounding, I was running with sweat, like the first time I heard 'Anarchy In The UK' or 'Straight to Hell'. My father clapped his hands: 'That's just how it was! Everyone went a bit crazy at sea, the best sort of crazy ... I'm sounding like Stan! I mean it was fine if you didn't mind the blood and guts.'

We rewound 'All Over the Place' and watched it again. My father recalled that it came from a film, *Sailors Three*, identifying the old man as Claude Hulbert and the young sailor with a mass of oiled curls as Michael Wilding, who married Liz Taylor. Senescence and youth flanking Trinder, the man: grandfather, father and son united in a magical triangle – all over the place, coffined in steel, with a head height of twenty feet ... In the song's final chorus it was obvious that they were surrounded by real sailors with bad skin, gappy teeth, tufting hair – chums with their arms around each other's necks; their gaze, bold but shy, followed the camera as it swept by: I felt a jolt of contact as their eyes met mine, as if their souls were living on inside the celluloid.

We saw Trinder once, my father and I: at one of my first Halifax Town matches. When Fulham, led by the great Johnny Haynes, aureoled in brylcreem shine, scored the sixth of their eight we heard the unmistakable voice of chairman Tommy, his catchphrase, 'O you lucky people!' booming above our faltering cries of 'Come on, you Shaymen.' And my father remembered him guesting on the TV game show, *The Golden Shot*, rocking with cruel mirth as a sobbing Bob Monkhouse recounted the contestants' increasingly heartrending and hilarious hard-luck stories, so that, unable to hold the crossbow steady on the prize target, he'd pinged the bolt into the studio ceiling.

'I saw that!' said Mr Siddiqui, who'd tacked gingerly across the ward to join us. 'Bernie, the bolt! ... Ann Ashton, the

Golden Girl!!' – he looked heavenwards, as if expecting her to appear.

The sound had drawn the ressies from the other wards. Even the smoking room emptied: a fat grey man covered in ash who I'd never seen before crashed down on to my father's legs, but he didn't seem to mind. I rewound it and played it again. And again. They began to tap their feet and to hum like drowsy bees and then, gradually, we – eleven dying men, the toothpaste nurse and myself – began to sing and then – on the slack, echoing lino – to stamp. The Pain Management Team appeared and started working out the hornpipe steps. My father – his hands steady again – was pouring everyone hits of Jesus Lethal into the bottle-cap.

The curtains around the next bed were thrown aside to reveal Coleridge in wrath at this army from Porlock that had apparently arrived. Index finger poised for the 'off' switch he shuffled agonizingly towards the screen, but then stopped as I froze Tommy again in that final transfigured pose. His face moved right up to Trinder's, as if getting his scent. 'That man,' he said, 'looks like a camel.' At the volleys of laughter that greeted this he blushed, blood rushing back into his face, then smiled – his mouth widening and widening until it hit the jaw line – 'A Bactrian.'

My Hard Friend

Those summer evenings My Hard Friend often called, to drive me back to the moors we'd walked as children. And so, that Sunday, after my usual struggle with the blank page, I heard his horn — on the last stroke of seven — sound out to save me.

'Noddy's come for Big Ears,' said my wife, passing across her book, Adorno's *Minima Moralia*. I read the passage she'd marked ready: 'The refined are drawn to the unrefined, whose coarseness deceptively promises what their own culture denies'. I flicked on and riposted with another quote: 'Love is the power to see similarity in the dissimilar'.

She hated him: he shrank from her like a snake from a mongoose. She said he was going to rip me off but I couldn't see that we had anything he'd want — even our money somehow seemed to be the wrong tender. For a while she probed around — she'd heard all about English public schools' crushes, beatings, hand-jobs in the shower — but concluded that my reversion was harmless, just one more vague disappointment: 'He's not exactly *Le Grand Meaulnes*.'

He'd got yet another car to wreck: already dented and sprayed with viridian grease, the floor shin-deep with ash, crumpled clothing and treadled maps, an arsenal of pills and bottles in the glove compartment. The tape was playing 'Wooden Heart' – Elvis, his hero, serenading a puppet in German, in *GI Blues*, made the year we were born. His hands, covered with indecipherable ink and pin prison tattoos, seemed hardly to touch the spinning wheel. He was supposed to be teaching me to drive, but we'd soon abandoned that: my arms were too long, my legs too short, my vision tunnelled in and out – whatever, I froze. From my schooldays I'd felt every word I read or wrote wasting my muscles, dulling my senses, scrambling my co-ordination – except perhaps for sex: my wife opined that only intellectuals know how to fuck.

I met My Friend on our first day at grammar school. We were the only two who reacted aggressively, moving towards each other through the white, frightened faces. My hip-throw riposted his corkscrew punch. Friends. There was something strangely familiar about the stumpy gait, the slab face with letterbox mouth and flat exiguous ears and nose, the straight or curling clumps of tow-coloured hair. We had much in common. When the boys sounded out each other's loyalties – Beatles or Stones? United or City? – we went for Elvis – dethroned, in semi-retirement – and Park Avenue – forever at the bottom of the league. And we both hated TV, preferring the radio because the pictures were better, and loved Marvel Comics, though his favourite was The Thing, while mine was Dr Strange. We had similar scars on our foreheads, were both on council scholarships and lived near each other, in the inglorious debatable lands beyond suburbia, on the fringes of the moors.

Although in the same form, subject streaming meant that

the only lesson we shared was Divinity, once a week: also allotted different lunch sittings, we hardly ever saw each other. It soon became apparent that his brute sporting potential had been noted: looking and sounding the way he did he'd had no chance. Teachers marked his work down, while opponents threw themselves under his trampling feet or ducked into his bouncers. I was classified as academic (Type 2: Arts) and slid from B to C to D team sheets. Occasionally I'd see him at break, marching by in army cadet uniform, either out of step or the only one in, while I sat on the wall puzzling over Ginsberg or Kerouac. His face was a mask of acne, crusting and cracking like an over-baked scone. Everyone laughed, but only behind his back, while I was joshingly embraced: nick-named Professor, I had to remember to be absent-minded. I felt that there was some malevolent power — not the teachers, not even the headmaster — making everything happen. I pictured it: brown and leathery, half-cockroach, half-school satchel, lathered in sweat or spittle, dragging itself along the nocturnal classrooms and corridors, imposing by laid enchantments our scenario for the next day.

Now, parking, he ran the car's nearside wheels into the ditch, leaving it looking stolen, used and dumped. Ignoring the stile as always, we vaulted the five-barred gate. Unseen from the road — through a curtain of aphids, past a rotting sheep carcass, beyond the sphagnum bogs and cotton-grass — was terra incognita. The forgotten south-west corner of Ilkley Moor, an expanse of thick purple heather, pathless except for the traces of our regular visits: in five months we hadn't seen another soul. After ten minutes we entered the kingdom of the birds: hearing the peewit's cry, like soaped hair rubbed, the plover's resigned one-note whistle, the skylark's scrabbling cadenza, the gabble of the red-polled grouse. The silent crows flocked with heavy emphasis from rock to rock. I realized that we were marching in step and that I'd begun to perceptibly ape his walk, like pushing through a succession of turnstiles.

It was here, the mid-point between our homes in Eldwick and Hawksworth, that we used to meet on Sundays, to sidefoot a dented football to and fro. We never talked about school — communicating mainly in the catchphrases of the various comic foreigners and sexual deviants from the radio show, 'Round The Horne', and the clipped, pained dialogue of its interminable 'Brief Encounter' parody. 'I know' ... 'I know you know' ... 'I know you know I know' ... 'I know you know I know you know' ... 'Yes, I know'. Oblivious to the flora and fauna, we watched the progress of our divergent metamorphoses, as if we were the mirrors in which we could still glimpse ourselves as we really were.

At sixteen he took his anger and acne off to the army. I left two years later for the first of a busted flush of universities. On my Christmas visits to my parents I'd hear news or rumours: his three tours of Ulster, his dishonourable discharge, his mercenary wanderings followed by monstrous if shadowy criminality. I had no doppelgänger dreams or Corsican Brothers flashes, just the feeling that he could have been here and I could have been there. When I finally returned to the area, having got tenure at Leeds, I discovered that he was 'away at the moor' — not Ilkley but Broadmoor.

I met him again when I sprawled my bike and myself across the icy cobbles of Haworth Main Street. He burst out of The

Fleece and lifted me up, straightened my handlebars and drew me inside. How had he known me, chubby and balding after these fifteen years? He hadn't changed at all, apart from the acne — a gargantuan toddler, dented and striated. The fingers of his right hand were bandaged together in a complex cat's cradle. There was a second pint of Ram Tam by the fire, as if I'd been expected.

He seemed to know everything that our contemporaries — whose names mostly meant nothing to me now — were doing, while giving the impression that he wasn't particularly interested. He'd even heard about my upcoming book on the French sentimentalists. When I asked what he was up to he just smiled: 'This and that, here and there, now and then.'

We'd thrown the bike in the back of his van and gunned over to the moor. As he led me across the frozen ground I discovered something new, his love of nature: 'I get up here as often as I can. Watch the birds come and go, the heather change colour. Whatever it's doing in the valley it never seems to rain on the tops'. Every time we followed this same four-mile circuit, always ending up in The Midland in Bingley, which had 'Suspicious Minds' on its jukebox.

He wouldn't let on where he was living but finally, reluctantly, gave me a Keighley telephone number: 'You might be able to leave a message for me there.' In fact, the few times I used it he himself answered on the second ring. One night I saw him on Leeds Headrow with two floridly-dressed Asians: he didn't speak, just looked straight through me. Whatever he did, I suspected that it wouldn't have been any more interesting than our funding crises, inter-departmental feuds, sexual harassment tribunals.

We crossed the marshy bowl under the fell-head, breeding place for a dozen pairs of curlews. I'd never registered these birds before, how beautiful and ridiculous they were: the long beak, combining épée and sabre, depending from a tiny head, all eyes; the colour gradations from gold to brown to white; their glorious landing glide, ending in a desperate sprawl, before, refolding themselves, they moved off in a waddling hop. The approximations of the composers – Warlock, Britten or Messiaen – hadn't prepared me for the sad sweetness of their cry, heard only in summer but the bleak essence of winter. At first they'd mimed broken wings, trying to decoy us away from their nests, but when they got used to us they'd meet us at the frontier of their territory and escort us through like a guard of honour, flying low over our heads. Their cries developed an increasingly interrogative note: were we looking for something? Could they help? When, eco-wardening, we pulled up by the roots a patch of leprous bracken that had started to choke the ling, they swooped around, whistling in encouragement or derision. And, later, after their unusually agitated flocking had led us to the rescue of a sheep tangled up in old fence wire, they landed nearby to watch us wrestling with it, rolling their bright satirical eyes, close enough for us to smell them – awful, a compound of rot and brown sauce. In time they displayed their fledgelings, moving around in synchronized peeping trios like Tamla Motown groups. Wary of anthropomorphism, I resisted My Friend's attempts to give them names.

But for the last week the curlews had no longer greeted us. They'd flocked and gone to the primal ooze of the West Coast mudflats.

'I miss them,' said My Friend. 'They'll be in Blackpool now,

tucking into their candyfloss and lugworms ... Are there any
poems about them?'

'About curlews?'

'Like there are for skylarks, nightingales and them?'

There weren't many. Fragments from Kinsella and Hughes.
MacCaig's pawky whimbrel. I remembered, from a school
anthology, the misprinted opening line of Gray's 'Elegy': 'The
curlew tolls the knell of parting day'. There was always Yeats,
of course: curlews galore, in Purgatory, at the Hawk's Well,
on Bailie's Strand. Haltingly, I recited 'He Reproves The Curlew' and 'Paudeen':

> '... on the lonely height where all are in God's eye,
> There cannot be, confusion of our sound forgot,
> A single soul that lacks a sweet crystalline cry.'

The words sounded weak, forcing my voice higher and
higher, to end in a squeak. He shrugged and made a wanking
motion: 'It's just all about himself.'

'I know.'

'I know you know.'

'I know you know I know.'

'I know you know I know you know.'

'Yes ... I know.'

I'd come to the conclusion that art plunders nature, never
reveals it. Indeed, it can even ruin it for you: I couldn't see a
hovering kestrel without thinking of Auden, so described in
Day Lewis' *The Magnetic Mountain*, having a last lofty elegiac scan
of war-torn Europe before winging it to the safety of New
York.

Each Sunday we acted as each other's press agencies. I genned him up on the brouhahas around Norman Lamont's sacking and *American Psycho*. He took out the *Sport*, with its masthead announcing, 'TODAY'S NIPPLE COUNT: 97!!' Among the drumlin fields of flesh there was usually a bizarre Elvis-related story: this time it was a cowpat which had miraculously reproduced – complete with sneer – the features of The King.

By the time we reached the trig point the wind had died. We watched the sun set: I always hoped the red disk would bounce back up off the horizon like a rubber ball, but it slid implacably out of sight. The sky was like a dab of jam being stirred into a bowl of sago by an invisible spoon.

As usual My Hard Friend produced a short dagger with an SS insignia on its hilt: his uncle, the area's last blacksmith, claimed to have hooked it out of a brewed-up tank in the Ardennes. Ripping it from the sheath, he flourished it self-consciously to north, south, east and west. I'd felt a bit queasy about this until he'd suggested that I bring along an icon I'd bought in Moscow – a badly warping copy of a Novgorod St Demetrius – and I realized that it had nothing to do with fascism or occultism. It just struck him as an appropriately charged combination of place, object and gesture.

'Do you remember Elliott?' he asked.

T. S.? George? Ebeneezer? Sir Walter in *Persuasion*?

'*Mr* Elliott. Took us for Div. Tall bastard with a shiny head.'

I sort of grunted, with a slight interrogative note. I wasn't sure which was the more unhealthy – my remembering nothing or his remembering everything: both were as bad, probably.

'Do you remember Manning at all? From that Divinity class?'

With some effort I could just recall Hurst, who threw a flour-bomb at the headmaster; the faces, though not the names, of a couple of teachers I hadn't hated; later, Garnett and Lievesley, who were stoned all the time; the multi-coloured chalk-dust that hung everywhere, suspended in the air; the weird acoustics, by which you'd hear voices whispering in corners where nobody was. And one good memory: sitting in the library, cutting the pages of first editions of Carlyle, Ruskin and Morris with a steel ruler – I knew they'd be good because no one in that benighted place had ever read them.

I broke off. He was looking past me, eyes narrowing as his mouth gaped. He pointed: shifting black flecks were outlined against the sun's exploding blues and greens. In a few seconds there was no doubt: fast-flying shapes – crows? bats? – closing. Then they were on us: a tight, improbably precise formation of curlews. It wasn't a passing flock, these were unmistakably our friends, mysteriously returning. There was the one with the enormous toucan-like beak, the one with the drooping wing, the dove-grey pair, the one that looked to have been ringed. Had they come back for stragglers? Or on some other unfinished business? Rhynchokinetic beaks curved into smiles, they wheeled around us with piping, antiphonal cries of welcome – sounds I hadn't heard from them before, as if they'd incorporated Warlock's cor anglais and Britten's flutes: nature imitating art imitating nature. I raised my hands above my head and felt or imagined feathers brushing my finger-ends.

My Friend stood soldier-straight, hands pointing down the seams of his jeans. His face clenched like a fist, eyes disappearing into their sockets. His breathing was normal, his shoulders didn't shake, his chest didn't heave: he just tilted his head back slightly so that his tears, conduited by the deep furrows at the sides of his mouth, rolled off his chin on to the rocks below. He stumbled aside, as if to flee, but they followed him, the ring tightening and descending, until they were circling him at head height, so that the blur of movement, like a propeller, almost obscured his face. The sound was deafening, strangely metallic, electric: I wondered if they were about to go into an Elvis medley. Then they peeled off and silently headed back the way they'd come, into the curdling sunset.

We didn't speak. We walked back in a silence I didn't care to break. I let him get twenty yards ahead of me. The darkness came down fast, as if it was blossoming out of the air. The birds were silent now: only the straying lambs and ewes called to each other in mock desperation. It struck me that the Pathetic Fallacy was, in fact, the only truth we know. Something white, fluffy and lethal hissed past and I recalled Hegel's 'the owl of Minerva flies only at dusk': knowledge is gained too late to make any difference.

When we reached the road I landed clumsily from the gate and he turned in the gloom and sprang at me. One hand caught my wrist, as if testing for a pulse, the other grasped my throat. His fingers seemed to wrap themselves round and round like tentacles, before beginning to agitate my Adam's apple, like a key in a rusty lock. His eyes, perfectly dry and clear now but with pupils heavily dilated, looked into mine: 'Don't ever tell anyone about this. Anyone at all. If you do I'll kill you.' He half-frog marched, half-oxtered me back to the car. He drove straight past the pub and turfed me out a full two miles from home.

What was he so afraid of? Who did he think I might tell?

I never saw him again after that night. His phone was always engaged: the operator told me that there wasn't a fault, nor was it off the hook — the line was in use. At last, after what had presumably been a month-long conversation, it blared as number unobtainable.

Through the long winter there was no escaping my doomed novel: about the foundation of the Independent Labour Party in Bradford — not so much *Fame Is The Spur* rewritten by Celine as *Mort à Crédit* rewritten by Howard Spring. One night I heard the familiar scream of brakes and a horn's impatient blare. I went to the window and lifted the blinds but no one was there. My wife smiled, without looking up from her book.

Then my mother rang and read me a report from the *Telegraph and Argus*: 'LOCAL MAN KILLED BY TRAIN'. They'd got his age wrong, but correctly identified him as a former grammar school boy. Suicide, by implication: it had happened at Kingham, a little station near Oxford, as the London express came through. What was he doing down there?

My wife cried off the funeral: I think she was worried about running into an old boyfriend there — God. St Mary's was packed. A phalanx of hard-faced men in cashmere mix overcoats — coppers and old oppos — sat at the back. In the middle ranks were a trio of rouged, ash-blonde heavily-décolleté women glowering at each other and glum middle-aged men with black ties — from his former regiment, I assumed. The rest of the church was filled by the hosts of his family, all with the same square heads on wide shoulders and his characteristic way of crying: The organist improvised on Elvis' 'Crying In The Chapel' in the style of Messiaen, with epiphanic crashings and massy chords.

I sat next to a grey-haired woman dressed in a torn slip and rubber boots: no one seemed to consider this at all exceptionable – I wondered if I was imagining her. I finished up pushed behind one of the potted-meat pillars, with a cold radiator digging into my ribs, under a murky painting, in which Christ and Simon seemed to be wrangling over the cross. 'Never have I seen such a wide variety of people at a funeral,' said the priest, '. . . only a special spirit could unite such disparate souls in a common affection . . .' I remembered that My Friend and I had promised each other a sky burial on the moor – the body to be burnt with petrol, then picked clean by the birds. I wondered if I should ask his family for the ashes but decided that they'd have other plans.

At the end of the service the surge of mourners bore me outside, straight across six lanes of frantic traffic, into the pub opposite and up the stairs to the wake. Already established were the two freeloaders who'd nearly wrecked my dad's funeral: one kissing everyone and telling ridiculous tales of himself and the dear departed, the other hiding under a table and periodically groping up for more food or bottle. My Friend's youngest sister – a once angelic child who now looked disturbingly like my mother – reeled up to me and whispered that the body – head crushed, identified by the wallet – hadn't been his, that he'd needed to disappear for a while. I knew, though I didn't tell her, that the police would have checked the fingerprints: it's hard to accept that some people are dead, like Elvis.

One by one the solitary men I'd taken for ex-soldiers came over and greeted me by name, identifying themselves by surname and initials. Old school chums, totally forgotten: Barrett, P. S; Lamonde, G; Stone, L. A. Q; Manning, P. R.

They stood in tongue-tied silence for a while before, after a
handshake, floating disconsolately away. Manning was tall and
grey, with a soft voice: after My Friend's last reference I had
to stop myself asking him, 'What — if anything — is your
significance?'

It was so depressing that I finally went back downstairs and
sat in the snug: the wooden panelling and the stained glass
were better than the church's. I sipped my Guinness and tried
in vain to locate and identify any emotion — grief, relief or
even indifference. Then I heard a clattering sound: Manning
was coming down the stairs. It took him a long time, as he
was badly lame in his left leg. He clung, sweating, to both
bannisters. His shoes, I noticed, were highly polished, horrible
but expensive brogues, pitted with whorls and chevrons. I heard
him pass through the pub, then down the street: it was some
time before he was out of earshot. I got another pint: everything
had come flooding back. I didn't want to, but I remembered
Manning, I remembered Mr Elliott.

It was the shoes that had done it. Before we started at school
we were told to buy a second pair of shoes to be kept in the
cloakroom and changed into, to keep dirt and wet off the
parquet floors. I remember my parents' indignation, and our
long search for the cheapest shoes in Leeds. My dad seriously
contemplated nicking a pair but the shops only had singles on
display — and those all lefts.

On the fourth day, My Friend and I met up again at our
shared Divinity lesson. We chose a double desk at the back
but fell silent as the master entered. Mr Elliott was impossibly
tall and seemingly loosely hinged at the waist, glaucous-eyed,
with a gleaming, faceted bald head like a pig-pink diamond.

Weak on theology, he coached the First XV and gave more detentions than anyone else. His first words were to ask a small, pale boy at the front – Manning – why he wasn't wearing indoor shoes. I don't know how he knew they weren't: they looked perfectly clean – he must have had a photographic memory for feet. Manning stuttered that he'd left them at home. My Friend and I looked at each other: we knew that his parents had done what ours so nearly did – jibbed at the cost, said 'no one will notice if you just pretend to change them', given him a rag with which to wipe them off. Although Elliott merely said, 'I shall expect to see them next week', something told me that he knew this too.

Next Thursday he called Manning forward, then looked down at his feet and smiled – wider and wider, as if his face was splitting in two. Manning was wearing gym shoes. I could hear his mother saying, 'Use *them*. They cost enough for an hour's use a week'.

'What are those?'

'My indoor shoes, sir.'

'But surely these are not shoes? . . . Shoes are leather, perhaps even suede or, at a pinch, plastic . . . but these would appear to be . . . canvas. And surely shoes are black . . . or brown . . . but these are . . . what colour would you say, Manning?'

'White, sir.'

'A trifle grubby perhaps but yes, white . . . and canvas. White canvas. Almost like . . . gym pumps. Where are your gym pumps, Manning?'

'At home, sir.'

'On your *feet*, sir. I suppose we should be grateful that

you're not wearing your rugby boots. Or ice-skates. Or crampons.'

The class bayed with laughter, which redoubled when Manning, sent back to his seat, burst into tears and Elliott made one last observation: 'People shouldn't send their children here if they can't afford to dress them properly.' My Friend and I looked at each other, stone-faced. Elliott chalked a map of the Holy Land on the board and we copied it: Damascus, Bethlehem, Tyre and Sidon . . .

That lunchtime My Friend and I went into the cloakroom and unloaded all the shoe-bags in a corner, selected a pair at random and presented them to Manning. No one said anything about it. Manning just wore the shoes – with some difficulty, as they were a full size too large . . . The only other thing I could remember about him was at the next Divinity lesson when, as he entered, Elliott threw a rugby ball towards him and, when he caught it, shouted, 'Bravo, Manning! There's the boy for the line-outs!'

What should we have done? Risen in a body – twenty-eight twelve year olds – and, swarming, beaten Elliott to a pulp? Perhaps My Hard Friend had spent the rest of his life hopelessly trying to do just that? I abandoned my novel and, to my wife's bafflement, started to write about Manning, how his life might have been before and after the indoor shoes, and what that week of waiting was like . . .

In spring I pedalled out to the moor again. No birds sang. Our path was now bafflingly wide, deep and rutted, with little yellow plastic arrows staked into the ground every ten yards and, next to the ginnel of the dry stone wall, a laminated sign, TYKES' BIG EASTER FUN WALK. There was no sun, just a weak phosphorescence that was suddenly cut off as if by a thrown switch. It began to rain. Then one large, draggled curlew flew past, calling, calling, a peremptory whistle like the crack of a whip, and I knew that My Hard Friend was indeed dead. And that I was now able to tell you about it.

Mr Personality in the Fields of Poses

Immediately inside the gallery the woman who was beginning to think of herself as The Wife of The Tooting Mapplethorpe was confronted by a wall of photographs of herself – or rather, parts of herself: the planes and folds of her own body, greased and shadowed ... mercifully unrecognizable, even as flesh. Beyond were more walls of other bodies: men – their scars, tattoos, scars of removed tattoos.

Adam's newest stuff was upstairs: shots of public monuments, dirty and mutilated. Chads peering over the Warkton Roubiliacs: a toilet seat draped round John Lennon's neck: Dublin's Molly Malone sprayed scarlet; forgotten municipal worthies furiously chipped and squittered; Our Lady with lipstick, monocle and moustache ... This touring exhibition would swell Adam's growing reputation, if only through imminent prosecutions for criminal damage and desecration.

Much of the show was a mess. The videos flared and buzzed and light glaring through the transoms had converted the Physical Energy sequence into a line of mirrors. Two of the Fisted Rosebuds were upside down but Adam had just smiled and rehung them himself. The catalogue was full of misprints: Barth for Barthes, What's? for Watts, 'never trust the artist trust the table', and his beloved team renamed Wet Ham Unted . . . He welcomed these as improvements, Zeitgeist edits. And he even decided to keep a shot left over from the preceding show, of The Guarantee Photo Studios in twenties Harlem: a Baptist congregation in their best furs and high-dicers under a Jacob's Ladder of zig-zagging tenement fire escapes.

Adam had changed. With his fire and tinder nature, she'd never thought he could give up his lifelong hobby of violence, in hot blood or cold: but he'd never lacked willpower, only taking up junk, she suspected, to show the world he could kick it. After thirty he'd felt the thrill of conflict fade, watching as his old oppos went strangely stiff, mutating from skinheads to slapheads, their clenched diaphragms holding back avalanches of flab, their dulling eyes dreaming of pipes and slippers. And there were too many undercover cops nowadays, too many Prince Hals, too many Arthur Cravan wannabes, too many people like himself; she'd expected ulcers, weight loss or gain, even coronaries, but he thrived. Smirking, he thanked her for redeeming him but she was disappointed that redemption had taken this particular form. Art Vandal! Couldn't he do something more constructive? With another smirk he'd offered to go to Russia and reinstall those overthrown statues of poor old Vladimir Ilyich and Uncle Joe.

After Adam had vouchsafed an interview to nervous local reporters – announcing a plan to sail up the Nile and take on the old gods themselves – they went for lunch. In the sunshine, children were tumbling down the steep grassy motte of a gleaming white tower, where in the twelfth century York had massacred its Jews. She had been at college here and was now somehow surprised, returning after ten years, to find everything still in place. She led Adam along the walls, down to the river, then past dear old Whip-ma-whop-ma-gate and up The Shambles where he bought a lovat wool tie, Belloc's *Collected Poems* and an armful of CDs. The English madrigalists: when they'd met all he'd listened to was The Ruts and Crass.

The city felt strange: one moment artificial, like a Potemkin Village, the next somehow too real, as if she was recreating it out of her own memory. For an instant a grey mist seemed to hang in front of her eyes before the golden waterfall of the Minster's west front blotted it out. In her last year, living alone in Marygate, she'd come here almost every day. It was the only place where men didn't try to pick her up. She'd sat for hours tracing patterns in the Five Sisters' dense grisaille. There was always something new, or rather something she hadn't noticed before: it had taken months for Lord Burlington's silver- and grey-lozenged floor to register. They walked down the nave: beyond their voices she could hear the sussurating echoes that always made her imagine benevolent snakes or lizards. To Adam's discomfort, she told the story of St Cuthbert, rattled through the kings of England on the pulpitum and, with a conjuror's flourish, revealed various carved misericords. In the gloomy choir aisle, poor Nick Wanton's shocked, choleric statue – the iconoclasts' one victim before General Fairfax pulled them off – stretched out its handless arms. 'What have you done?' she asked Adam. 'They were there a minute ago.'

'Bastard' – Adam whispered in the alabaster ear of Archbishop Sterne – 'Wasn't living and dying enough for you?' The dreamy, reclining figure, eyes fixed on eternity, made no reply, but the mouth above the drooling chin-beard seemed to blow a kiss. His crozier was clipped to the plaster behind, like Exhibit A, and his two attendant baggy-arsed putti were recoiling, indignant and weeping. One had lost a wing – a symbol perhaps best left unanalysed. An Episcopal boot slid from under the robes, ready to slyly foot the little sneak. He was Laurence's granddad, after all. Adam just didn't get camp, didn't get religion.

Leaving him to gloat over a flaying of St Barnabas she slipped into The Chapter House. She didn't want him ruining one of her favourite things in the world, a six-inch capital frieze of seven animals concealed among oak-leaves, including a she-bear suckling its cubs and a snub-nosed rabbit in pursuit of an acorn. She ran her finger down the tanged spine of the tiny boar half hidden round the back of the pillar. Red and yellow sparks flickered like insects over the empty niches which had once held silver statues of the Apostles. Stretching, she examined the small carved figures that decorated the Chapter Seats' canopy. She remembered counting them once: 237. Old friends: the man asleep on a prancing ram's back, the two lions french-kissing, the four-faced queen, the sabre-toothed pig riding on a king's head like a Vespa, the fearless flying lovers, the eagle feeding on a woman's face. And, among the belching, danger-tongued demons, were the masons' self-portraits: the one laughing like Kenneth Williams, the ardent one with the strong, nervous hands, and the falling apprentice, casually held and saved by his bearded master, attention still fixed on the next gleaming block of Purbeck marble.

There was one figure she didn't remember: a small, expressionless head, sex indeterminate, eyes shut, mouth a letterbox slit. Its blank presence, in the middle of an unusually undecorated expanse, disturbed her: perhaps it had been rubbed down for recarving and then forgotten. A group of tourists entered, led by their guide's raised, duck-handled umbrella. 'The highest unsupported vault in Europe': the hydraulics of fifty necks creaked to log the central boss' lamb and cross, then out they went, like swept leaves. Thirty seconds for the House of Houses. 'Look,' said Adam, putting one foot on a stone's worn scoop, 'the irresistible force of fat priests' arses.'

'If you ever do any of your stuff on this,' she said, 'I'll kill you.'

Adam left her outside the tea-rooms, after she'd directed him to the statue of Etty. 'The Yorkshire Rubens'. He was carrying pots of green and silver paint in case its birdlime needed touching up. Perhaps one day the statues would come for him, like Don Giovanni.

On entering, the aroma of fruit and spices hit her, and that unique tea-room sound of discreet mastications, genteel gossip and rattling teaspoons combining in a firestorm roar. The deco glass, silver cake stands and propeller-sized ceiling fans swam momentarily as nostalgia filmed her eyes. It was crowded, as always, but a prime window table had just cleared and, blindsiding two disorientated Japs, she bagged it. All eyes were on her. Most of the customers were old ladies, dressed predominantly in tartan, like Bill Haley's Comets. All their mouths were moving, shredding her. She pulled her skirt down, then, defiantly crossing her legs, let it ride up again. The plate glass windows were interspersed with mirrored panels, confusing the flows of room and street: people seemingly on collision course would vanish and then safely reappear further on. A restful soughing of silk stockings announced the waitress and she heard her own voice give the old familiar order: 'Tippy assam, fat rascal and a pot of strawberry jam.'

A chubby man got up from a table to her right and, carrying teapot and cup, moved towards her. Dressed in a collarless silk shirt with a shimmery grey suit, trousers tucked into scuffed brown cowboy boots, he looked vaguely familiar. He slammed the teapot on the table and, flicking up his jacket's long tails, plumped down opposite her, panting as if the journey had exhausted him. Glaring up at the ceiling, he made a vague circling gesture with his left hand and spoke:

'Has anyone ever told you that your ear lobes are like clits?'

'Pardon?'

His red-rimmed eyes worked their way around her face.

'Clitorises. You know, love buttons. You've got one between your legs, or should have.'

'Do I know you?'

'You asked for me,' he said.

'No I didn't.'

'I heard you. You ordered a fat rascal.'

Was he some old college boyfriend gone to seed? He wasn't really fat, just sort of inflated-looking.

'Look, do you know me?'

'Perhaps you've seen me on your television. My name is Søren Kierkegaard, but they call me Mr P, Mr Personality ... because I missed a personality.'

She was confused. His voice kept changing, like Peter Sellers' Quilty at the beginning of *Lolita* before James Mason shoots

him. Starting out as a fruity buffer Mr P had veered into
cracker American and finished up mitteleuropean.

'Cigarette?' he asked her, as Humphrey Bogart.

'This is a no-smoking table.'

'True.' He tossed a tipped Gitane high in the air and caught
it in his teeth, then chewed and swallowed it, crossed his eyes,
threw back his head and loudly impersonated the cry of a
peacock. The old ladies broke into polite applause.

Now she placed him: he was one of those 'alternative' comedians who'd risen to fame by slagging off a comedy establish-
ment from which they rapidly became indistinguishable.
Channel-hopping recently, they'd come upon him doing a one-
man show before an audience of minor celebrities – weather-
men, TV chefs, ex-Page Three girls. The more he insulted
them the louder they laughed. He had tremendous energy, but
then so did Norman Wisdom and Hitler. Adam, she
remembered, had fantasized about ripping that centre-parted
moustache right off, with his top lip along with it.

A waitress brought over her rascal – a large, well-baked
scone, its golem face studded with cherry eyes and jagged
almond teeth – and another brought Mr P more tea. Then
they hovered, giggling and blushing.

'Would you like my autograph?' he asked them. They
nodded. He flourished a cake fork: 'Bend over, then!' They
fled, squealing in mock terror. In a single movement Mr P
poured and drank the boiling liquid, without milk or lemon,
talking the while in a bubbling voice, his eyes locked on hers.
His pupils were pinpricks: Could you have a tea high? As Adam
said, if you take enough of anything you'll get off on it.

'Scottish, aren't you? You take the high road and I'll take

the dirt road. I've got this nice St Andrew's cross in my play-room. I'm going to strap you to it and tickle your little buns with a tartan tawse. Och aye the noo!'

She looked round for hidden cameras. Maybe Adam had hired him from a lookalike agency, although it wasn't, as far as she could remember, any kind of anniversary. A quartet of maiden aunts at the next table had turned their chairs to watch, smiling and nodding. Even if he was to whip it out and roger her right there they'd just smile and nod, nod and smile. It was only that funny man off the box. Should she leave or complain? Or maybe grind the rascal in his face?

'That's very interesting. Suppose I was to call the police?'

'I *am* the police. Look' – with difficulty he fished a bulging wallet out of his back pocket – 'I've got a warrant card. Honor-ary pig, like Elvis. I'm on the Police Heroes Committee, putting up statues of swatted bluebottles.'

Those would be just Adam's style, she thought, and so would Mr Personality himself. She'd always hated violence but in this case, she had to admit, violence was the only thing that would do. It was like when firefighters set alight a second area of forest to burn out a smaller but out-of-control blaze: poetic justice, a good hoisting with a bigger, nastier petard. She had to keep Mr P there until Adam arrived: she remembered what he had done to the workmen who'd mooned at her, to the kids throwing snow-rolled stones at them on The Heath. Mr P rattled obscenely on, Margaret Thatcher segueing into . . . Ian Paisley, was it? She smiled sweetly, which seemed only to inflame him further.

Adam was the only man she'd ever met who didn't seem to hate or fear women: maybe he got it out of his system by

beating the living daylights out of perfect strangers? She sometimes wondered if it was her own perspective that was skewed.
Was it possible that Mr P thought he was being friendly,
mildly flirtatious? Was the surprising suggestion that she pull
a pony-cart harnessed to her nipples his equivalent to 'thou art
more lovely and more temperate'? After her initial shock she
was beginning to find his tirade oddly relaxing: perhaps tapes
of sexual threat could be played to relieve tension at East
London derbies or in airport departure lounges? She'd always
found sex a subject of limited interest: how disappointed she'd
been when, shy virgin, she'd discovered there were only half-a-
dozen or so things you could do. There was a wasp-like buzzing:
Mr P had placed a large, flesh-coloured, absurdly noduled
vibrator on the table.

She didn't like the rascal's dry, sour taste, but then she never
had. She went for things because the names appealed to her:
smoking Camels, drinking Campari, wearing Aquascutum, reading Montherlant, listening to Hindemith, eating fat rascals. The
sight of her tongue fetching the last crumbs from the corners
of her mouth made Mr P halt and stutter: 'B-b-b-bad doggie.
They should have given you a bowl on the floor.'

She felt a sudden disturbance in the air . . . then Adam was
there, pale as death, with the blue scar running along his
stubbled hairline, cameras swinging, fifteen stone of sharp-edged
bone, six-four in clogs and ankle-length duster. Other people
struggled with the heavy revolving doors but he'd just smashed
through, leaving them a spinning blur of desperately recombining atoms. His burning eyes swept the room in challenge. Enter
the Monarch of the Glen – all that was missing were the antlers
and roar. He gave her an almost imperceptible nod and began,

with incongruous grace, to manoeuvre between the tables. An awful silence fell but Mr Personality, oblivious, was embarking on a new theme.

'Do you like snooker? I'm going to lay you out on my table but I don't know whether to start with the red or the brown.'

It was like a cartoon: Tom looms over Jerry while Butch the Bulldog tiptoes up with a mallet.

'One thing. I think I might be needing,' he slavered noisily 'the cue extension!'

'Hello darling,' she said, 'I've just had half an hour of this.'

Mr P swung round, then froze. Adam carefully placed one hand flat on the table next to the vibrator. His expression was refined, abstracted, as if he was considering some grave theological point. Slowly, like a tortoise, Mr P's neck retracted: he plunged his face into his empty cup as if he thought he could hide inside it. The next instant, she anticipated, the teapot's spout, like a rhinoceros horn, would be ripping open his nose, before he was force-fed, one by one, the complete works of the English madrigalists.

Then something happened to Adam's face. His mouth spread into an unfamiliar wavering smile, emitting a funny little tee-hee-hee snicker; his shoulders sagged, then fast-shrugged in a parodic cringe; his body seemed to recede inside his clothes: he muttered something – was it 'Excuse us'? Then the huge hand reached across, plucked her from her seat and carried her away, pausing only to slam a tenner on the cash desk, not even waiting for change. She looked back as she was borne through the door but Mr Personality had disappeared: the only expla-nation appeared to be that he'd dived under the table.

Adam silently dragged her for a hundred yards, then ducked

into a shop doorway. Leaning his head against her neck he let his breath out in a great explosion, nearly deafening her.

'Thank God,' he said. 'He does Comic Relief. He was at the Royal Wedding. They do what they like, these people. You can't touch them. Thank God I didn't hit him.'

'Thank me for redeeming you,' she said.

'Still, you can't blame him for trying it on, sad bastard. With your hair pinned up like that: Looks great.'

This was the first real compliment he'd ever paid her: it hurt worse than a blow.

He was still holding her arm, dancing them in tight little circles. Her muscles corded and spasmed, breaking his grip, sending him careening across the pavement. On Adam's face was an expression she'd never seen before. It was like that of the rubbed-down figure in The Chapter House: no expression.

It took an age for them to get through the crowds in the market square. She noticed the tourists from the minster: they weren't buying anything, just staring at the fruit and vegetables. Adam took her arm again and her skin crawled as she realized that he was clutching it with both hands, like a child. They saw that black and grey cables were snaking through the doors of the gallery: the television cameras had already arrived.

Coddock

Opposite the derelict Moravian church – blackened stone greening with moss, squat like a huge toad – was a lock-up chippy, long since boarded up: they said the owner had died in an avalanche of grease. One day it re-opened: clean, tiled, gleaming, with new steel-mounted fryers, Design Centre salt and pepper dispensers, fans whirring at three speeds on three levels. On the wall was a Brangwynish mosaic of triremes clashing at Salamis, incorporating a pinned-up Pirelli calendar and a Fulham fixture card: and, below, nose projecting out and over the marble counter like a chad's, was a tiny, ageless man, like a nut-husk sculpture of Stravinsky.

Maltese Eddie. He could cap every story: wherever you'd been, whatever you'd done, he'd been and done better. He'd heard Maggie Teyte sing Melisande, seen Parker at Minton's, climbed Ben Nevis from the Carn Mór Derg, played twenty-nine seasons on the wing in the Isthmian League, and once clean bowled Bill Edrich – admittedly drunk – in a charity match. He'd been a Café Royal chef, with some good Frank Harris tales of the Casanova-Munchausen's mass deflorations in the upstairs rooms – initiating Virginia Woolf . . . both the

Pankhursts ... Mrs Thatcher. I suggested that this last was unlikely, as she was born in 1925 and he was dead by 1930. He winked: 'Perhaps, my dear sir ... but did I specify *which* Mrs Thatcher? ... Or even which Frank Harris?' He was shy of the middle fingers of his left hand: he said that they'd frozen to the rail on the Murmansk Convoys but, another time, that they'd paid off a Yakuza debt.

His fish and chips were the finest I'd ever tasted. I watched him, moving with a dancer's unhurried speed and economy, enfolding the blue-white fish in sheets of glossy batter mix, like ectoplasm. The chips were edged and grained like wood, with a long smoky aftertaste. When your knife breached the batter – jewelled with faceted sea-salt grains, rosetted by an acidic vinegar – a short ichor flow escaped the cavity, along with a sigh like a departing soul. The boneless, flaking fish, buttering in its own heat, tasted bland at first but then seemed to move at bewildering speed through every possible gradation of savoury and sweet before establishing and holding on the palate a deep, chthonic resonance. One strange thing: as I told Eddie, the cod and haddock looked, tasted and cost exactly the same. He laughed, like Christoff doing Mephistopheles' 'Song of the Flea': 'Best of both worlds! ... Coddock!'

But no one from the blocks would use the place. It scared them: anything new always does. His fast, hard words rattled against their eardrums; the blinding lights and cleanness, like an operating theatre, made them think of death. They missed the comforting mediation of grease – the chips didn't ball into wet white fists, the fish wasn't skinned by its paper wrap. The razor-sharp chips slit their gums, crowbarred fillings; the fish retained its heat, scalding their tender insides all the way down, then lodging like a burning coal in the furthest reaches of the gut. It was as if the food was eating them.

They muttered about the seemingly endless supply of large cars in which Eddie appeared each morning, blocking the carriageway at a steady 18 mph, and about his three sons – giant, silent lizards in sheepskin. The chippy just had to be a front for something. All the locals decided to crawl miles to The Fishcotheque or switch to pizza. Only the boldest kids came in, hunting for scraps. He told them: 'They're only free if you buy something,' and – extending his gappy hand in malediction, smiling his capped smile – 'for nothing you get nothing.'

Eddie certainly put a brave face on it: in fact, he seemed to revel in disaster, as if he'd only opened up to have the pleasure of not serving people. If anyone hesitated by the door he'd move them on by leering terribly and beckoning with a crooking finger. He always sighed when I appeared – 'Here's the person from Porlock' – as if I'd just ripped some complex, irrecoverable skein of thought. He treated me with a mixture of complicity and contempt, as if I was a madman with an *idée fixe* that he was a chippy and who, he felt, it was best, on balance, to indulge. 'Can't you find someone who'll cook for you?' he grumbled.

Perhaps it really was a front. Eddie's radio pumped out static, with distorting voices fading in and out, like a police frequency. Maybe some supergrass or IRA turncoat had been resettled locally with a new name and a new face, with his one remaining identifying characteristic a crazed yen for fish and chips, so they'd set up the world's best chippy and were waiting for him to show. The three terrible sons were probably playing cards out back, tooled up ready.

One morning I saw that workmen were replacing the steel shutters, boarding up the windows. The inside had already been stripped. Maltese Eddie was never seen again, but we were regularly reminded of him when the shop alarms went off, usually in the middle of the night, loud and booming like a submarine's dive-warning. Once they sounded unbroken for twenty-four hours: I noticed that, in passing, the woman from the post office took one hand off her daughter's wheelchair to cross herself. Suppose the Devil had dropped in, offering fish for souls, but hadn't found any worth the trading — not one worth even a shovelful of scraps, or a bag of chips, let alone a coddock?

Tony Harrison

In my whole time in that block I never had much luck with my neighbours. When I arrived it was all old ladies, twitching their curtains and squawking disapprovingly: I heartily wished them all dead and then regretted it two years later when they were and the animals moved in. First there was Aubrey the crack dealer: desperate petitioners would serenade his window at all hours of the day or night. 'Aubrey! Aubrey!' – by the end of that summer the starlings had picked it up and were joining in. Then there was The Recluse, whose sole pleasure in life was to tip his dachshunds' shit on to the heads of people walking below and, next door to him, that bus driver whose stereo outgunned even mine but who apparently owned only one record, Neil Diamond's *Greatest Hits*. One night, after months of polite requests ignored – I'd offered to lend or even buy him something, *anything* else – I walked into his flat, ripped the stack off the wall and caber-tossed it through the open window ... the purest act, the best feeling of my whole life. He didn't lift a finger, didn't even blink, just moved straight out. He was succeeded by Magda's Punishment Parlour: her clients limped and tottered in but went out – after an hour of theatrical yelling – nice and spry. I liked Magda – a motherly soul who, considering me gaunt, would rustle up trays of salty, over-cooked scones – until she got religion. I couldn't stick those Sunday night prayer meetings: real cries of real pain, the sound of her tawse on The Holy Spirit's flabby backside.

It had struck me that I myself might not be considered to be a particularly desirable tenant. Whenever Jane came round one or both of us would, for various reasons, be making a lot of noise for most of the time. And then there was the music: I'd recently been going through a big piano trio phase – playing Haydn's E major over and over for long stretches. There was this jumping dance that I used to do to it: after the first couple of hours I'd levitate and The Recluse would stop banging on his ceiling.

My last next-door neighbour had been the worst yet: a feral-looking cove who only ever went out to the off-licence to restock with flagons of Merrydown cider and boxes of cheese straws. Whenever I ran into him he always pretended not to know who I was. Every time I came in I could sense the eyes behind his door's spyhole boring right into me. One night I sprang across and jammed my tongue into it, while simultaneously rattling his letter-box: I heard him fall backwards thrashing and cursing. Otherwise – except for the odd two-hour coughing fit – he was completely silent. I reckoned that he was working himself up to do something terrible. I started to walk Jane to and from her car and spent hours at my spyhole watching his spyhole across the landing – but then, a year to the day after he had appeared, he quietly moved out. The council's clean-up crew were reeling in and out of that place for weeks afterwards. 'What's it like in there?' I asked one of them. 'We should have brought the fucking exorcist,' he replied.

I thought things couldn't get any worse until I heard that Tony Harrison was moving in. He was something of a professional Northerner, of course, but it did seem strange that so celebrated a poet and dramaturge should choose to live in the third-worst inner city area in the country. 'He's had some little problems but he's a good lad at heart,' said the lettings officer but that was a matter of opinion. Those early sonnets about his Leeds childhood were everything that I wished I could have done myself but with the years he'd become increasingly bardic and pompous. I imagined him hammering on my door at all hours to share his latest blinding insights – that religious bigotry was a bad thing or that Hitler and Stalin weren't very nice men. And his wife – that Theresa Stratas – would be for ever practising her scales: her as Berg's Lulu under Boulez was one of my favourite pieces but it just didn't seem right to have her next door drowning herself out all the time. Who would be next? Ted Hughes with a glooming menagerie of savage dogs and raptors? Ginsberg with his harmonium and finger-cymbals? I'd spent my life hiding away from people like that: I knew they'd rumble me at a glance – a small-town autodidact, at once timorous and wildly aggressive, mute and inglorious but definitely no Milton.

When Tony did move in – carrying all his worldly goods in three Asda shopping bags – he proved to be a full forty years younger than his poetic namesake. Lacking any trace of Dantescan gravity, he obviously wasn't even a distant relation, although he *was* wearing a scruffy blue anorak similar to the one that the poet appeared to favour for his first nights and premieres. Tony's chief little problem was written on his face, which was all nerve and bone, seemingly tight-wrapped in dirty grey clingfilm, giving off the junky's usual dull, yellowish aura. His lips had receded to reveal the full set of teeth — remarkably tiny except for two tombstones at the front, like a cross between Bugs Bunny and Nosferatu. On the evening of his arrival he knocked at every door in the block in turn, introducing himself and borrowing one household item from each. He was casing the place: in the few seconds that it took for me to fetch him the requested chair, I felt that his sleepy glance had scanned and conned every corner, that he knew how many shirts hung in my closed wardrobe — seven — and the colour of my tooth-brush — black. He carried the chair out and stood on it to reach the landing trapdoor, disappearing through it up into the roof space — in search of possible exits and entrances, edges and angles. During that night he prised open the main electricity cupboard, jamming his own meter but setting everyone else's spinning crazily like fruit machines. Then he ripped away the automatic entry door's metal casing, enabling anyone to get in by simply putting together the bared brown and blue wires.

Tony had remarkable charm. In the months to come, when-ever I tried to take him to task about the drugs and thieving, it would rapidly become as if we weren't talking about him but someone else — a mutual acquaintance who, although he might be doomed, Tony's shrug and shake of the head implied, you couldn't help but like, could you? The nurse in the next block would never believe that he'd stripped her car because he continued to smile and greet her in the same irresistible way. Most people just accepted him, as if burglaries were like acts of God or dirty weather — to be endured until the wind changed. Tony had quickly assembled his own posse of local

Asian teenagers who spoke in parodically bad yardie slang and wore their hair in tight little dreadlocks which they'd untwist when it was time to go home to Mammy-Ji's for tea. Soon, virtually all the ground floor windows had been boarded up: The council stopped putting new glass in — it was cheaper to let Tony prise the chipboards apart every three weeks or so.

'Don't worry. We've got our eyes on him,' Dave the Community Policeman told the tenants' meeting with a wink. Maybe it consoled some of those robbed to hear that at least it was all somehow official. 'Why don't you just fit him up?' I asked but he just glared at me. Even ten years ago it used to happen all the time. We didn't complain when the coppers who'd just kicked our doors down made sure they found what they'd come to find. What else would you expect? — It wasn't a game, after all. When the police start respecting the law you're in serious trouble. I began to think that I should do something myself: Jane was all for squirting petrol through his letter box and gutting his flat. She might have been a social worker but off-duty she was as merciless as Tamburlaine. When her dad worked at the abattoir, she explained, he hadn't felt the need to come home and slaughter the family cat. Care and compassion were just a job to Jane: That was why I loved her. By the time I'd talked her out of the idea I found that I'd talked myself into it, so then she had to talk me out of it and so on . . . In the end we did nothing: as Jane said, 'He probably wouldn't notice, anyway.'

Just about everyone on the estate had at least one unwelcome visit from Tony and his friends, except for me and the wheelchair-bound old lady in the sub-basement. Her security was like Fort Knox's and if Tony ever had got through she'd have shot him with her crossbow. I knew the reason I'd been spared. His eyes had flicked dismissively over the dusty piles of LPs and books read and unread: nowt worth nicking. I wanted to tell him how wrong he was, that my copy of *The Golden Legend* would fetch at least a thousand, though not from any of the fences he'd know along the Manchester Road.

One night I discovered Tony, having lost his key, kicking down his own front door. I was amazed at the power that his puny frame could generate when necessary: I wouldn't have liked to take him on, if I'd been a door. The key turned up two days later in the map-pocket of his Berghaus waterproof, ram-raided from Allan Austin's. There was nothing in his flat except for an enormous multi-stained mattress that mysteriously came and went. Once, just before dawn, I'd heard the gang moving in a load of furniture – tables, armchairs, even a Welsh dresser and a grandfather clock – but then, after dark, they carried it all out again. Tony had even stripped the carpet underlay, prised the tiles off his kitchen wall, and ripped up the toilet and bathroom lino. Through his splintered doorframe I'd often see him sitting alone, cross-legged in the middle of nothing. If someone doesn't move or speak for long enough, I'd noticed, they begin to grow or seem to grow in presence – unless, of course, they happen to be dead. Perhaps junkies were the new ascetics – I doubted, though, that Maitreya or The Stylite ever had their central heating on so high. Tony had somehow contrived to crank up the radiators until they were too hot to touch, their paint beginning to flake and peel. The windows were fogged, their ledges running with condensation and there was always a strange smell – like metal and sugar, burning.

After a few months, Tony's creditors came looking for him. A slight disturbance in the air preceded them, like a thunderstorm: for a full minute before I laid eyes on them I knew that there was trouble around. There were two of them: not serious criminals but the kind who deal drugs or lend money to folk that they know will default so that they can batter them with impunity. They were serious about battering, I suppose. One of them was ginger and stringy — the very image of American choreographer Merce Cunningham, except that he bristled and raged like a hornet and babbled an endless stream of obscenities. But it was his mate that really worried me: Mr No Distinguishing Features. He always wore stonewashed jeans with a knife-edge crease ironed in, mirror-polished black brogues, a clean white shirt and a narrow brightly-patterned tie: I don't think Dante mentions it but that's the uniform of all the demons in Hell. They always contrived to just miss Tony: I knew when they were coming by the rotivator noises of their beat-up scarlet Cadillac — presumably they'd decided against pink on the grounds that villains should drive inconspicuous cars.

I felt I had to warn Tony: although he pretended unconcern, he knew who they were all right. A couple of days later I heard a tremendous banging at my door: 'Leg-up! Leg-up!' Tony was yelling. Although he gave me his usual smile and shrug he looked like a frightened child. Below I could see the red Caddy making its usual hash of parking. Kneeling, I put a hand under his left foot, took the right on my shoulder and then straightened up, thrusting him into the roof space. He was surprisingly heavy: I'm not weak but I nearly buckled under him, like Christopher under Christ. I knew that it would have saved everyone a lot of grief if I'd let them have him but I just couldn't do it. If, on some Day of Judgement, I was to encounter Hitler and Stalin running in terror before millions of vengeful ghosts I knew that I'd have no choice but to give them a leg-up too.

I think Mr N. D. F. and the Hornet must have seen a light or the white flash of Tony's face at his window. They went into his flat gang busters-style, then sprang across to beat out a complex tattoo – maybe they were Freemasons? – on my door. N. D. F. began telling me that they were Tony's uncles, sent by his worried mum – he didn't even try to make it sound convincing. The Hornet hopped from one foot to the other, as if desperate for a piss. I told them that I hadn't seen Tony for ages and that when I did I'd wring his thieving little junky's neck – I didn't try to make it convincing either. I met N. D. F.'s gaze with the full unblinking Death Stare: you tilt your head back, bug your eyes slightly and then, while talking, let them slowly cross – I'd copied it from the Belgian shepherd dogs that my auntie used to breed. It usually worked: I seldom had to bark and almost never to bite. I really had them going or at least enough to make them careful: if I was serious about anything it was bluffing. On their way out the Hornet punched the stair door's shatterproof glass: it crumbled into a pyramid of tiny granules, leaving only the wire grid, like a rabbit hutch.

When I was sure they'd gone I climbed up on a chair and called and called into the black hole. Tony didn't reply, so I went up after him. My eyes soon adjusted as I crawled along: Moonlight filtered through various fissures to reveal protruding knots of jagged metal, splintering wooden struts that didn't seem to be supporting anything, electrical cables partially submerged in rainwater – the sight didn't inspire much confidence if you happened to be living below. Although the roof was flat there felt to be a pronounced gradient. It suddenly struck me that, grown-up, I had completely forgotten the pleasures of crawling in confined spaces. I flashed back to those solitary childhood games in which I had been John Mills or Kenneth More pluckily tunnelling out of previously escape-proof stalags. I had a strange sense of being watched – but benevolently. There was a faint sound like pigeons cooing: I wanted to close my eyes and sleep ... but then I felt a chill wind down the back of my neck and, raising myself to my full height, I stepped through an open trap on to the roof. Tony was standing at the far end, his back to me. He was looking down, with his toes right on the edge. 'Don't do it!' – I called, only half-jokingly. He glanced over his shoulder and smiled, then waved his arms wildly, as if losing his balance. 'S'OK,' he said, 'I think I can fly.' As we crawled down again I felt as if we were tunnelling away from freedom back into durance.

That night was the first time I let Tony into my flat: he asked me if he could listen to his favourite tape – Black Grape's 'It's Great When You're Straight – Yeah!' He was in awe of Shaun Ryder but his great hero in the band was their dancer, Bez: 'He can't play nowt but if he weren't there jumping around and that in the studio they'd never be able to do a thing.' I liked the idea that Beethoven, Rembrandt and Shakespeare – although history doesn't record it – must have had the best jumping-around guys. Watching Tony eyeing my bowing book-shelves – with a little smirk that he kept having to tuck back into the corners of his mouth – I felt as if I was being weighed and found wanting in some unknown balance. It was as if I was being judged not by ignorance or illiteracy but by some different, older wisdom — by whatever it had been that had kept mankind going even before the cup and ring carvings up on the high moors. He stared long and hard at my framed photograph of Tennyson, as if he recognized him from somewhere. 'How much do you owe those two clowns?' I asked. 'Four thousand' — he shrugged — 'Three? Five?'

From then on Tony acted as if on borrowed time. He broke into places that he'd cleaned out only the night before — working in broad daylight, as if trying to get caught. He was doomed: The Mirpuri rastas shunned him now — he was reduced to running with the kids from the children's home. They were less than useless, he confided: all they wanted to do was to raid the fridges and shit on the floors. For some reason Tony had become obsessed with getting into the empty fish and chip shop: I'd watch as he and his new oppos — twelve-year-olds with the faces of old men — haplessly rattled its steel shutters, throwing themselves against their own watery reflection.

'Leg-up! Leg-up!' — I could hear him screaming even over the 1962 Karajan 'Ode to Joy' at full bore. Before the darkness had enveloped his kicking feet I could hear his nemesis clattering up the stairs. This time they didn't bother with his flat or mine. Either they'd worked it out or someone had been talking: N. D. F. went straight through that trapdoor like a shell and then, one-handed, pulled the writhing Hornet up after him. There was nothing to be done: I turned the music off. I could hear the two of them moving along above my head: it felt as if they were crawling through my brain. I looked outside: all the windows in the other blocks were dark but in most of them I could see people standing to watch this final act of The

Tony Harrison Story. It was better than the telly, unless you happened to be living in the middle of it.

Then, as if in slow motion, Tony came past my window. If not actually flying he appeared to be at least gliding. His body elongated, then his limbs spread-eagled to assume a swastika-like shape. I could have sworn that his head glanced back over a shrugging shoulder to give me a last, parting wink. I watched as he landed on the scrubby patch of grass, ducking forward into the impact and then double-rolling across the rubbish-strewn parterre ... and then he was up again, evidently unhurt, and beginning to run, head back, arms pumping high. His pursuers had begun to bellow from the roof: without losing speed, Tony gave a couple of lamb-like skips. The Hornet's scuffed brown cowboy boots came bouncing down the street after him – first the left, then the right. With a final leap and a sideways kick, Tony disappeared in the direction of Wakefield Road. I knew that he wouldn't be coming back: that he was going to keep on running, running clear out of this world.

The Hands Reveal

At midnight, as I was escorting Jane back to the car park —
after six hours of tender lovemaking alternating with violent
arguments about nothing — a dark shape slid out of the shadows.
Although the pavements were only slightly wet, it came towards
us with a splashing sound, breathing heavily, like a horse crossing a ford. I bunched my large, strong hands into small, feeble
fists, but then saw that it was only a girl — although a girl of
disquieting aspect.

'Jane, I can't get me gas to light': the voice had a slight
wobble in it, like a record playing on a crooked spindle. She
was enveloped by a fur-hooded fishtail parka that she must
have borrowed or stolen from some retro-mod Goliath. The
sleeves covered her hands: her tiny bare feet, peeping under the
hem, had settled — unconsciously I supposed — into the third
ballet position. An expanding inverted triangle of blue-grey
flesh, its apex at the navel, suggested that she was naked under-
neath it but the effect was not enticing. The neck joined the
shoulders as if the head had part-melted then solidified, like
wax. The yellowish hair was short and ragged, appearing to
have been singed to a stubble above the right temple; the eyes

were like a doll's – big, blue and goggly behind three or four pairs of false lashes.

'I've just moved in and I can't get me gas to light.'

Jane didn't answer, just opened her car door and began to struggle with the wheel lock's faulty spring.

'I can't turn it off: me flat's filling with gas.'

Jane replied in an even tone, very slowly, without looking up: 'Piss off, Pam.'

Wailing, the figure began to back away into the darkness:

'You're supposed to be my social worker.'

'Not until nine o'clock tomorrow morning I'm not,' Jane yelled after it.

'Ought I to check this out?' I asked.

'No,' said Jane, starting the car at last. 'Just don't light that joint.'

She had a moral courage or a mean-spiritedness that I just couldn't match. Her clients seemed to like her all the more for it: at least they knew where they stood with her. It was the same with me: when we were in bed she loved me – outside, well, at least I knew where I stood.

Pam's flat didn't blow up. Next morning I deduced that she must be living in the next block to mine, as I watched the dipsos, the perverts, the wannabe pimps, the Care in the Community Boys, the Christians, the bores, all beating their paths to her door. The no-hopers always get put on the ground floor. They all trooped in but none of them re-emerged. All day I entertained the fantasy that she was laying in wait for them behind the door with a chainsaw, and then stacking their limbs and torsos up to the ceiling. No such luck: at six o'clock they came spilling out with the silent, disconsolate air of a football crowd that has just seen their team get a hiding.

Client confidentiality meant nothing to Jane: she told me Pam's entire history. After her mum killed herself, she'd been left alone at twelve with her father. He hadn't sexually abused her, just kept her away from school, forcing her to scour and sterilize their house like an operating theatre and to cook him four separate dinners every evening. She had to write them out on a card and after he'd chosen one she'd throw the other three dishes away. If anything on the menus was misspelt he'd beat her terribly with a dog lead. Jane said that he seemed genuinely baffled when they came to take her away. He said he'd been educating her: 'All they teach girls at school nowadays is how to be lesbians.' He was a used-car dealer. 'How can anyone say I'm a bad parent?' he'd asked, waving a roll of twenties half as thick as his head. 'And this is nothing. This is just my small change.' When they left he'd started to foam at the mouth and was trying to eat his money. Due to a mispagination of her social enquiry reports, the children's home had Pam down wrongly as a pyromaniac: for the next few years she'd had no idea why the staff followed her everywhere, barred her from the kitchens and regularly searched her room to confiscate any matches – the other girls had to light her cigarettes. Now – Leaving Care Grant all spent, stuck in a damp flat, surrounded by the mad and the sad, she was – apart from a monthly hour of aftercare, ruthlessly timed by Jane – out on her own in the world. It didn't look as if it was going to be her oyster.

Pam was even stranger when seen in broad daylight. Her eyes, unblinking, seemed unable to move from a fixed forward stare: she had to twist, tilt, lower or raise her head to see anything. Her hands were even more disturbing, though. My dad always told me to ignore people's faces and watch their hands: 'Yes' with a closed hand means 'No', 'No' with an open hand means 'No (regretfully)' and 'Yes' with an open hand means 'Maybe'. I didn't like to think what Pam's hands might be saying: I watched them wrestling with each other like Robert Mitchum's in *Night of the Hunter* — except that they didn't have LOVE and HATE tattooed on the fingers, only strange blue dots around the wrists that testified to some ill-advised DIY. The nails were long gone, the quicks too: the finger ends were white and flaking, as if she'd started gnawing into the very bones — when she touched anything she left traces of a fine chalky powder. I never actually saw her chewing on them: it must have been the consolation of her solitary hours. Once she wore a pair of open-toed sandals: her feet were in the same state — either she was double-jointed or she'd got someone or something to bite them for her. The last two toes on either foot appeared to have fused.

'I can't stand to watch those hands,' I told Jane, which wasn't strictly true, as they held a horrible fascination for me. She flinched, as if from a blow, and tucked her own — well-bitten, orange with nicotine — behind her back, Napoleon-style.

Pam had a series of boyfriends, none of whom lasted beyond a couple of weeks. She even enjoyed a short-lived romance with Tony Harrison. Late one night I became aware — even over 'The Creation' at max ten/bass full/treble neutral — of a noise from outside: loud regular blows with a dull echo, like someone chopping down a tree. The landing light was out: all I could see through the spyhole was a swaying dark mass, like a bear. I flung the door open and my torch revealed Pam and Tony, locked in a long clinch of greeting or farewell or something in between. Pam's back was to me: the sound was her kicking each of Tony's shins in turn with the sixteen-eyeletted Doc Martens that she favoured – worn with baggy denim cut-offs and a red gingham shirtwaister. I stood transfixed: Tony wasn't even wincing. I met his eyes: he gave his trademark shrug and said, 'Eh ... they're funny, lasses, aren't they?' I wasn't about to disagree. Junkies make bad lovers, she told me later. 'They don't even feel it when you kick them.' The day after they'd broken up, Tony burgled her place, but only to get his own stuff back – she'd commandeered the blue anorak that he'd be needing for first nights and premieres.

Sometimes late at night she'd come knocking at my door.

'Is Jane here?' she'd ask, although she must have known she wasn't by the absence of the car – and that if she had been, she'd have just been told to piss off again. Sometimes I'd let her in. If she accepted a coffee or beer she'd only leave it untouched: if she took a cigarette, she'd refuse a light and I'd watch as her hands tore it to pieces – when she came to leave she'd stare in bewilderment at the heap of crumpled paper and tobacco in her lap. If I tried to start a conversation she stared at me as if I was speaking in a foreign language. One night I put on Tony's Black Grape tape but she didn't react. I asked if she ever saw him these days but she just looked blank.

'You know. Tony. You used to kick him all the time.' She smiled wanly, as if I was making some stupid joke that she didn't get. I rather envied her: I wished my own life had been either so exciting or so boring that I couldn't remember anything.

I thought she wanted me to fuck her. I weighed it up – I'd

never before fucked anyone that — if only for those few
moments — I hadn't wanted to. One evening I leaned across
and put my hands on her shoulders. She shrank back, her eyes,
moving at last, went strabismic and she petrified into a sort of
foetal position, muttering get lost get lost get lost for a full
ten minutes, like a mantra. I never tried it on again. We'd just
sit there in silence and I'd watch the hands, as bruised and
calloused as a boxer's, pursuing their perpetual contentions —
caressing or tearing, intertwining. There looked to be considerably more than ten digits involved. Once I observed that fresh
blood was appearing on her knuckles, as if something invisible
was nibbling at them. Just before she'd get up to leave the
hands would always go into a frenzied washing mime, like
Pilate or Lady Macbeth.

One day Pam just disappeared from her flat. Jane told me
that she'd stopped coming to Aftercare: no one knew where
she'd gone. I wondered if we should tell the police. 'No point,
she's been a missing person all her life,' Jane observed, with a
noticeable moistening of the eyes — but maybe that was only at
the pleasure of a nicely-turned, if rather sentimental, aphorism.

We did see her again, though, a year later. I'd videoed a
documentary on inner city problems for which Jane had been
interviewed. 'The Real Band of Gold' it was called: a true-life
follow-up to a witless TV thriller that had traded on being
'socially aware' — in that the prostitutes were shown ludicrously
'bonding' with each other in between being stalked and slashed
— from the usual gloating camera angles — by the regulation
serial killer. Jane was terribly excited, but when we sat down
to watch it soon became apparent that only her senior — Smiler,
a woman whose features were set in a permanent concerned

smirk — was shown talking out of the twenty-strong discussion. In just one tracking shot there was a glimpse of Jane's left ear. Freezeframing it, I assured her that it had been The Star, the most beautiful ear in the world. All through the car and lager ads that followed I slobbered over it, blew into it, trying to persuade her that it was a shoo-in for the oreille d'or at Montreux.

Then in the second half of the programme, the scene switched to a pale waif sobbing in a filthy basement. Sitting next to her on the ripped mattress was Pam — silently giving a survivor's tacit support, having presumably by now seen everything several hundred times. Unblinkingly she was staring down someone or something out of shot stage left. The cameraman was obviously getting excited by her impassivity: that silence was much more expressive than her friend's torrent of words. Pam's great tragic profile slid into the frame like an iceberg, then the camera moved inexorably down to her lap, to the hands which, on cue, began to writhe. Either I stopped listening to the voice or the sound cut out: for what seemed an eternity the hands filled the screen ... the hands, locking, breaking apart and then coming together again in a remorseless dialectic ... the hands, like nameless sea creatures fighting or mating in some bottomless oceanic trench ... Yes, the hands — Jane and I had to admit — made for great television.

The Kingfishers ... The Distances

> ... Hunting stones in the wrong places:
> Not epsilon on the omphalos
> But mere egg-box cups and rings ...

Inspiration! As usual when I'd hit the summit ridge the lines
had begun to come.

> ... In the valley the jungle
> Leaps inwards to create
> Keighley, twinned with Macchu Picchu ...

They were coming all right but whether they were any good I
had no way of knowing: as always, it felt like the whole universe
was dictating them.

> '... "La lumière de l'aurore est devant nous":
> The draggled curlew has a halcyon hue ...'

As the lines came my right leg went – disappearing thigh-deep
into a sphagnum bog. It held fast, as if it had found the home

for which it had been searching the earth these thirty years —
the Great Mother's green womb? – but I didn't feel like Antaeus
as I dragged it back out, just ridiculous. Why was I always the
most embarrassed when there was no one there to see?

The path had vanished into a morass. Although there'd been
no rain for months it would never dry out. More than erosion
had ruined the drainage: during the war the RAF had used the
area for practice strafing. One cluster had overshot or fallen
short a mile to the north, chipping the Bronze Age Badger
Stone, carbonizing its carved swastikas and roses. The smell of
burning persisted but now it came only from the lower slopes
where the heather was being razed, so that the grouse chicks
would feed on fresh green shoots to provide fat targets on the
Glorious Twelfth. I never saw anyone up here but then I always
avoided crowds: at weekends I moved between the spaces they'd
left in the city. By the depth of the footprints, heavily-burdened
men had been floundering to and fro – there were even hoof-
marks, although horses were banned by local ordinance. Maybe
the folktales were true and the vanished Ninth Legion was still
trying to find its way off the moor: it was as easy to get lost
on such high and open spaces – where you could see too
many possibilities – as it had been for Varus in the tangles of
Teutenberg Forest.

The words had stopped coming. It struck me that all my
poems were thematically linked: apologies and excuses for not
being better, for not having been written by somebody else. I
became what I read: I was currently six inches taller than usual,
American, myopic, seventeen years dead. After beginning 'The
Distances' on the Ilkley train that morning I was now shadowing
Charles Olson, rewriting his 'The Kingfishers' with a Yorkshire

slackerish slant. 'The pool is slime': he'd been right about that
– I shook my drying leg which felt stiff and not quite mine,
as if I'd plagiarized it. I was a pallid English version of the
Americans I admired: I'd be, at best, *Jimmy* Olson – Superman's
straight man, catamite or adopted son.

I plunged into the valley, digging my heels into the scree to
keep my descent just the right side of headlong. Friends had
dubbed this my Beer Run: far below I could see the glitter of
The Grinning Rat's roof slates – show me a pub and I turn
half-golem, half-greyhound. My sinuses tingled and my palate
ached in anticipation of that first mouthful of Tim Taylor's:
the boiling organ intro to The Small Faces' 'Tin Soldier' on
the jukebox was already sounding in my head.

The car park was empty as always, apart from Barry's rusting
Vespa. I wondered why he bothered to open at lunchtime –
or at all. The other equally remote pubs were packed with
drink-driving office trade: maybe the name was a problem –
who would pass up kings, queens and constellations in favour
of a rat? Or was it that while they'd been sandblasted honey-
gold, its stone was as black as the mill chimneys that had once
lined Airedale? Or that it appeared to be listing like a doomed
ship? On the signboard the rat and its grin had long since
vanished into a Rothko-like blur.

The interior was Stygian: I shuffled towards the sole light-
source – Barry's flour-white face, floating above the counter
like a leaking balloon. I'd almost reached him when my eyes
adjusted and I realized that the room was full of silent figures.
Twelve women and twelve teenage girls were paired off at the
tables, leaning forwards as if over invisible chessboards. I could
feel their eyes raying through me with casual hostility as if *they*

were the regulars. I knew that they must be social workers and their clients booked in at the nearby outdoor centre for intensive time-out counselling sessions but I'd never seen them here in such numbers before. It was always just women and girls: the boys – and the men – were presumably considered to be beyond redemption. Barry, as he served me, rolled his eyes like a maddened horse: he hated them. He claimed that one group had arrived carrying kayaks, demanding directions to the non-existent rapids: Barry had pointed to the ladies' toilets. Today he seemed to be somehow smaller than usual and to be turning weirdly hunchback; a cartilaginous ridge was pushing through the ash-grey toggled cardigan that, for some reason, he always wore back to front.

In a sing-song voice, as if telling a fairy story, the nearest woman – self-parodically spoon-faced and brush-cut – was genning up her bored-looking charge on the evils of the patriarchy. Whenever I hear of this malign conspiracy I always think of my old maths teacher, Mr Patriarchi, recalling his jug ears and sad eyes, his peppermint breath and soft, trembling, rose-petal lips. I wanted to tell her that I was pretty sure that he could have no designs on them. Suddenly they were all talking at once: confronting and comforting, disarming and empowering, sweeping the boundaries, getting to the nitty-gritty, peering through Johar's window – I knew the routine, I'd been in that game once myself. 'Fucking kayaks,' mouthed Barry, passing me my pint. The hope appeared to be that those kindly moorland winds would blow away all the years of damage and abuse. Most of the women were wearing sensible Kickers but the girls favoured six-inch stacks: they'd get fifty yards before – zinged by our super-aggressive bees, patriarchally stared at by sheep, frozen, frightened by the absence of anything very much — they'd have to repair for more crisps and treble Britvic shots.

Having thrown the first pint straight back — only pausing halfway for my customary sneezing fit — I made for the jukebox. But one of the girls — a skull with rouged or well-slapped chubby cheeks set atop a black LA Raiders jacket with COMMITMENT TO EXCELLENCE picked out in fraying silver — got there before me with a sprint and a lunge and, wiggling, straddling it, began to pump it with money. Resisting the urge to boot that part-fat, part-bony arse, I withdrew to the consolations of my second pint. Then a terrible noise began, like a jumbo-jet crash-landing in the car park. It was a while before I even recognized it as music: 'Doctorin' The Tardis', a version of Gary Glitter's clubfooted thumpalong 'Rock And Roll', with inserts from Sweet's 'Blockbuster' and a substitute chant of 'Doctor Who-oo-oo-oo!' It was by The Timelords a couple of self-styled situationists who hadn't played on the record, although they claimed that their car had been the lead vocalist. Their invocations of Debord and Baudrillard were, I suspected, merely a ploy to hoover up the cash of would-be intellectuals, along with all the other mugs'. Dumb shit wasn't shit anymore if it was ironic: maybe such benevolence might extend itself to my poems? I wondered whether I would — for a million quid — drag up in a silver cape and make a prat of myself: No, I was already doing it for free. I couldn't blame The Timelords for giving up the struggle: at least their witless row was drowning out the patriarchy rap.

Skull-face was about to suffer instant and condign retribution through eating one of Barry's pork-pies: that I chose to sit at her table was, however, not solely due to the prospect of watching her die. I was trying to get as close as possible to her social worker. She was the best-looking person in the room — or, at least, I thought she might be. A long-fingered hand had yanked across a glossy curtain of blue-black hair to conceal the face but the clavicles were good and those tiger-stripe stretch leggings usually meant that the wearer has some grounds for confidence. I wasn't looking for a pick-up, though. I'd only recently begun to realize that my obsession with beauty just had to be about more than mere insecurity or lust. I was still hoping, even after so many years, that Erato or Melpomene — or one of the other Muses whose names I always forget — might finally show up. I riffled the pages of my notebook: I certainly needed some help — if only from the Muse of Legible Handwriting.

Having rolled a cigarette I took out 'The Distances'. It was a Grove Press Reprint, its cover showing a dark grid fuzzing into barbed wire on a peacock field encroached by acid-green bands — minatory colours like those sad pills that have no recreational applications — overlaid by delicate fern-like traceries that proved on examination to be cracks in the laminate. I read on. 'In Cold Hell, In Thicket':

> '. . . So shall you blame those
> Who give it up, those who say
> It isn't worth the struggle?'

It's an even worse feeling to discover that you've been nicking things you haven't even read yet.

The woman opposite had turned sideways on. I still couldn't

see her face, although the hair did part enough to admit the rim of a glass of lethal sweet red cherry beer, the level of which then dropped alarmingly. Her sweater's black triskele patterns went badly with the tiger print. During the few seconds of blissful silence before, to my annoyance, 'Doctorin' The Tardis' came on again, I discovered that her name was Hilary – or rather, in her client's assumed lisp, Hiwwawwy. The Skull was deliberately infantilizing herself; kicking her legs, pouting and sighing, blowing impressively large spit-bubbles. Her inner arms were criss-crossed by purple stitched exclamation marks, with a blue raised circle like a steam-press button on her right wrist. She kept lighting Hiwwawwy's Gitanes, taking one puff, then violently mashing them into the ashtray. Hilary didn't object: I supposed they'd be going on expenses. The other clients were also performing variations on this naughty ickle girl routine: one was trying to eat a packet of peanuts by ricochetting them off the ceiling back towards her gaping mouth – the closest she came was in nearly blinding her left eye. Refusing proper drinks, they clamoured for owinge jews, although they subsequently topped it up from bottles of T-Bird under the table.

The scene was all too familiar. After college I'd done three years temping for a social work agency in Manchester. Residential: locked up with the tigers in their cage. Every day had been a battle; they came at us relentlessly, in waves. The staff worked twenty-five hour shifts: the residents stayed fresh by organizing themselves into eights, slipping regularly into and out of the mayhem. The only lulls were when the soaps came on. Two kids would quit tearing at each other at the sound of 'Corrie's' sig tune, spar fitfully again during the ads, then re-engage at full intensity as the end credits rolled. Mind you, I'd rather have watched someone spraying the walls with their arterial blood than the event-crammed but lobotomized proxy lives on Ramsay Street or Albert Square. There were no sanctions; fourteen year old girls would walk out through the fire exit at 2 a.m. and get into cars full of laughing pimps, mooning or wagging their cocks out of the windows, and we weren't allowed to restrain them, only to observe that we thought it wasn't a very good idea and then, after they'd gone, call the cops. I arrived for one shift to find that a crop of magic mushrooms that I'd earmarked for my own use had vanished from the home's front lawn: the kitchen was ablaze, the bathroom was flooded and from upstairs came the sound of the residents trashing their bedrooms. As always, I felt that I was on the wrong side, that I should have been up there with them – out of my head, burning, smashing, pissing on things, giving myself a bit of stick. Then the next shift never showed and the next . . . when the Emergency Duty Team finally got through I'd done seventy-two hours straight and had lost the power of speech. All that came out was a kind of whistle.

It damn near killed me: off-duty, I couldn't write or read or sleep, just eat and drink, but I didn't get fat, couldn't get drunk. That I stuck it for so long was down to my sheer cussedness and the pay-rates; if Night Disturbances kept you up it was time-and-a-half on top of the sleeping-in allowance. 'You've got a natural aptitude for this work,' one seen-it-all officer-in-charge told me, 'The rarest gift, the best edge of all.' Patience? Compassion? Empathy? I prepared myself to modestly demur. He grinned: 'You don't want to fuck any of the kids.' He was right: I didn't fancy any of the ones in The Rat either. Paedophilia – active or repressed – was so pervasive that I began to think there was something wrong with me. Incipient sainthood? – I tried to console myself that if I didn't want to fuck them then I certainly, much of the time, felt like hitting them.

My feet had started shuffling in time to 'Doctorin' The Tardis': maybe they were responding to subversive subliminal messages, revving themselves up to bear off my imagination – along with millions of others – towards its seizure of power. Then, for the first time, clear through the clamour, I heard Hilary's voice: 'So why do you keep cutting yourself, Tracey?'

I felt a shock of recognition and then a second, even greater, as the hair fell back to reveal her face. What was a woman who looked like that doing being a social worker? But then what was a woman like that doing being anything, anywhere? She was like the star of a perfect film that could never be made: Sophia Loren, maybe, playing La Pasionaria, directed by Tarkovsky. In spite of my reaction I knew that I'd never seen her before: it was more as if she had fitted perfectly into an empty and waiting space.

Tracey considered her question with the gravity of a zen master wondering whether a rozsin was advanced enough to handle a spot of direct pointing. At last she spoke: 'So I'll remember stuff that happens.'

'Why don't you just keep a diary?' asked Hilary.

Choking on a mouthful of beer, shielding my face with 'The Distances', I tried to pass off my laughter as a coughing fit. In the silence after the music ended, Hilary spoke once more: 'You need a bigger book: we can still see your ears shaking.'

'Doctorin' The Tardis' began yet again. 'I've put this on fifteen times,' said Tracey, 'just to piss you off.'

I told her that on the contrary it was my favourite record and that she'd merely saved me three quid. After sticking out a grey and startlingly spiked tongue she went over to join a couple of her friends who were starting up a game of miss-the-dartboard.

Hilary's eyes locked with mine, becoming even larger and darker. 'Are you Charles Olson?' she asked.

This threw me so much that my mind went blank for a few moments, as if I was unconsciously weighing the possibility of impersonating him. There was no jacket photograph and, after all, he was unlikely to walk in.

'I thought you might have been advertising your own book,' she said, apparently taking my silence as a negative. 'You kept sighing and smacking your lips as if to show how good it was, like Bisto or something.'

Discovering that Tracey had emptied her cigarette packet she rolled herself one with my Samson, without asking. Although her fingernails – unpainted but unusually long and well-shaped – had picked out a roach from the beer-mat it still fell into wet, burning fragments on the second drag.

'Are you having a day off work?' she asked.

'This is work' – I drank a mock toast to the papers on the table – 'I am a writer, although not Charles Olson.'

Her eyes flickered over me and she swallowed her half-smile. I wondered how many times people had said that to her. Everybody I knew claimed to be '(really) an artist' of some sort – out of the mistaken belief that it individuated them or as a signal that they might be game for anything that might be on offer. At least I tried, at least I pissed away enough hours to make myself miserable, even if the end result was about the same. I told Hilary about my poems in little magazines, my book reviews for *Artscene*, my appearance on Radio Leeds, managing to sound boastful and ashamed at the same time.

'But I used to be one of you lot' – I mimed fangs and claws – 'Lapsed social worker.'

'I thought you might have been when Tracey didn't freak you.'

'Not caseload, though. Residential: the hard stuff.'

'I did a two-month placement in a kids' home,' she said. 'There was so much cooking, cleaning, doling out pocket money, rowing over TV programmes that we never got round to doing any proper work. It was nearly impossible to get one-on-one. Playing happy families is a waste of time: at least this way' – she glanced at Tracey, who was trying to blow the dart at its target – 'you get to tackle their problems head on.'

'Problems?' I said. 'Tracey? Look at her' – Tracey and her friends, catching my eye, dropped their hands to their groins and began vigorously frigging themselves – 'Little angels. On their best behaviour. You don't know them at all. After all they've been through they bury themselves deep. At first they're polite – scared to death of your adult's power to hurt them – but then when you show no signs of doing so they despise you for what they can only conceive of as your weakness. They can't work out what your angle is: that you're being paid to do it never seems to occur to them. Once you've got through their initial defences – the minefield, the fence, the dogs – it's only to be confronted by a seeming infinity of minefields, fences and dogs. You have to pretend that you don't know what they're thinking and feeling, that you haven't read their files, that you haven't seen it all before: like a vampire you have to wait for the invitation to come in. Then their alarm bells begin to ring. Life was easier the way it was before you came: all their psychic energy concentrates itself on provoking you to finally destroy them, to finish the job. They piss all over you and you have to just take it: you give them, for the first time, the power to control, to hurt – so that they can renounce it in their turn. And at last all their pain comes pouring out and the full extent of the devastation is revealed. Then you can start to work with them. Once someone has accepted that their position is hopeless it's amazing what they can achieve. If you're getting anywhere with Tracey then it's only because her keyworker's been through all the shit – and all the boredom, all the squabbles over food, money and telly – with her already.'

Unphased by this tirade, Hilary paralysed me with her full smile: 'You obviously miss it a lot.'

'I miss the money. And it was easier than writing. Nothing's as terrifying as the blank page – except maybe when you read back what you've gone and filled it with.'

Hilary's mouth closed with an audible click, then opened again, her lip curling, as if about to deliver some definitively damning retort but all it said was: 'Can I see something of yours?'

I handed her my still-untitled poem. She furrowed her brow for a full two minutes and then pointed to the first word.

'I can't make it out,' she said, 'it looks like rubblesome.'

'It is,' I said. Taking it from her I proceeded to read it aloud, pausing occasionally to change things as they struck me – although most of it seemed pretty good all of a sudden. Hilary kept disappearing behind her hair: without her head seeming to move, first one wing would sweep across, then the other, like synchronized twin scythes. Peek-a-boo, like my dad's old favourite, Veronica Lake. With a green biro she played rim-shots on the table's edge, with no relation to the rhythms of my words or The Timelords, as if to a different tune that was playing in her head. I now considered the poem to be almost perfect, except for its ending. 'That last line's shit,' I said, 'I'm going to have to change it' – then I had the blinding insight that what I'd just said was itself the perfect last line.

'I can't make anything of it,' Hilary shrugged and mimed washing or wringing her hands. 'Names and places I don't know, things I don't recognize. Could anyone other than you understand it?'

'I don't understand it either. Would you say that you understood the world or your own place in it or anything very much at all? Perhaps you should just try to walk into it – like a room, like this pub – and see if you can live there?'

'I'm sure I don't understand anything but I do know that I've got quite enough confusions of my own, without taking on yours as well. Where's the fun in feeling like I'm back at school, having not done my homework? If I'm not interested in a book I know it's because the book isn't interested in me. Writers should write about what everyone knows with the words everyone uses but in a new and magical way.'

I told her that I loved stuff that I didn't get at first, that I had to ferret out, break down – new worlds, new words.

'Most people,' Hilary said, 'just don't have the time. Why don't you make a list of things that your readers have to know or have a questionnaire so they can find out in advance whether they're worthy to read your poem.'

Her knees, straining at the fabric, had formed the faces of twin tigers. I decided that I'd have just one qualification in my suitability test: to be able to tick a box marked 'Beautiful'.

'You don't need to tell me,' I said. 'You thought it was elitist.'

'No' – as her smile widened my heart felt as if it was dangerously inflating – 'Just sad, after all the things you were saying before.'

'So, do you ever find the time to read anything yourself?'

With a magician's flourish she opened her bag – an old-fashioned reticule, battered and stained, with a tarnished silver fleur-de-lys clasp – which was almost filled by a one-volume Penguin *Clarissa*, with a tasselled bookmark halfway through. 'Have you read this?'

'Of course,' I lied. 'I'm sure you can really *relate* to that. Very relevant.'

'No,' she said. 'It's a totally unfamiliar world but Richardson tells me everything I have to know about how it works. And it also' – she clean-jerked the book above her head – 'keeps me fit. And it also' – she swung it at lightning speed past my nose – 'serves as a handy weapon.'

Cringing in pretend fear I retreated to the gents' toilet. Although I was still too dehydrated to piss I felt I needed time to regain my composure. My hands were shaking and a warm glow in my gut was gradually spreading north and south. In the mirror I tried to select an appropriate expression but none of my three smiles would do – the best, the supposedly charming, roguish one, might have served as a good model if Barry had needed a new signboard. Out on the moor wind and sweat had spiked my hair into five horns, framed by a frizzy nimbus

of split ends. I tried to tamp it back down but the damage —
unless Hilary went for anarcho-punks — had already been done.
Through the wall I could hear gigglings, splashings and crashes
from the ladies': it sounded as if some of the victims of the
patriarchy were shooting the rapids.

None of what Hilary had said was new, of course. Concerned
friends and relatives had assessed my character — parasite, waster,
fantasist, coward, idealist, snob — many times. I used to play
up the louche exquisite to annoy them. 'My dear, one doesn't
write *about* anything, one just writes,' I lisped at my reflection.
Even my longest-suffering girlfriend used to introduce me as
'the writer manqué' — I'd always scratch and gibber at her
pronunciation. Was it because they'd come from a stranger
that Hilary's words had so hit home? I remembered that when
a weeping madman had once dogged me through Sainsbury's
shouting 'SCUM!' I'd taken it to be a divine judgement and
felt like Ishmael for days afterwards.

Back at the bar I ordered another pint. The dumbstruck
Barry gave me an agonized smile, like a damned soul roasting
on an adjoining spit. Tracey and her friends had lost the darts
and were now picking their noses and flicking the bogeys at
the board: I still didn't fancy any of them. An elderly couple
in reddish tweeds entered, their faces florid and animated from
a retirement crammed with nice little excursions. They took in
the scene and then wordlessly spun, linked arms and walked
back out again. Despite their considerable girth they slipped
neatly through the narrow doorway: I was most impressed
— they were obviously well-attuned after all their centuries
together.

I was surprised to see that Hilary was still sitting there, as if my brief absence had convinced me that she was, if not imaginary, then a somehow internal presence. She was reading 'The Distances'. I'd never seen anyone holding a book that way: in front of her face, very close, right hand on top, the other below, thumbs hooked over and under, index fingers overlapping mid-spine. As I approached she lowered it far enough to reveal one saltily-raised eyebrow.

'Has anyone ever told you that you walk like a womble?' she asked, in an execrable Irish accent. It was presumably a quote from something I didn't know. She rapped me lightly twice on the head with 'The Distances': '"La lumière de l'aurore est devant nous",' she said reprovingly. Her French was even worse. 'It's here in "The Kingfishers": the same as yours. You nicked it from Charles Olson!'

'Well, he nicked it too. It's a quote from Mao Tse-Tung.'

'What's he doing in a poem?'

'He was a poet.'

'Oh, I thought you meant *Chairman* Mao.' I decided not to pursue it.

She propped the book open on the table: it seemed to disappear, consumed by the strobing bands of her sweater: 'At least yours is as good as his. Or as bad.'

'Everything I write is full of whatever I'm reading at the time,' I told her. 'People like Olson swallow me whole, like Jonah, and I have to write my way back out only to get swallowed again by the next passing whale – or flounder or cod.'

'Why don't you stop reading and just write?'

'I need to know what's been done, what it's been possible to do. Where's the point in duplication? Besides, for some reason I feel that when I've read and imitated everything all that will remain will be my own original style, my voice – that when I've been everybody else I'll finally be able to become myself.'

'Why should being original matter? We're all pretty much the same. You may say some pretty unusual things but you're just like everyone else really. You breathe, walk about, wear clothes, smoke and drink, try to pick up girls in pubs.'

I became aware that my knees had locked themselves tightly around hers. Maybe she hadn't noticed: when I tucked my legs back under my chair her expression didn't change. I reminded myself that, if anything, I'd hitherto fancied social workers even less than their clients.

'I suppose you were born,' said Hilary, 'And I suppose you'll die. Nothing's original: not being kind or being cruel, not even not caring.'

'But that's life,' I said. 'Art's different. It was easier for your friend Richardson – being one of the first he had nothing to judge *Clarissa* against.'

'For some readers you might be the first. Yours might be the first poetry they ever read.'

'They'll get mad later when they find out how much Dante and Shakespeare have ripped me off.'

'Who cares about people stealing things? Even if you and someone else were to by chance write the same poem, word for word, most likely nobody would notice – or if they did, they'd just think it was intentional in some smart way.'

'Maybe The Timelords have never heard Gary Glitter,' I said. 'I've always believed that somewhere there's one reader who reads everything, a critic who weighs and places every book, every line, every word. He reads all my stuff and he just knows — and I can feel him knowing.'

'If he does exist he should get himself a life. I've always believed that whatever happens is happening for the first time. Everything is unique. Although there are millions of people they all have different faces.'

'Not different enough,' I said. 'What we need are more third eyes and second noses. New holes and new protuberances. Lots of major self-surgery, like Tracey's on her wrists.'

'That's my point. Where's Tracey in all this? What are you and Olson and Mao doing for her?'

'If you'd like to commission something I'm delighted to oblige . . .

> Don't let the patriarchs mess with your head:
> Stop cutting yourself — buy a diary instead . . .

How's that? No charge.'

'If you didn't care you wouldn't joke about it.'

'Who's joking? Me and Mao are doing Tracey our biggest favour by keeping well out of her life.'

'So you don't believe in helping people any more?'

'No one can. If Tracey does change it won't be through some Care Action Programme but because of something unforeseen and trivial that pulls some subliminal trigger and fires her off in some other direction. It's random: no one controls it.'

'That's easy enough for you to say, with everything you've got.'

'No it's not easy for me. And what's this everything I'm

supposed to have? A well-stocked mind? The gift of the gab? Whatever, it's nothing that Tracey could need.'

'You've got it all. You just don't know how to use it.'

'What have I got? What is this it? What is this everything?'

'No, you just don't have the guts to use it.'

'What the fuck is it? What is it?'

Hilary's face had become a grey blur. We'd stretched across the table until we were only inches apart, shouting into each other's open mouths. She drew back and took in a great breath that seemed to suck all the air out of the room. When she came back into focus she had once more hidden behind her hair.

Now I saw that the others had gathered around us, a cluster of pale, intent faces, like students at an anatomy lesson. I wondered how long they'd been listening and watching.

'Well –' said Hilary, getting to her feet and draping an arm round Tracey's shoulders, 'I'll leave you with a funny story. On my first day in that kids' home we took them out to London Zoo. After half an hour the lot had disappeared. We looked everywhere. I thought the tigers had eaten them. When it got dark we gave up, only to discover that they were hiding under our minibus in the empty car park.' She tossed 'The Distances' back on to the table: 'Enjoy the rest of your book.'

I saw that Tracey's face had unclenched, bone melting into flesh, and that she'd begun to cry silently, as if in dreadful anticipation. The tears didn't drip, just lay there in suspension like a gravity-defying lake. The girls and the women exited two by two – messily, unlike the old couple, jostling and stumbling with an edge of panic, as if they'd smelt smoke. Hilary let them get well clear before she pushed Tracey through and then turned for her Parthian shot. 'Although the creatures of the earth are numberless,' she half-whispered, 'I vow to save them.' She dropped me a mocking curtsey, threw back her shining hair and was gone. It had obviously been another quote, although presumably of a different provenance to the earlier womble one. The last echoes of 'Doctorin' The Tardis' died away. Silence: I was sure I'd counted only fourteen plays.

Getting in the next pint I was relieved to find that Barry had returned to his normal size and shape and recovered his voice. 'Fucking psychos and dykes,' he grumbled, 'lowering my tone. I fancied yours though . . . I could screw that . . . nay, shag it, even.' In a previous conversation − about synonyms that are really antonyms − we'd concluded that, locally at least, 'shagging' was the term favoured by irredeemable romantics like ourselves.

I sat for some time and watched the dust in a shaft of sunlight move forwards, then backwards, then settle. Then I returned to Charles Olson:

> . . . magic, my light-fingered Faust
> Is not so easily sympathetic
> Nor are the ladies worn so decoratively.

I closed the book: I didn't need him scoring off me as well. The silence was oppressive: I wasn't sure that I could face life without an attendant chant of 'Dr Who-oo-oo-oo!', like some-one living under a flight-path, whose blood has begun to circu-late with a turbo-charged roar. When I put The Timelords on again − five consecutive plays − Barry started screaming and bombarding me with beer-mats, flicking them backhand, like kung fu death-stars: he was astonishingly accurate, but then he'd had years of practice. As I ducked and flinched, it struck me that throughout our conversation Hilary hadn't blinked once — or if she had it could only have been at the exact same moments as me. To my horror I realized that I'd already forgotten her face: I could picture the hair all right but when I forced it to part it would only reveal Tracey in tears, her features twisting and corrugating as if an invisible hand was squeezing her like a sponge.

Next morning, after a sleepless night, I concluded that Hilary had indeed been my muse: it was for me to take up her challenge. I was through with reading: 'The Distances' went back on the shelf, unfinished. I determined to write a book after which there would be no more Traceys. It wouldn't be a bestseller like *Uncle Tom's Cabin*, shocking and shaming the world into changing its ways and means but rather a magical act that would somehow alter reality itself. For the next two months, slumped over my splintered, rocking desk, I devoted myself to this hopeless task. Tracey's face — an individual face out of millions, covered with its individual tears — was a starting-point from which I could go no further. What were those things that everyone knows that Hilary had talked about? Where were those words that everyone uses? How was I to deploy all this everything with which she'd informed me I had been blessed? I spent much of my time in front of the mirror, interrogating my own face: it stared sullenly back, an expressionless slab that now couldn't even manage its grinning rat smile. I tried to adapt my previous novel-in-progress, about a Chelsea boot-boy who murders Arab oil sheikhs that he suspects of trying to take over his club: it was dreadful, written alternately in the styles of Hemingway and Baron Corvo — although there was a nice pastoral interlude in Brompton Cemetery and at least it wasn't entirely autobiographical. As for my poetic oeuvre, the last line I'd written had been its unwitting epitaph — it was all shit but there was no changing any of it. I tried to write about Hilary, but her face was still lost to me.

I was sick of everything. The only creature of the earth that I'd been trying to save had been myself and I'd even failed at that. I was sick of the cats and the countryside, of drink and drugs, of painting and music — even my failsafe Coltrane albums now sounded limp or tinny. I didn't like any of my friends — I never had but previously it hadn't seemed to be a problem — and nor could I work up much enthusiasm for the women who would probably, in whatever order, be my next few lovers. I gave up and moved from the desk and mirror to lie numbly on my unmade bed. I did finally tackle *Clarissa*, though: I felt I owed it to Hilary, as penance for my lie. I read it in one terrible forty-eight hour stretch: I didn't feel transported to another world — more that the ingested mass of words was impacting me into this one. At the end I found that I'd lost the power of speech — once again, all I could do was whistle.

After a day and a night of dreamless, death-like sleep, I arose and rang my old agency. Although it had been five years they still remembered me. Even the secretaries came on to say hello: 'We knew you'd be back: you were one of the best we've ever had.' I didn't divulge my secret, my strange paedophilia deficiency. One asked how my writing was going: I told her that I was researching a book on the care system and wanted to recapture the feel but I knew all that was finished.

They didn't even bother to take up fresh references. That evening found me once again sitting in a TV room watching *Neighbours* with half-a-dozen evil-smelling adolescents, pretending to ignore me. It was as if I'd never been away: nothing much had happened on Ramsay Street except that a character I'd previously seen drowned had in the interval been miraculously restored to life. I was filling in a form the kids had given me: they were developing their own bureaucracy – although the information they wanted to elicit was such things as my favourite singer, animal, cartoon character. To almost all of these questions I answered ME.

My colleagues were the usual sinister or well-meaning boobies: I went native almost immediately, although I made sure that not even the natives noticed. During the next ten years many of the numberless creatures of the earth passed through my care: I saved none of them. All the faces were different, all their problems were the same – insoluble. In their sorrows and rages I saw myself mirrored, without my palliatives and accommodations. Once again I had to acknowledge that it is always the best of us that go under – the ones who see things, who feel too much and understand too well and, refusing to forget, remember. I used to believe that we'd be back in kilter if the universe was to be turned on its head, rendering the first last and the last first but now I accepted that there were only the last, fast or slow – that the only difference was between quarry caught and quarry still pursued. These kids, doomed, were at least standing their ground. I felt like one of the invisible angels in *Wings Of Desire*: powerless to intervene, able only to bear witness to who was being destroyed and – to some extent – why. It was a privilege: after the testing-out period they'd trust you with their deepest, darkest secrets – I knew them better than I'll ever come to know my wife. Sometimes I'd glimpse the same fleeting expression in their eyes, as if there was one common spirit or soul hiding within. Then I'd sit in the office and fill the logbook with confused metaphysical speculations, somewhat in the style of Thomas Traherne: my colleagues passed over them without comment, as harmless eccentricities. When the residents' Leaving Care grants arrived I was always the one to move them out. I'd first repaint their drab council flats with ultra-brilliant white gloss. High on my ladder, dizzy from the fumes, I felt like a God creating a new Eden: as I left I'd see that the serpents were forming a queue down the stairwell.

Successes and failures were hard to distinguish. A girl who'd seemed miraculously unscathed died later with her head in a plastic bag, submerged in the bath of a house she'd set on fire; a Billy Budd-type had, it transpired, only joined the Navy in order to throw himself overboard. Then there was Michael, the most damaged kid I ever worked with, who was in the habit of extracting his own teeth. We got on OK – communicating solely in lines from the *Terminator* films – until one day he vanished, for some reason taking the unit's front door with him. Five years later, as I was boarding a train at Shipley station, all the air was suddenly knocked out of my lungs. I was being hugged by a bear in a railwayman's uniform. Michael: when he smiled his teeth looked real – maybe they'd somehow grown back? He said he often thought of all the great laughs we'd had: I couldn't recall any of them. He produced a creased photograph of his wife and baby, posed in front of an immaculate semi, like an insurance company ad – too perfect. Such was his enthusiasm that the train, a tiny navy and white Sprinter like a foil-wrapped chocolate bar, seemed huge and epic, a mettlesome steed from the Age Of Steam. I forgot about my destination and allowed myself to be borne off, all the way up to Carlisle and back. Michael let me open and close the automatic doors on to Steeton's empty platforms and I went on the PA to introduce the startled passengers – in my best Viv Stanshall tones – to the prime features of the frowning profiles of Ingleborough and Pen-Y-Ghent . . . But in the driver's cab – as we swung out of the Blea Moor Tunnel's six-minute darkness and seemed to bank like a plane to squint down the vertiginous green walls of Dentdale – our eyes met and we silently acknowledged that, all appearances to the contrary, there would be no happy ending.

Then there was Christine: the second-worst of the girls. After she'd moved in, her room had gradually developed a terrible smell of putrefaction. During her frequent absences we tore it apart but could find no source. At last, on the fifth search, we discovered that she'd taped a well-rotted chicken leg under one of her bedside drawers. On her return she attacked us with nails and teeth, as if we'd stolen her child. The next time I saw her was in the Red Light District: she was a walking corpse in a pussy-pelmet, trying and failing to ascend to the cab of a cruising German lorry. She obviously didn't recognize me, even when I gave her a leg up. I'd filed her under Dead Or Worse Than until I encountered her again, long afterwards, in Scofield's furniture department – she was radiant and tanned, with gold at her throat and wrists. 'I can hardly remember those old days,' she said, bouncing experimentally on a green chesterfield. 'Like a bad dream I once had.' What struck me was that the scars – even better than Tracey's – where she'd slashed at her arms and neck had magically disappeared. 'So what are you doing now?' I asked. Christine beamed and stood ramrod-straight, like a guardsman at attention: 'Stripping,' she said proudly.

I often day-dreamed about seeing Hilary again: not only to show off my recovered sense of social responsibility so that she might lift the anathema of frivolity from my shoulders but also to thank her – every time I looked at Gemma and our children I felt as if they'd been somehow her gift. Sometimes I'd run my fingers down the creased spine of 'The Distances' where she'd held it. Suppose she really had been a Muse – materializing to show me that I was wasting my life, to turn me back from a road that wasn't mine? Or maybe she'd even been the Muse of social workers? I'd returned to The Grinning Rat the day after we met and every day after that for quite a while . . . then once a week, then once a month. Even many years later I still dropped in whenever I was passing – and I managed to pass that way surprisingly frequently. I'd park and walk up on to the moor – to the second stile, about as far as I felt that social workers, as opposed to poets, were permitted. Barry still wore his cardigan and, when provoked, still pelted me with beer-mats, but 'Doctorin' The Tardis' had gone straight off the jukebox the day after Hilary's and my brief encounter and no amount of pleading – that it had for me the same significance as Rachmaninov Two – could make him relent. I always asked out of town referrals if they'd come across a social worker called Hilary, although I still had trouble when they asked me to describe her. One of the T-Bird girls from The Rat had occupied our emergency bed for one night but she wasn't helpful. 'I've been a lot of places,' she yawned, 'and I've had a lot of social workers.'

For three years I'd been filling in as OIC at a teenage hostel – although still on a dep's salary. Then, over my head, they inserted someone with diplomas and a squint – a dead ringer for The Rat's patriarchy woman. Increasingly the council were sacrificing good practice to the balance sheet: we were assessed by the extent of our food bills and damage repairs and by the number of emergency services involvements. If a resident so much as said 'boo' it was to be move 'em out, lock 'em up or foster 'em. We'd soon only be allowed to work with notional clients who wouldn't need us: all ours failed the acid test – there were good reasons for their being in care. I'd started applying for other posts – in the grim knowledge that anything else would only be at best an earlier stage on the same terminal line – when Child Concern headhunted me to set up an independent adolescent unit. Lottery funded, it would have a one-to-one staff client ratio and was housed in a converted mansion – mullioned, finialled, georgianized – in the Durham countryside, with an ivy-smothered cottage for myself and family. This was my rollover jackpot, my Booker, Pulitzer or Nobel . . . After the interview, however, as I toured the bosky grounds, watching huge melanistic rabbits trampling the magic mushrooms, my exhilaration faded. It felt as if we were about to embark on some weird experiment – the creation of a utopia or of a new race – that was bound to go horribly, chiliastically wrong. I wasn't happy that my official designation was to be Matron: would I have to drag up in starched cap and apron, to loom and boom like Hattie Jacques in the Carry-Ons?

That night on the TV news I watched as The Timelords,

now metamorphosed into art terrorists The K Foundation, burnt a million quid in a household grate. There was a clip of them doing 'Doctorin' The Tardis': 'Dr Who-oo-oo-oo!' — Hilary's cataract of hair, still without a face, flashed through my mind. So they'd hoovered up all that cash only in order to burn it. I thought of all the sports facilities — the Durham Project's sole deficiency — that it could have provided. Why hadn't they just given it to us? Then, for some reason, I thought of Winston and the rats in *Nineteen Eighty-Four*'s Room 101 . . . Do it to Julia! Give me the money! I felt as if, under some subtle examination, I'd been coming up with all the wrong answers — although I had no idea what the right ones might be.

We'd almost finished our packing before I approached the crammed bookshelves: evidently Gemma had long since given up dusting them. I rang Clive at Help The Aged and asked him to bring his van round and then started two piles — To Keep and To Go. Three hours later the solitary book in the former was 'The Distances' — and that only for the memory of Hilary's eyebrows arching above it: I didn't even want the ones I hadn't read. I opened it: there were three tiny red asterisks on the title page that I now recalled had been roving cat fleas crushed by my thumb-nail. My own faded marginalia to 'The Kingfishers' baffled me. God! The languages, histories and myths that I'd once known and now forgotten! And the names! Fenellosa, Volney, Plutarch, Rimbaud . . . and who was this ANW who'd apparently said, 'No event is not penetrated, in intersection or collision with an external event'? Another sad case who should go and get himself a life: Now, like Hilary I couldn't make anything of it.

The colour of the pages — yellow giving way to white — showed how far I'd read ten years ago: I must have been pretty grubby in those days. I riffled idly through to the end and shut it ... then opened it again. Something strange — a near-subliminal flash of green — had caught my eye. And so it was that at last I read on the final page the closing words of the title poem:

> '... that young Augustus
> and old Zeus
> be enclosed
> I wake you,
> stone, love this man'

'Love this man' had been heavily underlined then ringed twice in green ink. Below, in a rather childish hand, was written:

HILARY — 806–1398 (H)
254–8722 (W)

The first letter of her name looked more like an M, the last like a badly-notched hatchet blade. I made for the phone as if my haste — taking the stairs in two ankle-jarring leaps — could somehow turn time back a decade. I dialled the home number and then redialled and redialled but always got the unobtainable's flat-line blare. The other turned out to be somewhere in the Midlands: The Pelham Area Office. It sounded vaguely familiar: was it celebrated or notorious? I spoke to the Senior there. 'I've been here twelve years,' she said in the regulation bleached-out but soothing monotone, 'but I don't remember any Hilarys. But then, as you'll understand, staff turnover has been pretty high.'

A Short Cut Through the Sun

I was making my way through the rolling maul around the bar towards the exit when something hit me hard in the sternum. Soft hands moved across my body at lightning speed, cupping my arse, checking my pulse and heartbeat, running over my inner thighs. I looked down to see a tiny head with bleach-blonde hair smiling up out of a jacket of dark ragged fur. 'Does your mother choose your clothes?' she asked, while her hands – she seemed to be Shiva-armed – continued their exploration. As usual, I couldn't think of a snappy comeback: 'Er . . . No,' was the best I could do. Her smile widened, then she ducked away under my armpit: I turned round but there was no sign of her. She'd realized that she was wasting her time – my wallet was wedged unreachably between my right boot and sock – but had given me the twice-over regardless. Those two fingers teasingly measuring my cock's length had been most unprofessional, just for fun. I wondered how she could consider my black and silver, leather and denim to be a particularly mumsy combination: she must have had some unimaginably gothic experiences of maternity. Perhaps she'd physically divined that apron strings were knotted to my shoulder zips, marking me as a biker

without a bike, a road-agent on a bridle path. The Milky Bar
Kid dressed up for *The Wild Bunch*?

For the sixth time I walked out of the club to scan the
street. There was still no sign of Bryn: These days I seemed
to spend half of my life waiting for him to show. I hadn't
enjoyed the previous hour: I knew that the people sitting around
me were thinking that I'd been stood up – I wanted to tell
them that I was only waiting for an old college friend who'd
been having a few problems. Saturday! . . . Midnight! . . . Soho!
. . . Ronnie Scott's! . . . That's how Bryn, as star and director
of his own perpetual movie, would have seen it. Lights! . . .
Camera! . . . Action! . . . I just felt like the same old me in the
same old scene. I'd lost any capacity for self-dramatization:
while Bryn still saw Scott's as a cross between Pablo's Magic
Theatre and The Celestial City, invisible to all save walkers of
The True Path, it struck me that they were letting in anyone
these days. Even the Bradford dives of my youth had been
choosier, at least so far as dress codes went.

I went back up the steps. 'Do you have a reservation . . .
sir?' the doorman asked, just like on the previous five occasions,
as if all memory of my presence had faded in the intervening
thirty seconds. He made the muscles in his neck bunch into a
line of babies' faces: why did such people think that impersonating Mr T would make them frightening rather than laugh-
able? The bouncers I'd known in Bradford – like Beaky, five
foot nothing with pebble glasses and a racking cough – would
have ripped this Goliath apart. 'Do you know you've got pick-
pockets working the bar?' I asked him. He cracked his knuckles,
then joined his hands as if in prayer and began to sing in a
smoky baritone: 'Fish gotta swim, birds gotta fly' . . . I had to

admit that for repartee and musicality he had Beaky well-outclassed.

Although the support band displayed blinding technique and encyclopaedic knowledge of The Canon, it struck me that this wasn't a good period for British jazz. The pianist, a twenty year old from Camberwell, sounded in turn like Powell, Tyner, Monk, Jarrett and Taylor – in fact, like everyone in the world except himself. The double bass player embarked on an interminable solo, delving into the lowest reaches of his instrument like a man hunting lost coins down the back of a sofa. His scratchings went ultrasonic or were drowned out by the storms of conversation raging around the bar. I re-read the notice on my table:

PATRONS ARE REMINDED THAT THEY ARE <u>REQUIRED</u> TO
KEEP AS QUIET AS POSSIBLE WHEN ARTISTS ARE
PERFORMING. IF YOU ARE DISTURBED BY NOISE FROM ANY
OTHER PATRONS, WE WOULD BE GRATEFUL IF YOU WOULD
INFORM ONE OF OUR STAFF.
THANK YOU.

Maybe everyone was complaining at once about everyone else's noise?

When Bryn and I started coming here the audience had been musos and bohemians with a few lugubrious locals thrown in: now it appeared to be mainly rubbernecking tourists and brash kids who were starring not in their own films but in their own videos. At least the ambience hadn't changed: crimson light falling on red and white tablecloths, like a Sunday school picnic in Hell.

A beautiful woman was sitting at the next table. She seemed familiar: I had the feeling that she was a TV weather forecaster, although I never watched TV and rarely noticed the weather. Her companion was a rat-faced man who was chewing his way through a large chip sandwich, dripping golden grease. I didn't like the way he was looking at her: in a civilized society, you'd be able to decapitate such a creature on sight – but then you'd probably find that you'd killed a saint to deliver a demon. In front of me was a party of obvious criminals and their molls: they were finger-popping and putting on the hard stare but merely looked as if they should have been chasing Dick Emery in some terrible British comedy film. All those waistcoats, cuff-buttons and matching ties and hankies: their mothers had certainly been choosing their clothes. Up on stage the band was joined by a girl with beaded dreadlocks, in a shantung silk dress and zebra-leggings who sang a series of soft soul numbers, the lyrics of which implied that universal peace and brotherhood could be achieved by the general application of advanced frottage techniques. It reminded me of my first love: she'd convinced me that if we only managed to do all the right things in exactly the right order then we'd awake the next morning to find that we were Adam and Eve reinstated in the Garden of Eden. Bryn, I suspected, still believed in some such nonsense: I wished that I could.

Recently, Bryn's partner Sally and I had formed a conspiracy against him. His habits and little foibles – the drinking and doping, the rages and depressions – had gradually come to seem terminally threatening: a long-accepted equilibrium was seen to be horribly out of balance. He appeared to be eaten up by a bitterness towards the world – or, at least, towards the two of us. After he'd moved in with Sally his dole had stopped so that his only sources of income were occasional proofreading and reviewing for the *Fortean Times*. Sally would leave for work at 7 a.m.: when she returned home exhausted thirteen hours later she'd find him lying on the sofa, covered in biscuit crumbs, her breakfast things still unwashed. She worked as a PA for some Arab princes: they enjoyed humiliating her, Bryn told me – like in a bad pornographic novel but with the sex taken out. He appeared to find this amusing. One night I'd gone to their place for dinner: after I'd dragged the unconscious Bryn up to bed, Sally and I sat and discussed the situation. 'Please help me help him,' she said, 'I know you love him too.' Next morning Bryn asked me what we'd been doing downstairs for so long: when I told him I'd been trying to screw her he looked relieved. Only later did it register that he hadn't bothered to find out whether I'd succeeded or not. It had always been part of his credo that his current woman was the one that everyone else in the world wanted. He'd given Sally such a huge build-up – 'Like Bardot crossed with Susan Sontag, but with longer legs' – that when I arrived at the pub I'd been disappointed to see Bryn wedged into the far corner, apparently alone. Waiting to be served I got talking to a chubby nondescript girl who appeared to be chewing gum and eating crisps at the same time. When I finally made it through to Bryn I said how sorry I was that Sally hadn't made it . . . and he, of course, replied, 'What do you mean? You've been talking to her for the last ten minutes!' I never particularly liked her but she certainly loved him too.

She had rung me earlier that evening to tell me that Bryn was on his way: 'He's not touched anything in the last three weeks – not even the lagers in the fridge – but he's not sleeping very well and I think he's started smoking again.' She had started doling out his expenses: 'He's got a travel pass and small change for the phone in case of emergencies. And I've given him a tenner for the admission. Don't give him any more money. Don't let him drink. And make sure he gets on the night bus in Trafalgar Square.' 'Did you wash his face and hands before he left?' I asked. There was a long silence: in the background I could hear the voice of Cilla Black screaming something about 'nookie' above a baying audience. 'I don't think Bryn's happiness is a laughing matter,' Sally finally said. I asked why she didn't come along herself: she told me she was too tired even to walk downstairs.

The band's set ended with Billie Holiday's 'Strange Fruit', played as if it had been a song about a cocktail. A prickling at the back of my neck told me that Bryn had just entered the club: I turned to see him passing through the massed bodies as if they were smoke. His regal poise and the certainty of his progress revealed that he had slipped Sally's traces and was well out of his head. He was laden with carrier bags that appeared to have been hung on his outstretched arms to keep him from drifting away, like ballast on a balloon. On reaching me, he insisted on going through his usual high fives and bear-hug routine that was becoming increasingly like a covert assault. He shouted into my ear: 'Shopping, old man!' He'd recently started calling me that – like Orson Welles to Joseph Cotten in *The Third Man* – and I was retaliating with 'old chap' – like Bernard Miles to John Mills in *Great Expectations* – trumping his threatening condescension with infuriatingly loyal affection. Sally's tenner had stretched an awfully long way: there was a complete set of *A Dance To The Music of Time* and a mass of Kim Fowley LPs – including three copies of *Sunset Boulevard* and some weird-looking things that probably Fowley himself wouldn't remember recording – and a pair of black leather shoes, pocked with chevrons, laced and side-gussetted, with long arches culminating in irregular toe-caps like art sculptures.

'Handmade!' yelled Bryn. 'Best shoes in the world! My mate Laszlo in Camden Lock! As new! Punter tried them on, then died right there in the shop!' He slipped the shoes over his hands and walked them across the table, then up and down my body: 'Death Shoes! Les souliers de la mort! Los zapatos del muerte!' I poured the last of the Aussie red into my glass and pointedly ordered a carafe of still mineral water but before it arrived Bryn had slammed a half-empty bottle of Jim Beam on the table: maybe Laszlo's client had expired in the middle of it.

My first sight of Bryn had been at the beginning of my second term at college, across a candlelit room, through a ganja fog, he was the most slumped of a row of slumped figures. He'd struck me as being impossibly ugly – the face as long as a horse's, with lank black hair and huge protruding putty ears, like Nick Cave after prolonged incarceration – but then, after an hour – during which he had neither moved nor spoken – I suddenly realized, with a sort of religious awe, that this was the most beautiful human being that I would ever see. He was always deathly pale: sunlight only brought out a mesh of blue veins like a complex river system. The full lips and hooded eyes recalled the portraits of the Eighteenth Dynasty Pharaoh Akhnaten, the first monotheist, who had sought to immolate the rest of the Pantheon in the exploding Sun of the Aten.

Bill Broady

When Justine and I had recently visited the Cairo Museum the first thing we'd seen had been that massive one-armed statue from Karnak. 'Another nasty case of Fröhlich's,' she'd said, ever the diagnostician, 'Like Bryn.' While I'd lost hair and gained weight over the years he hadn't changed, except that his originally long, dangling ear lobes had gradually disappeared. In the flat we'd shared, our badly-weaned kitten had loved to sneak up and suck at them when he was asleep: Bryn used to run around howling, blood streaming down his neck, with puss, teeth locked, hanging on like grim death. Maybe it was a Faustian pact: the devil had let him keep his youthful looks and illusions but had turned down his soul as forfeit, preferring for some unaccountable reason to take his ear lobes instead.

Sally had been right about Bryn starting smoking again. I accepted one of his untipped Gauloises and he leaned forward to give me a light from his beloved Zippo. At the fourth attempt a little blue flame peeped out and then ducked back into its hole. I bent closer, only for a jet of liquid fire to sear my eyes: I fell for it every time. There was a burning smell: probably that was how all my hair had gone. Bryn sat back with a satisfied air: 'Guess who this is, old man,' he said. He appeared to be impersonating a senile toothless monkey struggling with some very tough nuts: whoever it was, the malice was coming off him like dry ice. My right leg had gone numb: when I rubbed it I discovered that a large cancerous lump was swelling out of the ankle. In rising panic I prodded at it without sensation until I remembered that it was my wallet. I'd always been good at concealing things – the problem was that I usually forgot where I'd put them. Bryn was now flubbering his lower lip and had begun to drool: I said I gave up, just to stop him.

'Why, it's Sally, old man! Haven't you noticed? It drives me mad. She does it all the time in front of the TV.' I explained that I'd never watched Sally watching TV.

'Gangstas! Gangstas, old mon! Gangstas!' he boomed, in that appalling rasta impression that had got us into so much trouble over the years. The gentlemen at the next table, though, appeared to be flattered by his attention: they simpered and then applied themselves to looking even more menacing. 'Like James Fox in *Performance*,' Bryn said admiringly. He was a real gangland buff, to the point of naming his two over-fed tabby cats after the Kray twins. 'More like Derren Nesbitt in "Ooh, You Are Awful!"' I replied.

The lights dimmed and the roadies made their final preparation. Bryn, forgetting the gangsters, motioned towards the piano stool. 'God's empty chair,' he said. I got the reference: Dean Moriarty to Sal Paradise in Kerouac's *On The Road*, but their absent deity had been, bathetically, a so-so expatriate Englishman — George Shearing — whereas we were waiting for The Great Sun Ra.

'Sun Ra! Sun Ra, old man!' Bryn kept saying, punching the soft flesh above my elbow, 'Sun Ra and His Space Arkestra!' He'd always been a hero of ours: we'd waited until the final night of the residency because we knew that it would almost certainly be his farewell performance. He was eighty and last year's stroke had reportedly nearly killed him. To the left and right of the piano were his auxiliary keyboards: a clavioline and his customized space organ, the mutant offspring of a farfisa and a mini-moog. At college we used to start every day by playing 'Nebulae', his electric celeste solo, over and over at mind-shattering volume, taking it in turns to crush each other's heads between the straining speakers. After a while everything would seem to go red, then redder – rose through to crimson – and we agreed that we could both smell burning toast. One morning we'd started seeing wisps of smoke as well and then hallucinated the sound of approaching sirens: this turned out to be the fire brigade – the hall and kitchen were ablaze. Whether it had been started by accidentally invoked salamanders or vengeful neighbours was never established.

It was Sun Ra's mystique that attracted us: his music was supposed to be unlistenable, so we put him into our pantheon before we'd actually heard any of it. When we did get hold of the ESP-disk, two volumes of *Heliocentric Worlds* each time we listened the bits we'd previously liked would now sound lame, whereas the lame bits suddenly sounded great – as if there was some presence swimming around inside the music, surfacing in different places. We bought some imported 45s on the Thoth Label – misconceived attempts to crack the pop charts which were so unaccountably exhilarating and disorientating that we could only conclude that do-wop was the secret language of angels or demons.

Sun Ra was often said to be ahead of his time – by a few thousand light years. Being black, queer and a jazz musician weren't enough disadvantages for him: to deter everybody else he claimed first to have total recall of previous lives in Ancient Egypt and then to have come from another planet altogether, being born not in Birmingham, Alabama, but on Saturn. He'd registered as a conscientious objector, on the grounds that extra-terrestials have no part to play in this world's wars. In the forties he'd anticipated the free jazz explosion of twenty years later but in the sixties he alienated that potential audience by playing distorted twenties swing. Norman Mailer, in *Cannibals And Christians*, described seeing The Arkestra while suffering from a bad cold: the anger of the music had burnt it out within five minutes — curative properties aside, though, he found the experience horrible. At about this time they were hired to play for the most severely damaged patients in a Chicago mental ward: a woman came out of twenty years' catatonia to demand, 'Do you call *that* music?' Sun Ra was also famous for banning all use of drink and drugs: Bryn and I decided that if they ever *did* get high they'd just sound like Mantovani. He was said to make band members sign a vow of chastity but it was also rumoured that he fucked them on a rota basis, first wrapping them in protective asbestos so that his revealed celestial nakedness wouldn't burn them to a crisp. Whichever, he consoled his musicians by reminding them that although all humanity was enslaved they at least were in the Ra Jail, the best in the world. He'd never been fashionable: even the avant-garde wouldn't go near him. He'd never got to work with Paul Simon or Sting: it wasn't so much integrity, more that he was too peculiar to be suborned — offer him money and he'd probably just eat it.

Ronnie Scott appeared at the side of the stage. Dressed in his usual black and navy, he had a pearly aura that I'd noticed always comes off saxophonists good and great, or the recently deceased. I'd spoken to him a few times in passing and got my head bitten off. I didn't know why he was so miserable: if I'd been him I'd have stood outside every night under that blue illuminated horn and shed tears of joy. As he was announcing them The Arkestra seemed to just materialize in their places. They wore vulture-wing capes or wedjat-eye T-shirts and beanie hats with spinning propellers or optical disks. God's chair remained empty – Sun Ra liked to make an entrance. An obscure rustling and muttering began, as if each man was brooding on his own private inexpressible sorrows. Then the sounds resolved into one note, held then smeared, after which India Cooke's violin arched a cadenza reminiscent of 'The Lark Ascending' until – bam! – the lark was hit by a runaway train loaded with badly-moored agricultural machinery. After a while this hellish din resolved itself into a lurching version of 'Astro-Black'. The four percussionists regularly paused to solemnly exchange identical masks but the rhythm was unbroken, as if the drums were generating their own momentum. The band slowed to march time, as if heralding the arrival of a triumphal car. Behind the skirling and hooting horns, cries of challenge or panic seemed to be issuing from no recognizable instrumental source: the lights waxed and waned, in synaesthetic relation to volume or key.

Now Sun Ra, heavily wrapped in cloak and scarves, was led onto the stage. Wedged under his left armpit was a table tennis bat studded with gold and silver milk bottle tops: the famous Attitude Adjuster – a paddle with which he used to spank recalcitrant or particularly attractive members of the audience. He was beyond all that now. Judging by the grey face under the enormous turban they'd already started the mummification process – dehydration, removal of brain and viscera – before he was fully dead. The change was terrible: two years ago at the Hackney Empire he'd still been doing his Ali Shuffle and singing 'Somewhere over the Rainbow' way off key. He breathed something incomprehensible into the microphone: maybe it was his old introduction, 'Some call me Mr Ra, some call me Mr

Ree, but you can call me Mr Mystery.' Half the band started to play one number while the others started something else, then everyone split off in different directions. Remarkably, for a man who had just had a stroke, Sun Ra played as if he'd just had a stroke – or, rather, was in the process of having another one. Some ghostly fragments of stride floated up out of the maelstrom, seemingly independent of his hands, both of which were visible, hanging limply at his sides: he must have been doing it by contractions of the diaphragm or shiftings of the gut. He was four years older than my father had been when he'd died of what the doctors had called old age.

The gangsters got up and made for the exit, cringing as if anticipating a thunderbolt or a pinioned swoop from above. One of them was in tears: had his delicate musical sensibility been outraged or had he contracted Mailer's cold, incubated in the band's vortex of sound and now rehatched? As they left, the Arkestra slid into a mocking groove that suggested water trying to go down a plughole blocked with slimy hair. My teeth and gums had begun to ache and a taste like wet metal filled my mouth: when the trumpet re-entered, somewhere way above high C, a series of sharp pains whiplashed from the tip of my nose deep into my cerebral cortex. It felt as if a phantom wallet was growing on my other ankle: I glanced at Bryn – he'd gone into his Sally impersonation again. At the end of the number there was something I'd not heard in Scott's for many years: fully twenty seconds of – stunned – silence before everyone yelled at once in a mixture of delight and indignation, as if they'd just been goosed or had their pockets picked.

Then a small scowling man with badly-hennaed hair – Marshall Allen – leapt to his feet and began wrestling with his alto saxophone, like Laocöon in the coils of the sea-serpent. Raging into its mouthpiece he pumped the instrument full of bad air which it in turn pumped back into him, like an unsuccessful exorcism. Turning purple, he embarked on a ten-minute barrage of reed squeaks: more punters left, hands clapped over their ears. Allen and tenorist John Gilmore were the longest-serving Arkestra members: they'd dropped by for a jam one afternoon and stayed for forty years. After Allen and his alto had fought each other to a standstill – he'd also broken off halfway through to part-melt a flute – Gilmore rose. Here was the man who had got John Coltrane off junk and then given him lessons: what kind of being could rescue a god? With impressive gravitas he raised the saxophone, rubbed elephant-grey through the lacquer, to his lips, then thought better of it. He looked over at Ra whose head was rocking back and forth, as if he was dowsing. Five more times his cue came round: each time he raised his instrument, glanced at Ra and didn't play a note. Finally he sat down again. It was like Lacan's acolytes used to say as they pushed the paralysed sage's wheelchair round, snaffling the appearance money: 'Silence is now his instrument.' Bryn and I cheered loudly: maybe this had been Sun Ra's tribute to Britain's greatest avant-gardists, Sooty and Sweep?

The Arkestra broke into an a cappella chant – 'Nep-tune, Nep-tune, Nep-tune!' – nasally sounding the two syllables so that they set up a sustained undertone that twanged at the bladder and kidneys. There was a concerted dash for the toilets: Bryn – who'd had retention problems since his hepatitis in Kashmir – got up too. 'Coming, old man?' he asked, miming a fierce double snort off the back of his hand. I told him that I'd stay and guard his Kim Fowley albums. I wondered how he could look so unchanged – apart from those ear lobes – and yet seem totally different. Maybe it was in his movements: had his head always swivelled on his neck like a tank turret? Whenever I achieved anything he somehow made me feel simultaneously that I was depriving him but also that he wouldn't have wanted it anyway. Perhaps he was simulating jealousy to spare me his true feelings of pity or contempt. He'd reacted to my poetry collection – delicate evocation of nature and childhood – as if it had been Boyzone's latest single: 'Hot themes, old man!' He seemed to be expecting agents and publishers to retrieve the brilliant fragments from his dustbin and for record company executives to hang from his drainpipe waiting for him to chance a few chords on the piano.

After only half an hour The Arkestra were obviously exhausted: Sun Ra lay athwart the keyboard, asleep or dead. They limped through 'We Travel the Spaceways', periodically announcing the names of the planets – Mars, Jupiter, Mercury – as flatly as if they had been stations on the District Line. A group of Norwegian youths, looking as if they'd moored their trawler outside, took the gangsters' places. They sat in unblinking silence, wide-eyed and bland as the Midwych Cuckoos. I realized that they were writing messages on pieces of paper and passing them to each other: they weren't mutes, though, as they all shouted 'Beer!' whenever the waitress came past.

I realized that whenever I took a drink the trumpeter was sounding the same little three note snicker: a demonstration of Ra's claim that his band played the audience. I got him, though, by raising the glass to my lips and then withdrawing it, John Gilmore style, choking him off: his glare burned through his Ray-Bans. They had segued into a funereal version of 'Prelude

To A Kiss' when Marshall Allen suddenly launched himself at
the ceiling again, squealing like a stuck pig. My dad, a big
Ellingtonian, would probably have attacked him. The only two
of the Duke's records he didn't have were the small group dates
featuring those feared modernists Mingus and Coltrane. Those,
of course, had been the only ones in my collection. Sometimes
we'd play each other things: I'd mime digging a grave while
he'd have a pretty convincing retching fit. It was only later that
I learned that Sun Ra had started out with Fletcher Henderson's
band and had got the idea of doubling baritone saxes from
Erskine Hawkins' 'Tuxedo Junction': there were only two categories of jazz – good and bad. Now I was catching up on
swing: I hoped that behind the veil my father was listening to
Ra's 'Magic City' or 'Blues in Silhoutte' and considering himself
to be in Heaven rather than in Hell.

Although, by any known criteria, The Arkestra's set was
a shambles, various subliminal effects persisted. 'The secret
vibration', Ra called it: my sinuses ached, my vision was
obscured by a mass fly-past of muscae volitantes and I had the
illusion of a second – and then, briefly, a third – heartbeat.
All the really dangerous stuff comes in antic guise: like in
Anger's *Inauguration of the Pleasure Dome* – just when you're smirking at the camp silliness up on the screen you become aware
that evil incarnate is smirking back at you. Sun Ra had always
said that he was running a selective service to find those who
understand The Creator: 'The audience is sitting an examination
and I'm here to mark their cards' – well, this lot – heading
for the exit in growing numbers, bewildered and annoyed –
were flunking. No one, except Bryn and I and maybe the
silent Norwegians, had come to be secretly vibrated: they'd just

wanted a nice night out – I felt a certain sympathy for them.

'Sorry I've been so long, old man!' Bryn said as he plunged back into his seat, 'I thought I might as well have a piss while I was there.' His face was covered with red blotches which faded as I watched, deepening his pallor. 'This crazy woman kept trying to dip me.' He grinned and with crossed hands yanked his feet up to eye level, as if they belonged to someone else lying under the table. He had donned the Death Shoes, which appeared to be far too big for him: his wallet was also rammed down his sock. 'She asked me if my mother chews my clothes' – he stretched his arms to reveal the rips and tears on his sweater with livid scratches on the skin beneath – 'It's Ron and Reg,' he lamented, 'I don't even feel them doing it.' The Norwegians were giving us dark looks: Bryn's legs had locked at that impossible angle – I bent them, like pipe cleaners, back into a more socially acceptable position. He threw a cigarette high into the air, catching it effortlessly in his mouth on the sixth revolution as it came down, but the hand that moved to light it was empty. The thumb went on agitating an ignition wheel that wasn't there: Bryn stared at it as if expecting his forefinger to ignite. 'Where's my fucking lighter?' he enquired of the world in general. He truly loved that thing: being his, of course, it was the best lighter in the world. It had an archery target design on its side and its metal casing was badly dented, hence the variable petrol flow. The man in 'The Magda' who sold it to him claimed that it had belonged to David Blakely and that it had turned aside the first bullet when Ruth Ellis had shot him outside that very pub thirty years before. I suspected that it had been one of many: in North London garages shifts of men were firing Webleys at Zippo lighters. Something told me that things were going to get nasty: the Norwegians had started openly – if silently – laughing at him. The human race seemed to be divided into those who wanted to kill Bryn and those who wanted to fuck him – with a roughly even gender split inside those categories. He was locking eyes with the biggest Norwegian: although he lost most of his fights he wouldn't back off.

John Gilmore again rose to his feet but this time without his saxophone. In a mechanical voice that seemed to be gradually slowing down as if to the rotation of a key in his back, he began to sing another of the Space Anthems:

> 'What do you do when you know that you know
> That you know that you're wrong?
> You've got to face the music
> You've got to listen to the Cosmo Song'

Bryn, however, was now more interested in the Norwegians. He took off one of his shoes and banged it on the table like Krushchev at the UN then leaned forward: ''Scuse me, Sven, but where's my fucking lighter?' I pulled him back: 'They haven't got it. Can't you see they're all deaf mutes and none of them are smoking.' Sven scribbled something on the back of one of the SILENCE PLEASE cards which the others then solemnly relayed to Bryn. There was a neatly printed message in Norwegian:

> VI VIL STIKKE
> SKOA OPP I ROMPA
> DIN ENGELSKE
> RAEVSLIKKER

Bryn sniffed at the card as if there was some olfactory means of decoding it. 'It's a traditional Norwegian greeting,' I told him. He knew that I'd once lived with a girl from Oslo. 'Meaning – roughly – "a million blessings on you and your wonderful country."' In fact, Britta and I had never talked much so I'd picked up very little of the language – but enough to know that this had something to do with arses and licking. Bryn frowned, unconvinced: 'I'll get it translated,' he finally said, folding it into a little square and tucking it into his top pocket.

The music continued, with raging crescendi when no one seemed to be playing and silences when everyone appeared to be hard at it. The Arkestra was like a well-beaten boxer, way behind on points but refusing to fall, insisting on going the distance. They'd gone into a clinch with the sound, wedging their chins behind its shoulder and letting it pummel away at their bodies. At last silence fell and Gilmore with a hollow voice addressed the nearly-empty club: 'Thank you. That song was called "A Short Cut Through the Sun". This is our final night. In a few hours we'll be heading home across the spaceways. When we travel to Saturn we don't go round the sun, we just go straight through it. You're all afraid of the sun because it's made out of fire but it's just an image: it's not real – it's just a big hole in the sky.' Sun Ra's shoulders were shaking with laughter or weeping: it seemed odd that his votaries should be so disrespectful of their God but then maybe even the greatest power needs to be reminded of its limitations. The two baritone players picked him up and carried him out as if he'd been a wardrobe. Not even Bryn and I were calling for an encore. Sven and his friends silently began to fight with one another: maybe it was a defensive measure to keep Bryn off them. He was readying himself to pitch in when I saw that he'd been sitting on the missing lighter. I held it in front of his face: it lit first time. Fists bunched, he obviously reckoned that I'd been messing him about until I showed him its shape still clearly indented in the black plastic of the seat. On the way out, he kept looking longingly back at the Norwegians: remarkably, even the impact of their punches and their falling bodies made no sound.

'Soho, old man!' Bryn shouted. 'Hazlitt! Blake! Nina Hamnett! Paul Raymond!' He had to keep pumping himself up otherwise he'd have deflated into a scrap of wet rubber on the pavement. We were standing in Frith Street under Ronnie's angel sign, drinking double espressos from Bar Italia, surrounded by people who were somehow contriving to loiter dynamically – twenty years younger than us and exuding an ease and certainty that we had never felt. They were probably thinking the same things about us. Old Compton Street was blocked by a mass of motor-scooters, their long aerials waving like lances. Was it a mod revival or another neo-Italian phase? I never saw anyone riding them into or out of the area: maybe they were hired out locally as fashion accessories or folded away to briefcase size. I watched the girls and boys, at once knowing and open-faced, thronging around them and felt a deep regret that I no longer had to agonize over such matters as the coolest way of leaning against a scooter.

'Love the Vespas!' yelled Bryn. 'Soho, old man! Mozart! Maclaren Ross! Beckford!' I'd never noticed before that directly opposite the club was a blue plaque marking a residence of Mozart: maybe he'd only stayed there during the last few weeks.

I felt a familiar pain, as if something was forcing its way into or out of my chest: that little blonde head was looking up at me again. The hair was now spiked with sweat, the eyelids red and swollen: she was clinging on to my jacket lapels while her feet worked their way up and down the outside and inside of my legs. It felt as if she was barefoot, going after my wallet with her toes: I jammed my left heel into my right instep. 'Does your mother choose your clothes?' she asked. 'Er . . . No' – three hours later and I still couldn't come up with a decent retort. She beamed again and seemed to vanish back into my body. Perhaps it had been my feminine element popping out for some air. I was glad that my anima was so winsome but wished that it would stop trying to rob me.

A blue-grey van – no, a white van evenly covered with dust – jerked slowly up the street. Its tyres were worn down to the wheel-rims, its engine sounded like the howling of damned souls loaded with heavy chains. The thousand conversations about money, art and sex tailed off as everyone turned to watch it. Et In Arcadia Ego: although there wasn't a caped skeleton behind the wheel, just a fat middle-aged man in a Tattershall check shirt and plaid tie. The van halted in front of us: in its nether regions the dust gave place to rust and its back doors were lashed shut by a child's skipping rope with green and red striped wooden handles. The driver lit a small cigar with a Zippo that looked to be dented just like Bryn's. Sun Ra's drummers appeared: after a struggle with the rope's reefs and grannys they loaded away the space organ, which seemed to be held together with masking tape. The bass player briefly waltzed his instrument around the pavement to scattered applause. Marshall Allen, still in the grip of a barely containable rage, threw in his flutes and saxes – hard, overarm – and then stormed off towards Shaftesbury Avenue, accompanied by John Gilmore, who had donned a pair of tan leather trousers that bagged dreadfully at the knees. There was the smell of burning clutch pedal as the driver kept revving the engine while the band, running to and fro, cast nervous glances down the street: maybe they owed somebody money. Cardboard boxes of space props were now carried out: ragged streamers and tinsel, swathes of faded purple velvet, raying silver moons peeling away from warping chipboard, a stern Horus falcon, part-sprayed with glitter. I was reminded of my mum sadly taking down the Xmas decorations on twelfth night. Even Bryn was subdued by the spectacle: 'There's no business like show business, old man,' he said.

I felt a blast of chill air and turned to see Sun Ra emerging from the club. His arms were outstretched, as if he was pulling himself along an invisible rope: I noticed that Mr T flinched away as he passed. His feet hidden by the hem of his robe, he seemed to flow like lava down the steps. Like a golem, his skin looked to have been baked out of clay that was now beginning to crumble and crack: some instinct made me turn my head away and mask my nose and mouth with my styrofoam cup. At the kerb the baritone saxophonists caught up with him, expertly folding his body – he seemed to be conveniently hinged at the waist – into the van's passenger seat. The driver turned and blew a mouthful of smoke into his face but he didn't even blink: his hands fluttered in his lap, making repeated passes like a conjuror's. The percussionists fitted the last of their kits around him, wedging him in place: as a finishing touch a leather-cased wide cymbal was shoved behind his head like a solar disk. Allen and Gilmore reappeared, running up the road at surprising speed and virtually spear-diving through the doors which the driver, with a lion-tamer's flourish, then slammed shut. After he'd retied the skipping rope and kicked down the handbrake the van began to inch forward. Sun Ra's eyes were closed but he couldn't have been asleep: it was part of his legend that he never slept but read through the night from ancient manuscripts previously believed to have been lost when the Alexandrian library was torched.

The van stalled three times before it disappeared into Soho Square: the engine was even noisier than before, as if its vibrations were setting off the cargo of instruments. Bryn was drawn to follow: he looked to be riding an imaginary unicycle for a few yards before collapsing. He'd always been good at falling elegantly and without damaging himself. I still envied his ability to lose control – beyond a certain point I'd start to sober up, no longer out of my head but, whatever I did, plummeting back into it. He lay there, clutching at his ankles: the shoes appeared to be no longer loose but agonizingly tight. Either his feet had swollen or the leather had contracted – summary punishment for a poor man in rich man's shoes. I prised his wallet loose and helped him to his feet: he seemed to have jettisoned the previous pair, along with Kim Fowley and Anthony Powell.

The stars over Soho looked brighter than usual: larger, closer, burning through the nimbus of the city. The Arkestra's reaching Saturn seemed a more realistic possibility than my getting Bryn on to his night bus.

Bryn had started out living in Camden but had then moved gradually across the city. He used to say that London had

swallowed him: he was now in the lower bowel – Downham
– on the point of being shat out into the satellite towns. 'Kill
me,' he often requested, 'before I get to East Grinstead.' I took
his arm and we headed south. At one moment his legs were
stilt-stiff, at the next they appeared to be melting – either way,
he was limping heavily. With perfect co-ordination he opened
a fresh packet of cigarettes, extracted one and lit it. 'Ruth Ellis,'
he said. 'Last woman to be hanged in Britain! Irreplaceable!
Fucking Norwegians!' I reminded him that he'd got his lighter
back but that obviously wasn't the point. 'Hanged for being
beautiful,' he continued. 'Think of those fat Yorkshire hands
putting the rope round her pretty neck, old man.' I'd told him
how my auntie had lived in Clayton a few doors away from
the executioner, Albert Pierrepoint: as a result Bryn seemed to
feel that the guilt was on my head. I saw that his jaws had begun
weirdly shuttling: presumably unconsciously, he was being Sally
again.

We passed through Theatreland. Bryn dragged me over to
look at some cast photographs: groups of blonde women in
top hats and fishnet tights glancing coyly over their left shoulders. At the front of the house four rough sleepers lay, each
under his own critical notice: 'STUNNING' (*Mirror*) – 'GO! GO!
GO!' (*Times*) – 'A HEARTWARMING SHOW' (*Mail*) – 'DIVINE
DECADENCE' (*Telegraph*). They were part-mummified, like Sun
Ra, but the two unswathed mouths were smiling beautiful
chrome yellow smiles, as if the attenuated dogs tethered to
their wrists were drip-feeding them dreams of that fabled lost
Saturnian golden age of plenty. They appeared to be sinking
into the Yorkshire Sandstone pavement as if it was a swansdown
mattress. Never pass a beggar, my dad had advised me, so I

always carried plenty of change. For some reason, I felt as if I
was buying something from them and, moreover, getting it dirt
cheap. Bryn – jokingly, I hoped – motioned to empty their
caps and tobacco tins: maybe this was how he was escaping
Sally's grip. They seemed to be dressed in old clothes of mine
– that multi-darned Gaelterra sweater and soiled Crombie coat
looked all too familiar – as if they were parts of myself that
I'd sloughed off over the years.

We made surprisingly fast progress: although he was lame,
stoned and drunk, Bryn was sweeping me along. 'London!' He
shouted again, 'Oscar Wilde! David Litvinoff! Dr Johnson! Dr
Dee!' He broke free and ran ahead, waggling his arms like a
tightrope walker teasing the crowd by pretending to lose his
balance; 'Biggest city in the world!'

'The twenty-fifth biggest,' I replied, 'just behind Istanbul,
Jakarta and Dacca.'

'The greatest! The city of the imagination! The city of the
soul!' He tried one of his playful shoves that were closer to
rugby hand-offs: I sidestepped, so that he nearly staggered under
the wheels of a passing minicab.

He greeted Trafalgar Square: 'The centre of the city! The
centre of the world!' He'd read some international survey that
established this as the most famous spot in the most famous
city in the world: I wondered what wild illusions the Eskimos
or Chinese could harbour about this empty space filled with
traffic and pigeons. Bryn saluted the most famous statue of the
most famous hero: 'Nelson, old man! The victor of Trafalgar!
The conqueror of the Nile! The Fucking Butcher of Fucking
Naples!' Each title was emphasized with a stiff-arm jab. I took
two quick steps sideways and saw him cringe back. I realized

that I'd been giving myself room to hit him. I hadn't made a fist, let alone raised it, but I'd felt my weight shift and my left shoulder dip and I knew that he'd seen or sensed it too. I might as well have beaten him to a pulp: the line had been crossed – I was finished with Bryn.

'Sorry, old man, I know he's a hero of yours' – he brushed imaginary dust off my sleeve – 'It was all that Lady Hamilton's fault, nagging on at him. Fucking apron strings' – He gave me a huge, false smile, 'Lend me twenty for a cab?'

'No.'

'We could go to a cashpoint.'

'I've got the money, old chap, I'm just not giving it to you.'

'Sally will be grateful,' – Bryn ran his tongue round his lips twice, anti-clockwise – 'You'll be getting a nice big reward.'

We crossed the square: even at that hour tourist groups were busy videoing each other. 'It's gone,' said Bryn when we reached his bus stop, 'I've missed it.' I just pointed to the 171 standing there. 'It's broken down,' he said. The bus was brightly lit and full of passengers. 'There's no room,' he said. 'There's room for one more inside, sir,' said the conductor: he looked vaguely familiar – with his mullet haircut and pearl-drop earrings. Maybe he was a glam-rocker making an ill-conceived comeback video. 'It's going to crash, old man,' said Bryn. 'It's like in *Dead of Night* – he says that and next thing the bus falls off Westminster Bridge . . . Remember, old man: The ventriloquist with the homicidal dummy.'

'Max–well! Max–well!' said the conductor through clenched teeth. 'Best British film ever made, except for *Colonel Blimp*, of course.'

'Where else but London' – Bryn hissed into my ear – 'do you get bus conductors like that?'

Personally, I was getting rather tired of everybody being *too* interesting.

'I haven't got the fare,' said Bryn. Not until I'd started to count it into his hand – in coins of the smallest possible denomination – did he produce his travel card. I could see a thick cartilage of banknotes in his wallet. Without further word he jumped aboard and clattered upstairs. There were half-inch gaps between his heels and the Dead Man's shoes: they were simultaneously too large and too small. The conductor shook his head and clicked his tongue sympathetically: that was another problem with London – everyone understood every-thing, at a glance.

I started walking away but then stopped and turned as I heard the bus's engine start. As it came past, I saw that Bryn was sitting in the front seat, waving vigorously at me. The expression on his face was different: one that I hadn't seen in a long time, if ever before. Its mixture of fear and blissful anticipation made me think of wartime film of children being evacuated. All the other passengers were faceless – turned towards each other, kissing. I knew that this would be my last sight of Bryn: disappearing into the darkness down Whitehall, a solitary figure on a bus full of lovers. I stood there for a while, listening: there was no splash – at least they'd made it across the river.

The buses and crowds had all gone: only their echoes remained. The sky was still full of stars and above The Strand was a full moon, so bright and perfectly round that I'd taken it to be an illuminated sign for some eatery or show. I looked up at Horatio: it wasn't for his victories that I admired him, nor even for being loved by the most beautiful woman in the world but for the way that, as a midshipman, he'd attacked a polar bear with the butt-end of his musket.

I had an hour to kill before the first tube would take me home to Belsize Park: there was no chance of sleep there because Katy would have already raised Justine and I'd be walking straight into the heavenly chaos of Sunday breakfast. While the ladies dribbled at each other, I would fry the bacon, with the cats — feral creatures absurdly named Bubble and Squeak — biting at my ankles. Afterwards, we'd push Katy's pram across the Heath to Kenwood House and stare into the 1665 Rembrandt self-portrait. He's proudly standing, holding palette, brushes and maulstick, between two perfect circles but somehow you feel that he's on the point of collapsing with exhaustion and despair. Then we'd sit in the beer garden of The Spaniards: Justine mildly disagreeing with everything she read in the *Independent*, me imagining how the pub's most celebrated patrons — Dick Turpin and Black Bess — would have scattered the minor TV celebrities, bright ties tucked into their waistbands, that posed around the bar — and Katy, sleeping, infolded like a rosebud, clutching her favourite toy, that elk-antlered koala.

Happiness: more than I'd ever dreamed of. I shut my eyes and, with a double catch in heart and throat, saw on the red field of their lids the faces of Katy and Justine, wreathed in golden light . . . then they gradually twisted and distorted to become duplicate images of Bryn, evilly munching and slavering as Sally at the TV. What kind of welcome awaited him in Downham? Beyond any sorrow or indignation, I still couldn't dispel the sense that his soul-sickness was a strange form of health, that his failures were, at some deeper level, triumphs. Suppose there were things beyond my hopes and desires — beyond even my dreams? Or suppose that I'd fitted together the jigsaw pieces of myself in the wrong order — revealing a perfect carthorse where there should, unfortunately, have been an orchestra? A sudden tension behind my eyes implied that those pieces were too tightly joined even to be able to be pulled out again. Bryn hadn't changed: he was merely having to fight harder and dirtier to stay where and who he was, desperately preserving that absence inside himself, so that into its jagged outline something unimaginable — the infinite, the truth, every-thing or nothing — would be able to fall or ascend. What would I do if that great or terrible destiny in which we had both once believed was to suddenly turn up? Even if I was still able to recognize it I was now all full up, without room for even one more inside.

Although I was flitting between the shadows along The Strand the cruising patrol cars and paddy wagons didn't even slow down. I was police identification type #7: Flâneur (harm-less). Even as a night wanderer I was a failure, unable to lose myself in the most labyrinthine and unfamiliar parts of the city; whenever I paused my head would swing unerringly to point due North. In a window displaying office furniture I confronted my reflection. What a thoroughly nice-looking man, the kind you wouldn't hesitate to ask directions of, so long as you weren't searching for Hell or Heaven. I tried to twist that benign half-smile into a snarl but only made it worse — posi-tively Pickwickian.

I cut down to the Embankment, then turned back towards

Bill Broady

Westminster, feeling a gentle wind on my face, although the trees in Adelphi Gardens didn't move, made no sound. The lights reflected in the river didn't correspond to anything on the far bank: a line of red lozenges bisecting a circle of silver circles seemed to be rotating slowly a few feet below the surface. Something dark loomed ahead: with a shock I registered the enormous arse and tail of a sphinx of dull brass, one of the attendants flanking Cleopatra's Needle. My first job in London – I stuck it for a week – had been franking mail at Shell Mex House: during my breaks I'd come and stroke the obelisk's rose-red granite, imagining that I could feel it vibrating with power and mystery under my hands. Since then I'd driven past it thousands of times, without giving it another thought: you know when you've become part of a place – you don't notice anything about it any more.

The Needle had been lugged here – via Cleo's Alexandria – from Heliopolis where, with its twin, it had flanked the gates of the Temple of the Sun. At least it wasn't in a museum but out under the open sky and still next to water, although the Thames must have seemed the merest trickle after the Nile – Bryn would doubtless have claimed that it was bigger because so many English poets had ruminated upon it. The twin had a far worse fate: it was taken by Caligula to Rome where I'd seen it, insultingly garnished with a cross, under the Pope's bedroom window. I'd consoled myself with the thought that one day St Peter's Basilica would bear a Sekhmex lion-head.

On the chest of the second sphinx, scratched and pitted by German bomb fragments, I traced the hieroglyphs of solar disk, comb and scarab. MEN-KHEPER-RA: the divine name of

Thurmose III, The Warrior Pharaoh who had conquered half the world only for Akhnaten to piss it all away, staring raptly into the sun while the borders contracted. I clambered up and sat astride it. I could now see, at eye level, leprous green ferns behind the pedestal's uraeii – bracken, growing anywhere, unkillable. Downriver the floodlit dome of St Paul's was peering over Waterloo Bridge. Bryn always used to shake his fist at it, reminded of the bald head of his hated father. I recalled how, during the Blitz, the writer and film-maker Humphry Jennings, revelling in the smoke and fire of Natural Selection in action, had claimed to have descried on it the features of Charles Darwin. Bryn had his own Theory of Unnatural Selection, undreamt of by evolutionists – that, while the brutish and ruthless got survival, the more awkward forms that couldn't or wouldn't adapt got immortality. And even on this earth, he'd say, there were rumours that the predators would finally fail, as the meek gradually smothered them, like bracken.

A dog-fox appeared, heading east, hoping for a slap-up breakfast round the back of the Savoy. It sat for a while observing me with its bright sardonic eyes, its tongue lolling into a pink question mark: presumably it felt safe with a man whose mother still chose his clothes. Then I watched it saunter away along the road's central white line, tail held stiff as a rudder. I couldn't make it symbolize anything: it was no Anubis-jackal – just an urban fox.

Faint shouts came from across the river. I couldn't make out the words but as they echoed along the concrete tunnels and walkways of the South Bank I gradually picked up a familiar rhythm:

> 'What do you do when you know that you know
> That you know that you're wrong?
> You've got to face the music
> You've got to listen to the Cosmo Song.'

The water seemed to ripple with the feeble sound waves of the silly, insidious chant that had unaccountably come into my head so many times over the years. Although the voice was unrecognizably distorted, I knew that it could only be one person. Sally would wait in vain in that chilly bed in Downham. Bryn had baled out of the bus of lovers and was wandering again, staggering along in the Death Shoes, in the absolute certainty that everything was going to plan, that the ridiculous position in which he had so long maintained himself was about to reach its intersection with the marvellous. The obelisk pointed him upwards while sternly admonishing me: he was an Akh-spirit, readying himself for transfiguration, while all my self-knowledge and self-control, my senses of humour, proportion and responsibility were merely condemning me to eternal darkness as a mut. There was no escape: even if I had kicked my heels and galloped the Sphinx all the way back to Hampstead, its only significance would have been the saving of my tube fare.

The first train out of Charing Cross came over Hungerford Bridge, its wheels rattling along in that same rhythm.

> 'You've got to face the music
> You've got to listen to the Cosmo Song.'

There were no faces at the windows: even the cab seemed to be empty. The rays of the rising sun struck an answering flare from the apex of the Needle, as if the gilded cap it would have worn at Heliopolis had been returned. Lazy silver jumbos were studding the sky, stacking up for the long descent to Heathrow. Far below, a smaller craft followed a shallow trajectory, jolting westwards, its driver's cheroot leaving a broken, wispy vapour trail: a dusty white vanful of broken-down musicians that only a knotted skipping rope saved from being hoovered up by infinite space. It was heading straight for the sun, that hole in the sky, their short cut back to Saturn or beyond. After a while the speck was lost in the glare: I turned my smarting eyes away. The shouting across the river had finally stopped. Goodbye, Bryn. Goodbye, Sun Ra.

Bouncing Back

... At about this time bears began to appear in the city. My first sighting – a startling orange-brown flash – was at the wheel of a rusty council van that was pulling out – without indicating – from the Shearbridge depot. I watched it in the mirror, closing on me. Its wedge-shaped head, fully two feet wide, was bumping against the roof: neckless, with ring-rolls of jowl fat melting into the shoulders, it vibrated like a blanc-mange. A matt-black central square – less a nose than a Hitler/ Chaplin moustache – was its sole distinct feature. I shaded into the cycle lane to let it pass. The hands on the wheel were swollen, seemingly fingerless: neither flesh nor fur, more like velour. It glanced down and across: in so far as it had an expression, it was contemptuous. Although I could see no mouth I got the impression that it had said something to me. I gave chase but it shot a red light at All Saints Road to shake me off. Whatever it was, the creature could certainly drive.

I was no stranger to hallucinations. There was an armadillo that I used to have some interesting conversations with and I still always held each new pint of Guinness up to the light to check that the little green lizards weren't once again sporting in its turbid depths. If there was the slightest flicker I'd replace it on the bar and walk straight out: they used to play havoc with my guts, those lizards. And there were more recent spectres that sometimes passed my house: a ragged crone carrying a pineapple and a limping fox-terrier with a child's doll, limbless, in its mouth. I'd yell for Cathy but by the time she got there they'd always gone. I decided not to mention this latest one and then reminded myself that she'd finally moved out three months ago.

That night I fell asleep on the sofa again, so that by next morning seven hours of subliminal TV images had erased all recollection of the creature. Unfortunately, when I stopped off at the cashpoint on my way to college I saw it again. Across the road, with its back to me, it was staring into a shop window, appraising convertible sofa-beds in chintzy fabrics or, more likely, watching my reflection. Naked, pachydermous, lumpen, it was stumbling in the bondage trousers of its own flesh. At least I could now confirm that it was a man wearing a costume. Then, from north and south, others emerged to join it, greeting each other with broad gestures and muffled shouts. I still wasn't certain that they were bears, though – the flapping, pouchy ears seemed way too long. Not elephants: no trunks. Nor rhinoceroses: no horns. Pendulous, wrinkled: maybe they were bloodhounds? At this point a fourth appeared who actually filled the suit: was it padded out with kapok or was there a real bear inside? So it *was* bears, then – but what were they doing here? Or, rather, why was I seeing them? As I fled, they had joined hands and were embarking on a clumsy quadrille. The collective noun for bears is a sloth, I remembered, but what about a group of people in ill-fitting bear costumes? – A sag? A slouch? A slump? Driving past the station I saw three more, with proffered leaflets wedged into their paws: the commuters all walked past, unblinking. Obviously, like Orestes with his Furies, the bears were visible only to me.

That morning my students seemed even less interested than usual: there weren't even any embarrassed shufflings when I essayed a joke – dead silence. I'd always liked it when, between ten and midday, the sunlight through the transom window dazzled me but now I sweated, my hands shook, and a series of black and silver circles, like eclipsing planets, floated across my vision. It wasn't the hangover, unless maybe it wasn't quite headsplitting enough. My lecture sounded senseless: as if the good old British Constitution – tacit, unwritten mysteriously insubstantial – was something I was making up, yet another delusion, like the swimming lizards. I wondered if my audience had sneaked away: against the glare I could only make out fuzzy, motionless shapes. I fought off the rising dread that I was addressing a sloth or a slump.

After lunch I walked back from The Castle with Mal, our Local Historian. He was updating me on his eternal work-in-progress – a vast history of The Bradford Alehouse, which conveniently enabled him to pass off his own alcoholism as research. He'd just discovered exhaustive records in the archives of the size, shape and number of spittoons used in four adjacent Manchester Road pubs between 1869 and 1873. This meant the introduction of a startling new category: IRISH(Genteel). I'd just begun to expound on my startling theory that, wherever and whenever, drink is drink and drunks are drunks when, in front of us, two of the bear-creatures tacked crazily over the mock-cobbles to disappear into the Physics Block. I could have sworn that I'd seen Mal's eyes following them, so I took a big chance. 'What *are* those things?' I asked, as casually as I could manage. He glared at me – as if I'd propositioned him or, worse yet, contravened every rule of good fellowship. 'The Bouncing Bears' – he doubled up as if something invisible had punched him in the stomach – 'The new campaign to' – he refilled his lungs with air – 'revive the city.' His eyes were unfocusing again: he seemed to be shrinking or, rather, receding, spinning back in his private time-vortex towards the safety of 1869 and his spittoons. Perhaps only the past should register in the true historian's visual field? My problem was that I was far too here and now: apart from the odd armadillo, I was strictly limited to whatever happened to be going on.

When I left work at five the bears had massed outside The Mannville Arms. The morning's waddling had given place to capering: only just born, you had to admire the speed of their development. Linking arms, they embarked on a series of high kicks as sickle-smooth as The Tiller Girls, then broke away into hand- or paw-stands. One could even do back and side flips, as if the cracked pavement flags were a trampoline. Each one had its own distinct personality: cheeky, thoughtful, menacing, sad – it was some sort of testimony to the impartibility of the human spirit. They gave off a strong smell, like sour milk overlaid by perfume: I recognized it as Estée Lauder – Cathy used to spray it on our cat. At least I was now secure in the knowledge that everyone else was seeing them too: my students turned their faces away, like they did from policemen, beggars and lecturers.

I drove fast across the city, as if in flight, to The Royal Standard. Betty began drawing me a pint of Taylor's Landlord:

I had no 'usual' but she somehow always knew what I was
needing. The aroma of its herbs unblocked my sinuses with an
audible click and I took my first clean breath of the day. A
mass of dust motes, like a kindly angel in mid-materialization,
escorted me to my seat. Although no one had fed it the juke-box
began to boom and rattle like an approaching tube train – the
opening to Blondie's 'Fade Away And Radiate'. I watched the
lights of the traffic bleeding kaleidoscopically through the thick
stained glass: poor devils speeding from ghastly jobs to worse
homes. I took my first sip of Landlord, lit a cigarette and,
closing my eyes, offered up a prayer to my nameless personal
god of tobacco, good beer, dust and wasted lives.

I picked up the Bradford *Telegraph and Argus*. A screaming
headline – BLAST-OFF!! – filled most of the front page, with a
crudely-drawn bear surf-boarding the hyphen from T to O.
The sub-heading ran: FROM TODAY WE'RE ON THE WAY BACK
UP! That very afternoon, I learned, Max Madden, the MP for
Bradford West, had tabled a Commons Motion congratulating
The Council and The Chamber of Commerce on the launch
of the Bouncing Back Initiative. Spearheaded by the famous –
already! after only a few hours! – Bouncing Bears, its aim was
'to attract the new businesses and tourism that the city so badly
needs'.

On the inside pages I read that there were THIRTY-THREE
REASONS TO PUT A BOUNCE IN OUR STEP. These included that
Bradford was now 'The Heart Of The Building Society World':
did this mean that it contained an unusually large number of
such outfits or that – in debt reclamation or mortgage-rates –
they evinced a higher than average level of compassion? . . .
That Animal Fibres of Eccleshill had developed a revolutionary

mix of cashmere and angora goat's wool, to be called Cashgora
... That Concorde could now land on Leeds-Bradford's newly-
extended runway, although it would admittedly only be appear-
ing on bank holidays to take local worthies — at £1,000 a head
— for an hour's Supersonic Champagne Superspin ... That
Spring Ram were producing one in four UK domestic baths
... That we had before us the shining examples of our 'great
Bradford achievers', such as Mandy Shires, Joe Johnson, David
Hockney, 'King' Kenny Carter — beauty queen, snooker cham-
pion, painter, speedway rider.

From every page Bouncer the cartoon bear fixed me with its
hypnotic, Manson-like stare. Why was it always saluting? Why
was it — apart from a wing-collar and kipper tie — naked? Why
did it have no discernible sexual characteristics? Why was it
heavily freckled? Why was it strabismic? Could it have been that
evergreen school assembly blasphemy, 'Gladly My Cross-Eyed
Bear'? I ordered another pint, stopped rationing my cigarettes
and tried to make some sense of it.

Bradford, as far as I knew, had no ursine associations at all.
It was obvious that, to enlist apt alliteration's artful aid, whatever mascot they'd chosen would have to begin with a B, but
why bears? Why not buzzards or bison? Budgies or bandicoots?
Why not bantams, the club badge of Bradford City? I supposed
that although these were fierce, brave and lion-affrighting, they
were also notably ill-fated, being favoured as a parting oblation
by Socrates and such ... and that recent memories of the Valley
Parade fire — of oblivious celebrants in Foghorn Leghorn suits
being cauled by the burning stand's molten bitumen cascades
— were all too sharp. But why not bats or bees? Bulls or bulbuls?
Baboons or babirusas? Badgers, beagles or boomslangs? Why

not boars? — A boar's head proudly tops the city's coat of arms, along with the hunting horn of the Rushworth family, who had been gifted Great Horton as a reward for killing such a beast. They don't *bounce*, I supposed, and they weren't cuddly enough. Those tusks might have frightened the children: all they did was rootle and, sometimes, gore. The choice of 'bouncing' was more comprehensible. Alternatives were limited — blooming? buzzing? blithering? blundering? beseeching? . . . But why 'back'? If Bradford had been away, where had it been? And where was it going? Where was it bouncing from? And where was it bouncing to?

Not even three more pints of Landlord, two packets of cashews or 'California Über Alles' and 'Love-itis' at mind-shattering volume could bring on any further insights. What the hell was it all about? Bradford's goose was cooked by the end of the nineteenth century, when the wool industry had gone into steady and irreversible decline: bear-suits, Cashgora and David Hockney weren't going to change that. There was nothing to be done . . . But then what did I know? Sitting there, fat and grimy, alone, soaking up toxins — the best I could do was rootle, I couldn't even gore, any more. What had I ever done to attract the new businesses and tourism that we so badly needed? Maybe everyone, everywhere could reinvent themselves by fiat? I was beautiful, I told myself, I was a sixteen-year-old hermaphrodite on another planet . . . by the look of my liver-spotted hands, the trick didn't seem to have worked.

Outside, on the empty streets, I felt a tension in the air as if the silence was about to be broken by the twang of a great bowstring, sending some huge, deadly arrow to strike at someone, somewhere. The dead city was about to be dragged unwillingly back

Bill Broady

into life: when Christ reawakened Lazarus, I wondered, did he have a bear-suit ready for him? My usual short cut through the alley behind The Boy And Barrel was blocked by a soft, heaving mass: Bouncer and the others were pouring pints of Tetleys into various gaps in each other's faces. When I finally reached my house – its darkened windows showing that I wasn't home – I had the sudden desire to put my foot down and just drive, drive until I was out of petrol, then get out and run and run ... Exit – Pursued By Bears.

I heard that their costumes had been bought as a cheap job lot left over from the last doomed Sugar Puffs promotion, just before their cereal-munching bears had been supplanted by the Honey Monster, a giggling subnormal puppet-hulk wearing a school cap. Whatever, from now on they were omnipresent: in every photograph, always looking somehow awkward and out of proportion, as if they'd been roughly inserted into the places where subsequently discredited elements had, in Stalinist fashion, been airbrushed out. They even appeared flying shotgun in the new three-million-pound police helicopter, the mission of which seemed to be to ensure that our inner-city crack dealing and ram raiding didn't spread to the most isolated and picturesque parts of the Dales. Healthy minds in healthy bodies: they were particularly keen on culture and sport. The corridors of the Central Library were lined with bear colophons, books temptingly displayed in their hollowed-out chest cavities: for some obscure reason, they favoured The Movement – John Wain novels and New Lines anthologies. Bouncer depped in white tie and tails for James Loughran at St George's Hall, waving a baton in front of the Hallé while they played 'Fingal's Cave', although he appeared to be conducting something quite different – 'Poème D'Extase', maybe. He also regularly guested on tenor sax with the Gordon Tetley Big Band: his solos were admittedly rudimentary, loud and one-note like Rudy Pompilli, but that note was interminably sustained, without a quiver, showing a mastery of circular breathing to rival Sonny Rollins.

Even on our college stationery, the old council logo – grey and black lower case b's merging into a domino mask – had given way to Bouncer, saluting smartly top right or sometimes even, bilocating, in mid-hurtle diagonally across the page, so that you had to fit your words around him. On posters he was represented inflating a word balloon which promoted the council's anti-racism and anti-sexism policies and then – in a second series a few weeks later – he celebrated its non-racism and non-sexism, implying that both these evils had been eradicated in the interval. Bouncer also starred on the AIDS pamphlet that they made us hand out to our students. The text – etched on to his sack-like torso, as in Kafka's 'In The Penal Colony' – reassured them that 'Bradford's bouncing ahead with its policies and actions over AIDS and HIV'. So we were actually *ahead* on this one: the subliminal message seemed to be that all-over velour was the best prophylactic. Or maybe it was that the bears themselves were infected? Was all that bouncing the first sign of the immune system's breaking down? Were those freckles the telltale skin eruptions? Were their skins' folds and pouches the result of the occupants' rapid weight loss? My students, forewarned, determined never to share a syringe or have unprotected anal intercourse with a Bouncing Bear.

I finally got to see inside one of them when he was interviewed in mufti on a local TV news magazine. He was anything between twenty-five and fifty: greying, thin and whippy, with angular protrusions from face and hands, as if every bone in his body had been broken and then badly reset. The eyes were strangely distorted, as if full of tears behind pebble glass: he looked a bit like me wearing a talcumed wig and ten stones lighter. His story was familiar but also, as the interviewer informed us, heartwarming: he'd been laid off by Manningham Mills six years ago and wasted away on the dole thereafter. He ate and ate but he didn't get fat; he drank and drank but couldn't get drunk. The more he slept the more exhausted he felt – finally he was unable even to summon up sufficient energy and will to put a fresh toilet roll in the holder: 'I looked at it all morning, then finally I just put it on top of the cistern' . . . But now, as a Bouncing Bear, attracting the new businesses and tourism that we needed, his life was back on track. His wife and kids had returned and he'd fully recovered his potency as a husband and his authority as a father. Moreover, he'd undergone a spiritual transformation through the discovery that the animal he was impersonating was, in fact, his totem. 'When I get into that suit,' he said, 'I can feel my bear-soul flowering inside me.' He'd taken his family down to London Zoo, where they'd spent six hours watching the bears: 'They definitely recognized me. They all came right up to the wire and just stared at us, making little whimpering noises' . . . Poor lad – if they had recognized him it was as a fellow creature trapped in a cage, not as another bloody bear.

Bradford's Bouncing Back: yes, it was perfect. Fighting back would have been too aggressive, implying the unacceptable possibility that we might actually have had some enemies in this world. Bouncing was le mot juste: knock us down and we'd rebound straight back off the canvas, not even waiting for the standing count but coming forward only to be decked again. And always smiling, too punchy even to know we were being hit, let alone who was hitting us. After all, we were out to underbid the workers of the third world to attract the new businesses that we needed: 'we speak slightly better American and we're even bigger saps – I mean, can you imagine the kaffirs and coolies standing for those Bears?' . . . Bouncer's perpetual salute was also, on reflection, perfect: the Good Soldier without a glimmer of Schweikian irony, the valiant little man ready for orders, cannon-fodder, the salt of the earth. Bradford was cring-ing back, tail between its legs, tongue lolling out ready to lick the hands that were striking it.

In order to attract the new businesses and tourism that we needed, the *T&A* resolutely accentuated the positive. Its political tone changed: no longer did it inveigh – or at least mildly jib – against free market capitalism and government spending cuts. Although the usual local atrocities, disasters and accidents were still reported, these stories were now relegated to the inside pages – starkly factual, shorn of unnecessary details, with noth-ing of the previous tone of gloomy relish. Feature writers ignored such inconveniences altogether, so you'd read of the two latest murders – wife of husband, son of father – then of the growing incidence of rickets and malnutrition on the Ravenscliffe Estate, then of the torture of animals on a chil-dren's urban farm before coming at last to an editorial that asked, 'How can anyone deny that Bradford's Bouncing Back when there's yet another DIY Superstore opening up?'

The moment that anyone did anything marginally noteworthy they were ludicrously over-lauded, installed as instant Folk-Heroes. I'd thought that the whole point of such figures as Robin Hood, Dick Turpin or City's last great centre-forward, Bobby Campbell, was that they had to be nominated by The Folk, not foisted on them by journalists. The Bradford Achievers — Kenny, Mandy, David and Joe — figured almost as prominently as The Bouncing Bears until it became apparent that to be so designated was a poisoned chalice. Only Hockney, far away in LA, about to embark on an epic portrait series of his pet dachshunds, appeared to escape a speedy and terrible nemesis.

Mandy Shires, Bingley's Queen of Beauty, was the first victim. Miss Bradford, Miss UK, then close runner-up in Miss World — they were about to appoint her as Bradford's Official International Ambassadress — leading the fightback, padded shoulder to padded shoulder with The Bears — when it was discovered that she had once posed topless for the *News of the World*. Once the councillors had established that her nipples had indeed been visible, they sacked her. Broken-hearted, Mandy left for a modelling career in South Africa. Next was Kenny Carter, the World Speedway Champion, a monosyllabic but pleasantly open-faced lad, although he was seldom seen to smile. One night, at his lonely moorland farm, apparently without warning or immediate motive, he took a double-barrelled shotgun and killed first his girlfriend, then himself. It took my neighbour, an avid Halifax Dukes fan, the entire morning to expressionlessly scrape all the KING KENNY transfers off the windows of his car and caravan.

Then there was poor Joe Johnson. The whole city had gone wild when he won the World Snooker Championship. Joe had hitherto seemed to be irredeemably small-time. He had as much talent as anyone – with the most beautiful cueing action imaginable – but, as the sneering Celts and cockneys who dominated the game loved to constantly remind him, he always bottled it. He'd never won a single televised match: the cameras paralysed him. He could feel them sucking his soul out of his body – he'd lose as quickly as possible to get away, to efface himself . . . Then, all of a sudden, the nerves disappeared, prompting rumours of hypnosis, religious conversion or, most likely, a switch from Tetley's to Taylor's. Right from the start of the tournament, he'd given the impression that he'd already won it and that the actual playing of matches was a mere formality. Steely, unblinking, playing at three times his normal speed, he slaughtered Steve Davis, the defending champion, in the final . . . But as soon as he had it all – success, fame, money – he discovered that he didn't want it. He didn't like having to endorse things, posing with Page Three Girls, opening supermarkets, being the butt of TV comedians' jokes. He hated having to smile: 'I just want to be ordinary', he said dolefully. I once saw him awkwardly manoeuvring a chocolate-coloured stretch Mercedes down Thackley Main Street. No heads turned: he looked – incredibly, even in his scarlet velvet suit – *ordinary*. He loathed having to travel: he only wanted to be with his lovely wife Teryl – an affectionate diminutive, I liked to believe, of Pterodactyl . . . There was only one thing for it: Joe happily reverted to losing every tournament in the first round. Pretty soon he'd become an unperson for the *T&A*, which started trying to raise the profiles of two fast-cueing young Thais who had recently settled in the area . . . but for me Joe Johnson – in freely choosing failure over success, in snatching back obscurity out of the jaws of celebrity – was an authentic Bradford Achiever, the perfect role model for the kiddies, a hero of negation, our Bartleby.

If the football or rugby league teams managed to string even a couple of wins together, the previously cynical local sports columnists would now pump up expectations. At fourteenth in the table, they'd opine, City were perfectly placed for that big promotion push: really successful sides always like to give themselves a twenty point deficit to make up, they find it concentrates the mind wonderfully. When, on consecutive nights at Odsal, Northern were to play the Australian tourists and City, in the Littlewoods Cup, Brian Clough's Nottingham Forest, there appeared – under twin portraits of Bouncer in the clubs' garish kits – the promise that 'Our Boys are about to tweak the kangaroo's tail and shut Cloughie's big mouth'.

Odsal Top – Britain's highest and largest stadium – has its own microclimate: there's usually a strange Cimmerian feel, as if you are entering a different geological age. That night, the torrential rains and the swirling pink and green fog-banks meant that we were not only spared witnessing The Bears' pre-match routines but also caught only intermittent glimpses of Australia subsequently beating Northern 38 – nil. Such fixtures are never cancelled because, with the tightness of tour scheduling, they can't be rearranged: the clubs would play through plagues of scorpions rather than lose out on their most lucrative game of the season. Somewhere in midfield, no doubt, the fabled Wally Lewis was working his magic: all we saw was the ball emerging from the murk four times for an Australian winger to flop over the try-line. The linesman kept sneaking on to the playing area, once disappearing for fully ten minutes: the referee had to come over to fetch him in at half-time. Another top night of Bradford sport: I'd paid ten quid for a drenching and the sight of a fat man with a flag running sideways.

The next afternoon I was in Rawson Market, stocking up on my favourite Roma Mix coffee and Black Diamond cheddar. Nobody else was buying anything: just standing and staring at the stalls or at one another. It didn't look as if they cared much about the commercial possibilities of Cashgora or being at the heart of the building society world: they all looked mad or in despair. I was getting dark looks for not being in rags and having the standard number and disposition of limbs – every second person seemed to be crippled. With extreme difficulty, an old man was pushing a wheelchair: its occupant was a youngish woman, her body terribly swollen, with a facial prosthetic that looked as if someone had rammed a pecten into her bloodied mouth. As always, there was a strange sickly-sweet blue-grey mist hanging in the air, like incense and the fumes from a chip pan fire . . . Suddenly, the bears were there, seeming to charge straight through the crowds as if they were substanceless, wraiths. The leading pair were carrying between them, like a huge chrome funeral urn, the Littlewoods Cup. A breastless, thyroid-eyed girl was running with them, her head thrown back like The False Maria in *Metropolis*, red satin bra and hot pants matching her kneecaps and nose-tip. 'Look out Cloughie!' she screamed in a blood-freezing coloratura like The Queen Of The Night, 'It's The Bears' cup!'

The skies above Odsal that evening had, astonishingly, cleared. The pitch had been thoroughly churned up by the rugby: through scrying the skids, stud marks and divots, I tried to reconstruct the unseen play in the previous night's game.

The ground staff and The Bears, in City's strip of fluorescent rust and dirty yellow, were busily engaged in roughing it up even more. Perhaps Forest's preening aristocrats would stumble in the ruts or reel in horror at the strange creatures — birds or huge moths? — that would periodically batter themselves to death against the blazing floodlights? Or freeze in front of an open goal as they were struck by the sudden realization that, far above, the stars were in a completely unfamiliar alignment?

The fastest that Forest moved was when they ran out at the start: the ball, treacherously, did all the work for them. Johnny Metgod stood with his domed head bowed, staring fixedly at the ground, as if lost in contemplation of unknowable things: when the ball interrupted this reverie he'd dismiss it with side-footed passes that would trundle sixty yards, provoking a series of abortive interception attempts, before picking up pace to slip perfectly into the stride of another Forest player, clean through. The more City chased and harried the more languid and unerring the opposition became: they sprang up in space like sown dragon's teeth. The man next to me thought that Nigel Clough roamed the pitch because he was terrified of our centre-backs: they lumbered after him but then he'd disappear, leaving them baffled, lost, nowhere. In contrast, Walker and Fairclough not only nullified our strikers but also somehow managed to get forward into our six-yard box to score from open play. The normal laws of space and time seemed no longer to apply. The previous night's merciful fogs did not return: five — nil and they hit post, bar and junction and our keeper, Litchfield, made at least a dozen good saves.

My neighbour was in tears: 'They've shown us up.' His flat

cap and Ronco big check jacket glittered with enamel badges and silver-wired pennants: with his tiny bright-eyed head bobbing up and down on his shoulders I was reminded of Robert de Montesquiou's jewel-encrusted pet tortoise. 'They should have played in the bear-suits. They've let us down. I thought we were supposed to be bouncing back.' 'Nay,' said his mate, who'd watched the proceedings impassively. 'We were all over The Forest. We fucking murdered them.' The chelonian stopped crying: 'So why did we lose, then?' 'Best team doesn't always win. A few lucky goals on the break. We've never liked playing against defensive sides.' I wanted to hug him: he knew that winning had nothing to do with scoring the most goals but was measured by his own personal standards of effort, heart, worthiness and sincerity. City, therefore, had never really lost, would never really lose. He was, like Joe Johnson, another great Bradford Achiever.

I couldn't remember when I'd last enjoyed an evening as much. There was a real pleasure — way beyond Eros or even Thanatos — in watching us get stuffed. This obviously wasn't the universal view: unprecedentedly, no one — apart from a few Forest fans, trying not to look too pleased — came into The Drop Kick for a post-match drink. They'd all gone straight home. I sat alone in the snug, lined with faded sepia photographs of behemoth pre-war Northern players — Dilorenzo, Gouldthorpe, Spillane — and unnamed munitions workers killed in the 1916 Low Moor Explosion. 'They've let us down . . . they've shown us up': the words of the tortoise continued to sound in my head. All this Bouncing Back, this pursuit of some impossible regeneration was merely destroying our ability to fail with dignity. For weeks now, asleep or awake, I'd kept imagining that little family at London Zoo, huddled up against the bars, whimpering with the bears. When the mirage finally faded, we'd no longer know who or where we were.

I'd also been thinking about the people behind the great initiative to attract the new businesses and tourism that we needed . . . the people who had dreamed up, commissioned and recruited Bouncer and the rest . . . who were claiming that with our baths, our building societies and our doomed Achievers, we were about to buck the iron laws of geography, economics or the gods. I doubted that they'd been shivering out on the terraces that evening to see whether their promises that City were going to shut Clough's mouth were fulfilled. I knew damn well where they'd be: nice and warm at home, hidden safely away up the valleys of the Wharfe and Aire. I imagined myself walking up a long well-raked gravel drive . . . I imagined the click as the security lights came on – along with tapes of baying Rottweilers – to reveal, beyond the triple garage, a converted farmhouse, its walls sandblasted to honey-gold . . . I knew that this must be the lair of The Master of the Bears . . . I peered in at a lighted window, double-locked and heat-sensored . . . Two children were playing with pale wooden educational toys between the slippered feet of the pater familias, his face hidden behind a newspaper – *not* the *T&A* . . . He hadn't even bothered to listen to the commentary on Radio Leeds – the result had been a foregone conclusion, after all: instead, beautiful music was playing – a Mozart piano quartet perhaps or that sublime 'fuck me' bit in Pergolesi's 'Stabat Mater' . . . His wife – why, under that cascade of ash-blonde hair, had I given her Cathy's face? – was choosing from the wine rack: Burgundy, Beaujolais or Beaune? . . . People like that always get away with everything and don't feel in the least bit guilty, never even suspect that there is anything for which they could be called to account . . . 'What's so wrong about bringing hope to the hopeless, harmless fun to the careworn and grim? . . . What's so bad about attracting the new businesses and tourism that we need? . . . What's wrong with being prosperous and successful? . . .' The Bear Master put down his paper and I found that I was looking into my own face – but unlined, calmer, content. And then, with a pitying smile, he mouthed at me through the glass: 'What's so terrible about being happy?' . . . At closing time the landlord forced me to leave my car in his car park and put me into a taxi home.

Nature abhors a vacuum: in the next few months, although there were still no signs of the new businesses that we needed, there was certainly a sort of galvanic entropy, a frenzied marking-time. Every half-forgotten sidestreet was suddenly adapting itself to the exigences of idleness. A thousand flowers bloomed: multi-coloured signboards pulsed and glowed . . . JOBCLUBS, TRAINING CENTRES, SKILL CENTRES, CATHEDRAL CENTRES, CENTRES AGAINST UNEMPLOYMENT, NEW DEPARTURES, NEW DIRECTIONS, NEW HORIZONS . . . So much novelty when nothing could change. So many centres when we had drifted far outside any known circumferences. The problem of unemployment, it appeared, was to be solved by treating it as if it was a full-time job. Soon, if there was any work to be done, no one would be available to do it, being far too busy acquiring new skills. Bradford's highly-motivated army of Esperanto-speaking, spot-welding jugglers would be primed and ready to bounce back into an inconceivable tomorrow. Most of these new training centres, though, looked suspiciously still derelict and never seemed to be open: maybe we did have one local success story, after all — POTEMKIN SIGNBOARDS PLC.

Large areas of the city were vanishing, their mills and chapels crumbling to dust at the very downdraught of the wrecking-ball, to be replaced — seemingly overnight, as if they'd been rolled out like carpets — by huge new roads. The Cock And Bottle — inviolately Grade 2 listed — now sat on a spur in six lanes of largely empty concrete. The heroically-misconceived idea appeared to have been that if you built roads then the cars — bringing the new businesses and tourism that we needed — would just appear, like blue-tits when you hang nuts out in the garden. The lovely old wooden pedestrian bridge — users of which would run the risk of falling through on to the railway lines below — gave way to the cross-valley Hammstrasse, named after one of our twin towns. No one ever seemed to drive on it: the local feeling was that it was reserved for Panzer Tanks. Who had really won the war? I was glad that my father hadn't lived to see this.

Half the city, it appeared, had been stealthily levelled, recalling the Domesday Book's entry for the Bradford area; after the harrowing of The North: 'Ilbert de Lacy has it — and it is waste'. VASTA EST . . . Then large display boards went up on every vacant site, heralding imminent office blocks, leisure centres, superstores, malls. The designs — enormous glowing Doric ziggurats — were like Albert Speer on a weird retro-Babylon jag. Two tiny figures — a male and a female — were always depicted gesturing in the foreground, like Adam and Eve welcoming their second Eden. None of these things ever got built, of course, although some Asians in Manningham did embark on a mosque, only to lose heart halfway through, leaving the frame, a fast-rusting orange spider. The last few brick chimneys in the valley toppled: the bears seemed to take a particular pleasure in sitting down on the plungers to detonate the charges. I remembered how, as the school bus came down Bolton Road on winter mornings I'd see the smoking chimneys poking up through the mist like the funnels of a great battle fleet bravely setting out for a doomed engagement. All that now remained were the silver organ pipes of the chemical works: whenever I passed them my backbrain would numb and everything would go dotty, a snowstorm of colours like walking into 'La Grande Jatte'.

I realized that Bradford had just lost its only real chance of bouncing back: the wrong buildings had been demolished. We should have turned the bulldozers loose on the CLASP police HQ; on the BT Centre, like the superstructure of a long-scuttled battleship; on the Halifax Building Society, ribbed and noduled like a sex toy for the stimulation of some ghastly alien orifice; and on – above all – the Council's Architects' Department, a brutalist grey slab with permanent damp swathes on its windowless end walls, as if giants had been – with good reason – pissing up against them. Thus cleansed, we could have relaunched the entire city as a historical theme park: 'The Nineteenth Century Experience'. We could even have changed the name: 'Revisit the industrial revolution in hands-on, inter-active Worstedopolis'. The old businesses would be trans-formed into new businesses by being now engaged not in production but in its simulation. Full employment would be immediately restored through faithfully recreating the last great boom of 1873. Once again, the air would have been unbreathable, the cobblestones slippery with suint, the IMR at 60%. All the newly-woven cloth would have to be thrown away unfortunately but not before all the lost souls of Rawson Market had been gifted walk-in wardrobes full of tailor-made kid mohair. Even such irredeemables would have their part to play – as muttering streetcorner fanatics, temperance or socialist. Mal could have been the technical consultant for alehouses, checking the size, weight and distribution of the spittoons: I'd have supervised the dust and smoke effects and taken care of the beer ... Instead, once again, VASTA EST ... But maybe there was another theme park possibility that might save us? We could all don rags and – cringing against the tourists' camera-flashes – pick around the rubble like rats ... 'Come to Post-Apocalypse City: A fun day out for all the family ...'

Instead, the place teemed with little plans and projects, such as reopening the long-dark Alhambra Theatre or turning the Little Germany area into 'the North's answer to Covent Garden'. So what was the question? Who could see in that ruined district anything other than a terrible warning? Next it was announced that into the gap between The Silver Blades ice rink and the Central Library was to be inserted the new National Museum of Photography, Film and Television. This completely baffled me: what connection did any of these things have with Bradford? And, further, what was the point of devoting a museum to such evanescences? Its exhibits would have to change daily, hourly, by the minute ... Then there was the reclamation project for Undercliffe Cemetery, its riot of celtic crosses, obelisks and mock-Egyptian temples etched against the city's northern skyline. Although all its paths had been newly concreted and its graves set straight, cleaned, scaled and polished like long-neglected teeth, the tourists we needed still stayed away. 'Unfortunately, of the 120,000 people buried here,' said a spokesman, 'none are famous. What wouldn't we give for a Brontë or two!' What's Ada Gilroy's armless angel against Oscar in Père Lachaise, Marx in Highgate or Kleist in the Wannsee? – in Bradford even the dead let you down. One day I noticed that a large banner – CATCH A MINIBEAST!! – was spanning the cemetery gates. The still-dense undergrowth was alive with schoolchildren brandishing nets, magnifying glasses and speci men jars. One teacher was leading her group away, white-faced or in tears – perhaps they'd happened upon a distressing strain of flesh-eating worm?

There was still plenty of optimism. On TV I saw our tourism officer, Maria Glot – under a sign, BRADFORD: SUCH A SURPRISING PLACE! – addressing the delegates at 'Confex', a conference of conference organizers. 'We're rapidly losing our old negative image because there's so much going on here,' I heard her say. 'We have so many good venues to attract confer-ences, it's unbelievable.' She wasn't wrong: the city – being nothing but voids – certainly had the room to host every conference in Britain, Europe, The World, The Universe. So that was to be the future, then: a perpetual conference. In this respect, at least, I myself had been – if unwittingly – bouncing ahead: after one ill-advised lunchtime reversion to Black Bush chasers, while I spent the afternoon dry-retching over my waste-paper basket I could hear the department secretary informing a succession of callers that I was 'unavailable – in conference'.

You can confer – or conference – anywhere. The previous summer Cathy and I had been rudely joined at the top of Beamsley Beacon by a dozen middle-aged men: they were a disgusting sight – nearly as fat as I am now – purple and wheezing in brand-new Gore-Tex, Yeti gaiters and pinching Zamberlans. Huddled between the summit's double cairns, they started to hold a business meeting, taping flow-charts and organograms on to convenient boulders. A. J. Wainwright meets John Harvey Jones. Even after twenty minutes of conferencing we didn't have the slightest idea of what they could be making and selling. Cathy was particularly disgusted that their unfortunate secretary, struggling with the weight of an enormous silver coffee thermos, was still parodically high-heeled, short-skirted, décolleté. To our great delight, their discussions of downsizing and economies of scale were abruptly terminated by a swarm of rock-wasps – that had earlier fled from our caporal tobacco smoke – now returning, enraged, to chase them down the scree.

Max Madden and the other local MPs continued to leap up in The House on the slightest pretext to hymn the praises of 'the city transformed'. The Bears even descended on London – 'taking our message to the country', as the *T&A* put it, above photographs of them joshing with Prince Charles and Denis Healey. They'd apparently also been roaming the Underground. An old college friend of mine had rung me after a five-year silence: 'I've just been trapped on a peak-hour tube with a bunch of bear-type things shouting about Bradford,' he said accusingly. 'All the way from Embankment to Burnt Oak. They smelt like shit.' I denied all knowledge but explained that it must have been a sloth or a slump, not a bunch.

There was one project that was realized. Two years after the Bradford City fire, the new stand at Valley Parade was completed. The day before the ground's official reopening, Prime Minister Thatcher appeared in the city. Although her visit had been unannounced we knew that she was coming

when a two-square mile area was cordoned off – not even
Bouncer could get through – the sky turned black with heli-
copters and sharpshooters appeared on the highest roofs. Inside
the stand she was photographed, waving a claret and amber
scarf, exactly in the middle of the empty tiers of seating. She
looked flushed and excited, as if she was watching a game that
only she could see: in which a crowd of Margaret Thatchers
cheered as Margaret Thatcher continually crossed the ball for
the centre forward, Margaret Thatcher, to head into the net –
goal after goal after goal. On the smoked glass of the bullet-
proof Jaguar that brought her was a BRADFORD'S BOUNCING
BACK sticker. 'Such a good campaign,' she cooed as she left.
Even before they hit the M1, I guessed the window would be
wound down and a clawed hand would release into the slip-
stream a screwed-up strip of cellulose.

Perhaps to restore flagging morale, Bradford's much-loved
Xmas lights – dim, fusing and cutting out, tangled round fascia
and streetlamps like dying creepers, spelling out indecipherable
messages, delineating unrecognizable shapes – appeared earlier
than usual this year. We were even having a celebrity to turn
them on: Bonnie Langford, the former child star now struggling
to resurrect her career as a singing, dancing – sexy, even –
all-round entertainer. Unless she married royalty, however, or
was unmasked as a mass-murderer, she was doomed to be
known forever as *Just William* and *The Outlaws'* paramour or
anima, Violet – or, as the *T&A* had it, Violent – Elizabeth
Bott.

The night of the lights was foul, with wind and driving rain
and a swirling ochre mist, as if the old gods were descending
from Olympus – or Odsal – for revenge. The crowd in the

Town Hall Square was tightly-packed and silent: there was an air of expectancy, as if they were waiting for something of massive significance – the return of Arthur, maybe, or the end of the world. Whenever the press photographers yelled at them to smile they duly obliged, some even feebly waving their arms, so as not to disappoint these poor wet lads with their nice cameras, but still remained resolutely silent. It was a gathering that didn't seem to fit into the crowd-typologies of Caneti or Le Bon: the dead crowd, the leaderless, centreless, directionless crowd, the powerless crowd. I was reminded of when Prime Minister Palmerston had come to the city in 1864, at the zenith of its prosperity, to lay the foundation stone of the great Venetian Gothic temple to Mammon, the Wool Exchange. As he'd recently definitively vetoed any Electoral Reform Act, demonstrations and riots were expected. The streets were lined with Peelers and hired thugs but the vast crowd that finally assembled just stood and watched the proceedings in stony silence. The silver trowel trembled in Palmerston's hand: he felt as if his body was being eaten away by the acids of their contempt. He was dead within the year. It was this same elo-quent silence that was said to have killed Sir Henry Irving at The Theatre Royal. This was notorious for being the worst House in the land: they'd watched unmoved as he'd raged and raved as Othello and Lear and finally yawned through his protracted death scene in Tennyson's *Becket*. Irving, apopleptic, spoke his own last words in character; 'Into Thy hands, O Lord! Into Thy hands!' But no beatification ensued: no real storm broke outside, nor did the earth gape to swallow his murderers as they mooched off home.

The Bears were circling the piazza, jiving and reeling to

the accompaniment of the UK-Championship-winning Alliance Conquest Marching Band. As the rain filled their instruments, it sounded as if they were slipping beneath the waves: as a tribute to the *Titanic*'s orchestra, they played 'Abide With Me', then segued through 'Mouldy Old Dough' to what might have been 'Ode To Joy'. The Bears, I noticed, had stopped capering: now they moved in slow motion, like convicts trudging towards some still-distant gulag. Their suits were saturated: one by one they stopped moving, as if petrified by the crowd's unblinking regard. A couple fell to their knees, as if in a final prayer for mercy: stewards in fluorescent tabards carried them away.

Looking disturbingly like Mrs Thatcher in a set of Bugs Bunny teeth, Bonnie Langford — with an electrocutioner's relish — threw the switch. The resultant watery illuminations elicited no cheers: it seemed to grow even darker, as if a black light was seeping out and spreading, like squid's ink. Then Kleig spots revealed The Town Hall's new installation: a thirty-three-foot-high inflatable Father Christmas, clinging precariously to the campanile. It was like a feeble riposte to the colossal pop-eyed reindeer that seasonally back-scuttled Manchester's bigger, better Lockwood and Mawson neo-Gothic pile. The band left off playing and the dignitaries ducked back inside but the crowd still didn't move. The rain no longer fell but now seemed to be coming upwards, as if from sprinklers under our feet. No one appeared to be breathing: even the small children were silent. The only sound was the gale's demonic howling, as it ripped at Santa's scarlet extremities. It took me ten minutes to get out of that square: it was like fighting, in mounting panic, through an overgrown birch wood.

With the wind seeming to come at me from every direction at once I ran all the way up Manorgate: I badly needed a drink. A large coach was parked athwart the pavement by The Royal Standard, in defiance of the double yellow line. It was covered with dents and scratches, as if it had passed through shellfire: on its side was written, in crude crimson letters of dripping blood, MYSTERY SIN TOUR. The pub was – unusually for this or indeed any other hour – heaving with trade: the high-pitched hubbub even drowned out the jukebox. Still more unusual was that it was full of women – and not even those occasional pallid whores on their mid-evening break. These were all dressed in bright, baggy jumpsuits, like chic mechanics; all were slim, extremely clean and healthy-looking, like dental nurses; all had similar short, bobbed haircuts of various shades. And they were all also extremely drunk ... or so I first thought before I realized that their extreme animation was something else – sexual excitement? Fear? Anger? I decided that it must be someone's hen night, with the boot, for a few hours, being on the other foot – a couple of red-faced men were hurriedly drinking up and leaving, to loud jeers.

A woman at the bar was ordering twenty-seven pints of snakebite, which seemed an appropriate drink for such maenads. I felt a gentle but firm elbow in my ribs: 'Which was The Ripper's seat?' she asked me. I pointed to the table next to the jukebox. Peter Sutcliffe had apparently been a regular in here during the New Wave days, before they took away its music licence, but try as I might I just couldn't remember him. No one would ever sit in his old place but, for some reason, none of the five subsequent landlords had seen fit to move the semi-eviscerated buffet and the small chipped table that was now so rickety that a full glass placed on it would slide straight off. While I was helping her to distribute the drinks my new friend told me all about their interesting day out on the 'Mystery Sin Tour' of the murder sites of West Yorkshire. They'd spent the afternoon being photographed outside 'The Ripper House', inside which Sonia Sutcliffe was still living: one of them had finally managed to get up the courage to ring the bell – then they'd all run back to their coach but no one came to the door. She and the others were the Rochdale Young Wives Club, meeting up every fortnight for outings and socials. I told her about a similar group in eighteenth-century Paris that I'd just been reading about in Mackay's *Extraordinary Popular Delusions*, who had all killed off their husbands by administering slow poison: she appeared to be seriously taken with the idea. I collected my pint and, although I knew myself to be too old and fat to be worth harassing, hid away round the corner. Didn't people in Lancashire ever kill each other, then? I hadn't realized that Rochdale was such a haven of brotherly love and boredom.

At this point it struck me: here they were at last! The new businesses and tourism that we needed! It was really happening! Before my very eyes, Bradford was bouncing back! The solution had been there all along: we had Third Division Great Men but Gold Medal Monsters. There was Sutcliffe, of course, but also both the Nielsens and Mark Rowntree, the shamefully-underrated 'Stab Spree Schoolboy' ... Even Brady and Hindley's moorland graveyard could be reached by a pleasant half-day's stroll along the Pennine Way. Bouncing back would require ruthlessness: the names of the St George's Hall crush-bars would have to be changed – from The Delius and The

Priestley to The Ripper and The Panther. Forget the Bradford Achievers and Folk-Heroes: it was time to celebrate those local lads who had followed their dreams, listened to their secret voices, knew that they'd been called, that they were special . . . I recalled a night in The Flying Dutchman when I was watching journalists pumping the regulars after the seventh Ripper murder. They weren't getting much response until an old gimmer stuck his head out of the Games Room: 'That London bugger, Jack, t'owld one – how many did he do, then?' On being told that it was five he smiled and said, 'Aye well, our lad's beaten yours already,' and returned contentedly to his dominoes and pipe. I submitted that to the *Dalesman*'s 'My Favourite Yorkshire Story' section but, for some reason, they declined to print it.

I'd heard that – as crime increased exponentially, every year bringing new atrocities to be commemorated – Scotland Yard's Black Museum was running out of space. Even with our anticipated confluence of conferences we could still fit them in. The Krays' crossbow, The Black Panther's noose and hood, Denis Nielsen's bath – made by Spring Ram? – and the clear plastic block that held flakes and gobbets of his victims' flesh, the very spade with which Colin Evans buried little Marie Payne (4) . . . All these things were ours by right. We'd even sired the last three British hangmen: The Pierrepoints of Clayton – Henry, Thomas and Albert – who killed for their country for fifty-five years. After Henry's debut topping of the anarchist Faugeron, his mentor Reaper Jim Billington had taken the kid's pulse. 'Normal. You'll do,' said Reaper Jim.

Never mind Photography, Film and Television: we'd have the National Museum Of Psychopathology! What a money-spinner that would be! The new businesses and tourism that we needed would fly to us like iron filings to a magnet. Think of the merchandising! Think of the spin-offs! I decided that I would make a free gift of this initiative to the city — or at least I would claim no more than a Bouncing Bear's basic wage. We could even keep the current slogan: 'Bradford, Such a Surprising Place' — over a series of portraits of Sutcliffe's thirteen victims, their neutral features staring unsuspectingly back at the camera. We could keep The Bears too: Bouncer, in a stick-on crêpe beard and gollywog wig would hand out rubber claw hammers and retracting screwdrivers to the thousands of tourists who'd day and night be prowling Lumb Lane ready to spring out on unwary working girls. They'd be prostitutes no longer but paid-up EQUITY members, finding in their writhings and simulated death-rattles a greater job satisfaction than their pre-vious provision of the local gourmet sexual fare — the celebrated twenty-second blow job with a champagne-flavoured condom. But why merely *simulate* it? We'd all have to make sacrifices to attract the new businesses and tourism that we needed. 'What do women want?', Freud once asked before providing his own short — six-inch — reply. Well, I've gathered that they're pretty keen on being ineptly fucked by drunken fools but isn't what they're really after — as all those well-versed in the modernist canon know — a violent death at the hands of a sexual maniac, like Wedekind's Lulu? Looking around, I decided not to embark on a straw poll of The Rochdale Young Wives.

When Sutcliffe finally dies in prison, I thought, his ashes could be brought back to Undercliffe for interment: the ne plus ultra — better than any Brontë, certain to attract the tourism that we needed. But what form should his monument take? A marble articulated lorry? Or a vastly-enlarged copy of Bingley's Zapolski grave from which, on a tape-loop, would issue God's momentous orders to young gravedigger Pete? Then I thought of the centrepiece of the necropolis: the light grey granite Smith obelisk, like a minatory finger high over Bradford. Joseph Smith had been the person who drew up the cemetery's contracts: the middleman, the gopher, had reserved for himself the prime site. After turfing out his bones we could chisel away the stone until it was reshaped as a lethally-sharpened Phillips screwdriver, Sutcliffe's favoured instrument. Then we could flank it with specially-commissioned statues of his victims, classically-draped in the style of Maillol, in attitudes of admonition or supplication. And the epitaph? Well, Sutcliffe — like Villon, Swift or Yeats — had provided his own: the notice he used to stick in his cab window when nodding out on the hard shoulder. 'In this truck is a man whose latent genius, if unleashed, would rock the nation, whose dynamic energy would overpower those around him. Better let him sleep?' How often had I wondered about the meaning of that final question-mark?

As I went up for another pint my buttocks were abruptly pinched hard from left and right simultaneously. I swung round in mock indignation — secretly flattered that my arse at least had proved to be still visible to women who, if I'd ever been to Rochdale, could have been my daughters — but there was no one within touching distance, no one smirking or blushing, no one even trying to look innocent. A man in the front bar, however, was giving me the hard stare: I met the gaze but his frown, like some Tibetan demon's, merely deepened. Then I realized that — not for the first time — in the mirror behind the optics I'd been eyeballing myself. At least that was one fight I might have had a chance of winning. I smiled but the reflection's expression didn't change. The face was a flat slab of tallow-coloured skin, except for its nose, squashed, pitted and strawberry red, and the beautiful Tyrian purple shadows under its hooded eyes.

I noticed that some reckless or oblivious soul had plumped themselves down in the chair by the jukebox. All the smoke seemed to have been somehow sucked across into that alcove, so it wasn't until I got up close that I recognized the figure as Peter Sutcliffe himself. He was dressed as in that best-known photograph taken on his wedding day – in frilly shirt, velvet jacket and floppy bow tie, like a croupier. There was a cigarette packet and a throwaway lighter on the table in front of him, but he didn't have a drink. He looked at me and nodded, so I stopped and came straight out with the question I'd always wanted to ask: 'Pete, why'd you hate women so much?' And he threw his head back and laughed for some time before replying, in that famously incongruous fluting voice, 'Don't be so daft. If I'd hated them I'd have had nowt to do wi' em.' Then he laughed some more while he vanished, back into the smoke. The cigarette packet was empty: I'd have taken the lighter as a souvenir, but its flint wheel was jammed. I had to admit that there was something seriously wrong with me – worse than seeing lizards and phantom dogs. I could imagine all the stuff in Sutcliffe's head – love gone wrong, desire all twisted up into hate and fear – but not in those of well-meaning, socially-responsible Councillors or Members Of The Chamber Of Commerce. Hacking up thirteen women – the darkest blasphemy against the most sacred of things – was still to me a recognizably human activity ... but I couldn't conceive what

sort of man could put people into bear-suits and let them be
– or pretend to be – grateful.

The Young Wives were beginning to drift away back to
their coach. They were apparently planning to stop off for a
last drink in Todmorden at a pub near the Leeds-Liverpool
Canal where the floating body of a little girl had recently been
found. 'It'll be her Dad that's done it,' one said. 'It's always
the Dads that do it.' I knew they'd be coming back here
soon . . . The National Museum of Psychopathology! And why
should we stop at that? Perhaps we could even top it with a
Holocaust Museum? Although there was virtually no Jewish
community in Bradford, we had plenty of Nazis – Estonian
and Ukrainian ex-Sonderkommandos and death-camp guards
– hiding out in the quiet sidestreets around the park. Those
charming silver-haired old gentlemen would make the most
perfect tour guides, while also providing a fresh and challenging
perspective. New revisionism: 'It wasn't six million,' they'd
whisper roguishly. 'It was twenty million . . . and counting!'
The tourist attraction to outdraw even Disneyworld: Bradford
– the Twentieth-Century Experience. It would have saved us
but we didn't have the guts to do it.

Now that the pub had cleared I became aware of half-a-dozen
men hunched over the table by the door. They were ashen, as
if the sun hadn't seen their skin all summer, and taciturn even
by Bradford standards – expressionless and totally silent. They
looked familiar but I couldn't remember where from: I'd never
seen them in here before. They lifted their glasses, drank and
then set them down again with perfect synchronization: the
levels of their beer dropped at exactly the same rate. Only when
one came wordlessly to the bar for a fresh round did I realize:

it was the poor devil who'd gone all shamanic inside his Bear-suit. They were drinking Hoffmeister, of course: it was The Bears — or, rather, their operators, sloughed of the skins. The cheeky one, the thoughtful one, the sad one ... they were staring into space, like a defeated army in an old newsreel, sitting at the side of the road as the victor's tanks roll in. They all took out cigarettes: each one gave the one on his left a light and then, as with one breath, they blew out each other's matches. Nowt had happened: Bradford hadn't bounced back, after all ... In less than a minute all my scorn and hatred for The Bears had turned to love. I'd been terrified all along that they might indeed succeed in attracting the new businesses and tourism that we needed ... but now that they'd failed they belonged once again to Bradford, belonged once again to me. I wondered if I should remind them that the best team doesn't always win — that the best team is the one that never wins, the one that doesn't even take the field — but I didn't want to spoil their perfect moment. I paid discreetly for their next round, threw back a double Drambuie and left.

I half-expected the silent crowd to be still waiting in Town Hall Square but it was deserted, except for three scruffy men propped against each other like rifles forming a tripod. They were pointing upwards and laughing. I assumed that they were mocking or marvelling at the great inflatable but when I reached them I saw that the roof was empty — perhaps I'd at last learnt how not to register things, like Mal. 'Santa's buggered off early doors,' one of them said. The North Wind had evidently torn it from its moorings and borne it away. 'It went bombing down Thornton Road then split in two' — he mimed a severing up from crotch to crown — 'Half went up the Aire Valley, the other'll be Haworth way by now.' 'No presents this year,' I said. 'Happy Christmas.'

Then the booze hit me. I was laying alongside my car for quite a while, not sure whether I was on my face or my back, whether it was the stars that were twinkling or just broken glass among the cinders. I wondered if I should just stay there and rot: rats, maggots, worms and crows would hurry to my corpse, so that at least I would be attracting the new businesses and tourism that we needed ... But then, the next thing I knew, I was driving, cold sober, at a responsible speed – if in a previously undiscovered gear, at once jerky and floaty – down the empty Hammstrasse. The sky had cleared and the pavements were riming up with frost but I was snug and warm in my new fur. My paws gripped the wheel, tighter and tighter ... my massive head filled the driving mirror. Dreaming or awake, dead or alive, more than or less than human, I was bouncing back ...

The Tale of the Golden Bath-Taps

The end of another crap gig: we'd played great music – badly – to the usual drunken doylems in a well-strafed WMC. They kept yelling for a smoochy one so we did 'Loco Mosquito' even faster than usual, then somebody took a swing at the bass player . . . It was getting like *The Blues Brothers* but without the car chases and hats, without the laughs.

We made for a pub at the edge of town that we'd heard had a late licence but the car park was empty and the building dark, walls and windows silted up with fine grey dust. The Cock and Bell, it was called: the faded signboard, swinging metronomically in the wind, showed a rooster and a bull – of equal size – seemingly about to clash over a neat pile of cannon-shot: there was no bell to be seen. Its local name, for some reason, was The Bollocks. Behind the grille mesh, multi-coloured glass flickered with fitful lights: we felt like divers peering into a long-sunken galleon.

I pushed one finger against the door: it snapped open like a trap and heat, glare and roar almost knocked us off our feet. Before my glasses misted over I saw that every face in the packed bar was chalk-white or crimson, as if about to either crumble or explode: they made our Goth pallor look like peaches and cream. There was something deeply familiar about the noise, like the rhythmical roar of the primordial sea: then I realized that they were singing along with Elvis' 'Suspicious Minds' from the jukebox. 'Never mind The Bollocks,' Dave yelled in my ear. 'Here's a fucking dangerous pub!'

Out of the golden nimbus behind the counter a slim, silver-nailed hand emerged, limning on the head of my Guinness a perfect shamrock. 'Suspicious Minds' finished and then started again: either the selector was jammed or it was someone's favourite song. 'I don't want to be sexist,' said Dave, 'but that barmaid's tits are unbelievable.' My haze had finally cleared: she wore a v-fronted cream silk blouse buttoned at the wrists, her thick underarm hair showing through, spiked by deodorant or sweat. Her firm, high breasts needed no support: out of tan aureoles ruby nipples, long and stiff, jabbed at the material, tautening it, forming twin pleats that finally converged in her deep, dark navel. On the contrary, I did believe these tits – I already trusted them implicitly. Her hair was in a chignon, honey-blonde; dorje earrings depended from her tiny lobes; her calm grey gaze flickered over us and she half-smiled – sadly, as if our attentions had slightly disappointed her.

From the back bar there came a series of hollow clacks, like kendo fencers: elderly Winstons in leather trilbies were playing dominoes at bewildering speed, slamming the pieces down. A man next to me struck up a conversation: his hands shook and across his brow there was a long, fresh cut – the blood didn't drip but kept on flowing in circulation, like an underground stream momentarily surfacing. 'Just had a barny with the wife,' he said. 'Nearly had me with the bread knife' – he jerked his head back — 'Just missed.' I felt I had to disabuse him: expressionlessly, he checked his reflection in the bar mirror, drained his pint, shook my hand and set out for Casualty. The barmaid smiled again and, unbidden, passed our drinks over the heads of the last orders scrimmage. I became aware that Dave and the rhythm section had their eyes shut: they seemed to believe, like small children, that it made them invisible.

They never came back, but I did. It was the sort of pub I liked. The main bar was lined with double benches like a slave-galley and part-ringed by confessional-sized snugs. Swarms of motes dimmed any sunlight, omnipresent grime took the hard edge off things: if the barmaid, Christine, was always cleaning and polishing, it was only to keep new dirt from obscuring the established, much-loved old. The carpet was a mixture of blacks, greens and browns, like a well-trodden bridle path. In the stained-glass windows, chubby doves, bearing in their beaks inspiriting Latin tags, perched atop a tangled thicket from which protruded a line of foxes' brushes. The ancient wallpaper was of a well-cured lung pattern: on the ceiling a century's nicotine had formed overlapping dark haloes. Blue smoke clouds hung perpetually in the air like incense ... My first impression had been right: this was one of the last remaining churches of the true faith. But for the fact that Ken the landlord was a bit too cadaverous and there wasn't a cat, it was perfect.

The band didn't understand that this was the safest place in the city. They were more likely to get hurt in the warm, cosy pubs up the valley, full of well-fed, well-off, well-occupied folk who should by their lights be happy but aren't — who, after a couple of drinks, start looking for someone to blame and, for some reason, usually choose me. People came into The Bollocks for relief from the conflict and pain of the rest of their lives: off-duty, they'd no more fight than doctors would listen out for heart murmurs or accountants tot up the burns in the carpet. Even the Care In The Community boys behaved themselves: it was literally their last chance saloon. If you fancy a quiet drink, seek out the violent: if you want aggravation go down to The College and hang out with the Peace Studies crew. Here, no one cared about anything: if you could open the door and breathe the air they assumed you must be OK. Most of the faces in the police rogue's gallery hanging by the bar were to be seen in the adjacent photo of the Sunday football team – middle of the league but last season's winner of the Fair Play Trophy. Naming and shaming hadn't worked in The Bollocks.

The only trouble I saw in the subsequent months was one night when the dominoes players all suddenly went for each other: it looked faked, like a John Wayne film with flying balsawood furniture and trick bottles. The darts boys kept on flighting their arrows through the ruck, with one caroming off a polished head on its way to double-top. In darts, I suppose you can overstep the oche or lunge halfway to the board, but how on earth do you cheat at doms? Without a word or gesture Christine came out from behind the bar. As she glided through the combatants they froze. She threw open the doors: a whistling wind blew in large flakes of snow. They lowered their hands – a knife that no one seemed to have used slid and clattered across the boards – and filed meekly past her, heads bowed, like rebellious souls being expelled from paradise to coldest hell for all eternity . . . Two days later, they were back.

It was a while before I acknowledged that I was only coming in on Sunday lunchtimes and alternate weekdays – when Christine was serving. She always wore the same outfit: the cream blouse with stretch blue stonewashed Falmer jeans and gold ankle straps. Her tan was an eighteen-tube sunbed job, too perfect – impervious to the light, like matt emulsion. Watching her I felt my simple delight in a woman's beauty rapidly turning more complicated. She was graceful – but, paradoxically, graceful in repose, as if her stillness contained in itself the fulfilment of all motion. As she sat skimming her glossy magazines it seemed that she was somehow shifting inside her skin. Just looking at her was hard work: my eyes kept refocusing as if she was constantly vanishing but then immediately reappearing. I always left The Bollocks with a headache, twin vectors of strain connecting at the bridge of my nose. At first I didn't think that this was about my feelings, more a natural if baffling phenomenon to do with light and time, space and mass . . . but when, as an experiment, I forced myself to concentrate as hard on other people or things it didn't have the same effect.

I was struck by the respect with which everyone treated her: at my dad's golf club the moneymen would have pinched her black and blue. She walked with her back straight, head high and still, hips shuttling as if to wrong-foot prospective tacklers. Even those who swore like troopers suddenly went sweet-mouthed as she dipped, bent-kneed, to collect their glasses. They'd stare down her deepening cleavage without lust or slyness – as if at an area of outstanding natural beauty, like Dentdale. Sometimes the old men would emerge from the snug to order a shot of crème de menthe: the bottle was kept on the highest shelf. Christine took her time about fetching the ladder and then, with much flexing and clenching, climbing it, while they grew redder and redder until finally they had to look away. The drinks remained untouched: some nights the bar would be lined with glasses, fluorescent green and sticky, until Ken, calling time, downed them as he passed.

She was always smiling at me: true, she smiled at everyone, but only as if they were ambassadors to her court who kept committing irritating but venial breaches of protocol. This was different: her eyes would lock with mine and she'd raise one eyebrow, then the other. She never blinked: she could have stared out the world — I was reminded of a cricketer I knew who'd ducked into a bouncer and couldn't close his eyes thereafter. Instead of dropping the change into my hand she'd press the startlingly warm coins into my palm, then slowly sashay through to the other bar. I'd watch that special smile gradually fading in the pub's hall of mirrors, like at the end of *The Lady From Shanghai*. Although she moved as if protected by a forcefield she kept brushing past or even bumping into me. One evening I suddenly felt her whole body ramming itself hard against my back. I didn't react, pretending that I hadn't noticed or that it was no big deal. I was desperate to love her but I also didn't want all the delicious preliminaries to end.

It was hard to believe that she had a terrible temper but so some of the regulars said. They also told me about her brother Terry — supposedly the most dangerous man in the West Riding. His face didn't appear on the banned poster: he'd be on the ones tacked on the portals of Heaven and Hell. No one had seen him in years but they reckoned that anyone who messed with her could look forward to his speedy rematerialization. Even Ken, in his fuddled way, warned me off her: I assumed that he'd tried it on himself and failed. I looked into his face, eaten away by spirits and secret disappointments: he'd probably been fat and sassy until he hired Christine.

The Bollocks wasn't an easy place in which to talk but I'd discovered that she was Taurean – of the most boring sign, like Hitler, Wittgenstein and I. We'd been born two days apart but at the same hour, between two and three in the morning: she seemed to consider this significant. She told me to call her Chris. I didn't tell her this was my own name – long since superseded by the hated Ginger.

Sunday lunchtimes were the best: a quid a pint or double short. Free Yorkshire puddings were served that, even flooded with onion gravy, somehow remained crisp . . . Then, like Tiresias, Gabe the pianist was led in. Blindness gives me the creeps, especially in musicians: I think of those bluesmen said to have bartered their sight to play the Devil's music – which still didn't stop them from shooting their rivals and battering their women. It felt as if, from behind his Big O shades, emanations were probing me like x-rays. He could play, though: while his whole body trembled, the huge spatulate pink and grey fingers struck the keys with precise articulation. He did these crazy medleys – once segueing from 'Stardust' to 'Dancing In The Dark' via Scriabin's 'Vers La Flamme' – but mostly he backed the singers: there was no karaoke in The Bollocks. The spirit of The King possessed almost everyone: there was the Asian Elvis, the Whistling Elvis, the Stuttering Scottish Elvis, the Elvis Who Didn't Know Any Of The Words, but there were no Singing In Tune Elvises. Even Ken – doing a better or rather a worse Dean Martin than Dino himself – got up on stage and so did Chris.

She had serious showbiz aspirations. Apparently she'd once been a dancer and still gave classes at community centres and retirement homes: I imagined her inflaming the old dears to spin their wheels, tap their canes, pogo on their zimmers. Singing was her great love, though: on Sundays she'd vanish into the ladies' for half an hour to return transformed – all in black, with silver-glittered eyelids and a dark bobbed wig – to give an eerily accurate impersonation of Karen Carpenter, her idol. Her voice even had the chilly echo that I'd thought must have been studio-engineered. I made the mistake of telling Chris that Karen's anorexia and sad end could have been predicted from that weird timbre, as if – having passed beyond love and hate, fear and hope, pity of self or others – she was singing her own death, so that even on the lollipop 'Please Mr Postman' it sounded as if the letter so eagerly awaited would have black edges, her 'Ticket To Ride' would carry her over the Styx. 'Nothing's sacred to you, is it?' she laughed, punching me playfully on the left bicep: my fingers were numbed and the bruise stayed for weeks. Maybe it hadn't only been fear of her brother that had quelled the dominoes players?

That night she turned up at our gig. I'd been woodshedding the solo on 'Goodbye To Love' in the hope of recruiting her – I aimed to Svengali a second Nina Hagen – but she said we'd have to smarten up first. The rhythm section mutinied at the merest suggestion of frilled shirts, wine velvet bow ties, personal hygiene.

Afterwards, as I was stumbling down the dark, dripping passageway to the Gents, Chris ambushed me. I crashed into the wall, thinking I'd been hit by a tidal wave or suffered a fit until her tongue – long and thick, with a slightly metallic taste

— slithered into my mouth. Its tip touched the back of my throat, then it snaked round mine and began tugging, as if trying to rip it out by the roots. I clutched her bum and lifted her, she clutched mine and lifted me — we seemed to float in tantric union for a while. Dave was right: her tits were indeed unbelievable: I could feel them getting harder and harder against my chest, hotter and hotter, in some strange volcanic petrifaction. She finally released me and, hooking a thumb over my belt buckle, led me out of the emergency exit into the car park. A taxi was waiting: without instructions it drove us away. She made a lot of noise and her hands were all over me. The driver wasn't looking in the mirror but I could hear him muttering to himself. I imagined his whole life — lonely, wretched — and how he must feel to be ferrying lovers. If we're momentarily happy we should at least have the consideration to be discreet about it. Chris bit my ear: 'I love you,' she whispered but she was still too loud. I resisted a sudden panicky urge to open the door and jump for it. I knew that my life was never going to be the same again.

I didn't pay much attention to the route but when we got out I knew where we were: in front of the mass of council blocks that clustered in the valley bottom. I'd observed them, like yellow-grey fungi between the railway and river, when looking down from the high moors — and I'd cursed them: flat roofs have always depressed me. After the Ronan Point disaster they'd switched to building middle-rises: these already looked decrepit, older than the Victorian terraces laddering the surrounding hillsides. Alphaville, I called it: most of the streetlights were dead, the shadows flickered with furtive movement but no one stepped forward — just as well, as I was no Lemmy

Caution. Forgotten washing hung from the balconies: it was raining and I became acutely aware of my continued need to piss. The wind's howl kept modulating, as if the blocks had somehow been tuned.

Chris suddenly began to run, as if she'd changed her mind. I gave chase, tripping over cracked and shattered flags, skidding on grass verges trampled into mud. Even in three-inch heels she outpaced me: a dark entryway swallowed her up. I followed up the stairwell: there was a smell of burning toast and the walls seemed to have been scorched red and black, as if by dragon's breath. It was sticky underfoot, like a fish dock, so that my DMs kept clamping to the ground. On each open landing the wind velocity increased: I could no longer hear Chris ahead: I had the feeling that I would arrive on the roof only in time to see her vanishing among the stars. But on the fourth floor there was a blaze of light. She was silhouetted in the doorway, already half-naked, her blouse crumpled in her hands. In kicking off her shoes she stumbled and I caught her. I gently stroked her back, then kissed her breasts: something scraped my tongue and there was a crackling sound – her nipples had been held erect by sellotape.

The flat had a strong, sour smell like bleach: I wondered if it was caused by the large fish tank in the corner of the living room. Chris immediately unzipped me and started to suck my cock. She kept butting my stomach, as if my aching bladder was a football: I suspected that she knew the effect that this was having. The room was full of things: TV and video, newish three-piece suite, music centre with good speakers. The walls were lined with steel-framed Post-Impressionist prints – Seurat's bathers, Renoir's umbrellas, Monet's lily pond. I noticed a white rectangle above the false fireplace — an empty space, as if a fourth, larger painting had been removed. After about ten minutes Chris took pity on me: she was laughing merrily as, trousers round my ankles, I shuffled off to the toilet.

The bathroom was enormous, half as large again as the living room: either the builders had screwed up or it had been part of some council cleanliness drive. Above the deep, chipped bath was a damp patch shaped like Madagascar: I couldn't piss. I checked out the pills in the wall cabinets: there were some old friends and enemies but they were all legal, prescribed. Tight rows of cosmetics filled the window ledges: beauty's army ready to march, with gleaming lipsticks arrayed at the front, like shells. I ran a tap, breathed deeply, danced on the spot: nothing worked, not a drip. Against the far wall was a big oak wardrobe, dotted with clips and screws which had presumably once held mirrors. It contained eight of her silk and denim work uniforms and six pairs of the gold shoes, a huge coat of dark fur with a torn sleeve, a fringed thing with lots of straps like a child's cowboy outfit and a strange, long, cowled garment criss-crossed with velcroed vents and panels. Something suddenly registered: the complete absence of mirrors. There was an empty hook in the window transom and by the door a perfect white circle with brackets still in place. I gave up any idea of pissing.

In the hall there was a radiant door-sized space where a full-length mirror would have been. Chris must have taken them all down: if I hadn't seen her in The Bollocks I'd have believed her to be a vampire, without reflection. I could faintly hear her voice in conversation: I tried the bedroom door but it was locked — maybe all the mirrors were in there? The front room was dark: she wasn't on the phone but down on her knees talking to the fish. Wanda and Moby: they looked to be floating rather than swimming, dead or dying. She turned and kissed me, her body blue-white from the tank's fluorescence, squirting red wine, warm and sour, into my mouth. The bottle on the table was empty – I presumed she'd already drunk the rest.

We lay on the rug: grubby white polyester cut to the shape of a steam-pressed polar bear. She didn't want foreplay or tenderness, pushing my hands and head away, but penetration, immediate and deep. Even through the prophylactic she felt tight and dry, pulling me in to the hilt and then straining, as if it was a matter not of pleasure but of life and death. She thrashed about at intervals, like a sleeper deep in nightmare, ululating as if urging hounds towards their quarry. Every two minutes she insisted on our changing position, announcing each one – The Scorpion, The Crescent, The Charioteer – in a flat voice, as if they were the stopping places of a departing slow train.

I'd never come across gymnastic frigidity before. She reminded me of Chuck Berry. I'd seen him the previous week at The Apollo: after a medley of all the great songs – two lines of each then a crude segue into the next – he'd done an interminable version of 'My Ding-A-Ling' and then stalked off. Twenty-six minutes and no encores. 'He's earnt the right,' said a daft old ted next to me. Maybe he had but had Christine? Even behind or on top I felt pinned and crushed: strange cartilaginous protrusions dug into my belly and ribs – I was being pulped. My cock was numb: I could no more come than I could piss. At last, without a word, she broke away and headed for the bathroom. I lay and watched Moby and Wanda blowing silent kisses at me like nervous hard men working up to a fight.

When Chris returned she'd applied fresh lipstick: that perfect coral pink phosphorescent bow must surely have required a mirror. She took me in her mouth again while I stroked her hair: no matter how wildly it was mussed it always fell back into place. She kept up a low, unbroken mantric hum. Then the small quartz alarm clock on the sideboard went off – it was 2.30 – and I came at last, profusely. I felt no satisfaction, though – it was like draining brain fluid. She spat it into a wad of apple-green Kleenex that she'd plucked from under the sofa, then sprang to her feet. 'Time to go, lover,' she said, 'I need my beauty sleep.' She switched on the CD player – Karen doing 'Jambalaya' at a volume that precluded further conversation.

I struggled into my clothes, which were oddly damp: the stairwell had left orange stains on my best leather jacket, fusing the teeth of its Aero zips. Chris was waiting in the hall: she quickly folded her arms, but not before I'd seen the purple and red scars on her wrists. She was still holding the tissue: I thought she was about to present it to me but she just bussed my cheek and shouted, 'See you Sunday, lover,' in my ear. As the door closed I could hear her chiming in, 'Son of a gun we're gonna have big fun on the bayou'. . . The taxi was outside waiting, engine off, interior light on. It was the same driver: I tried to start a conversation but he kept on muttering and giggling. Something told me that this was a regular run. As we drove through the deserted streets an image came into my mind – of Chris retrieving the mirrors from their hiding places and hanging them back up. I knew that I ought to have been feeling upset and disturbed but I wasn't. Whatever was wrong with her I was going to cure it: I loved her — I was like a fly drowning in syrup. My only concern was whether I'd ever piss again. When he dropped me off the driver wordlessly handed me a business card along with my change: it was inscribed, in Gothic lettering, ELVISCABS.

I knew things with Chris were going to get weird but I hadn't guessed how weird or how quickly. The next Sunday when she plumped down next to me — glowing with triumph as the rattle of applause for 'Yesterday Once More' subsided — and I moved to kiss her, she pulled away. 'Don't spoil everything,' she said. 'You're different, you're special. All that,' she fluttered her hands between breasts and groin, 'just messes things up.' She spoke with an American accent: her Karen Carpenter impersonation always altered her voice for some hours afterwards. 'You're the only one who understands me, who likes me for myself not just these,' she gestured again, 'and this.' I assured her that while I did indeed understand her, this and these were still pretty good. I put my arm round her shoulders but she prised it off. 'Let's keep it special,' she said.

'You're different. You're special.' She repeated this litany whenever she knocked me back. 'You understand me.' I realized what a disqualification this was: no one wants to be understood, everyone wants to be able to pass themselves off as their ideal or fantasy self, if not as something even better. 'Lovers come and lovers go but friends are hard to find,' she'd intone: as a friend I was now privy to progress reports on her period pains and wonky left knee. She said we'd moved on to a higher plane but I knew that this wasn't promotion but relegation. I tried everything: I argued, proving by inductive logic that she was in love with me ... then I ignored her, shunning eye contact,

ensuring that only Ken served me . . . then I wore lots of black
. . . then I started taking other women into The Bollocks.
Nothing worked – I was different, special and that was all
there was to it. I wheedled, I sulked . . . once I forced a kiss
on her but her mouth went sphincter-tight. 'Let's just remember
our one perfect night together,' she said, without apparent
irony. I began growing a beard: I hoped it would make me
look like Brad Pitt in *Seven*. 'Do you know who you remind
me of?' she asked. 'Jesus.' That's when I knew my goose was
cooked. Jesus has a lot going for him – even now – but very
few people, in my experience, want to fuck him.

Now that I was different, special, neutered, safe, I played an
increasingly large part in Chris' life. I hung in there in the hope
that this was just a hiatus before we moved on to the next
phase. I spent more time in her place than my own. The
same shaggy stray dog, greyish-white as if half-erased, pissed
perpetually in her stairwell. The flat, although full of stuff,
seemed bleaker than any junky's den. None of the windows
would open, their catches stuck in a gelid fall of gloss paint.
Although her light bulbs were all 150s it remained crepuscular.
I always felt uncomfortable, alternately agoraphobic and claustrophobic, as if the walls were expanding and contracting like
lungs. 'Poor ickle me,' she mimed wiping away a tear, 'I'll
probably die in this hole.' Since she'd bought it, the Mirpuris
had moved into the area and its value had plummeted. 'I'm not
a racist,' she said. 'But I hate them brown bastards.' I had to
admit that seeing the way the Asian kids' eyes followed her
and hearing their snuffling noises as we passed was beginning
to qualify my own previously easy multiculturalism. At least
she had a wonderful view: the smooth horizon sweep of

Rombald's Moor was only broken by the twin spiked radio masts at Whetstone Gate. When I suggested that we go for a walk up there she just shook her head — sadly, as if such things were far beyond her, like poetry and conceptualist art . . . as if you needed a string of qualifications to enjoy silence, clean air, empty sky, heather. 'You like looking down, I like looking up,' she explained.

Chris loved to cook but, despite a spice rack that filled the kitchen wall like a ship's wheel, her chillies and curries always came out muddy and bland: I compensated with draw and bathtub Esthonian vodka. On every visit she'd show me — with a disturbing excess of enthusiasm — some new household item that she'd bought. A spiky futurist-style plastic cruet or place mats of famous racecourses; a small print of a Hockney swimmer or a santa-suited toy moose she insisted was a reindeer. We had to spend one evening toasting each other, clinking the flawed Bohemian glass goblets long after the vodka was finished. Another night she was stroking a butter dish in the shape of a hollowed-out Guernsey cow, talking to it in a mooing voice that put my teeth on edge, while the butter, melting, ran down her wounded arms. Having filled her world for a few hours these fetishised objects never put in a second appearance: were they locked in the bedroom with the mirrors or did Elviscabs take them away?

Afterwards she'd sit in front of me on the hearthrug and I'd cradle her head in my hands while she told me her life story. I hoped she was making it up or was at least exaggerating but I suspected that she wasn't telling me even the half of it. All she remembered of her real dad was a voice like thunder: her mum was a pink and yellow blur from which sharp slaps periodically issued — always on her knees, prostrated by drink or prayer. Our Terry — who'd apparently marched out of the womb as Roberto Duran — had protected her but after he'd gone she'd run from her umpteenth wicked stepfather — only to have a succession of policemen, social workers and foster parents molest her too. So she'd run again, to the safety of the streets ... She rolled up her sleeves to display her old wrist-slashes — mandalas of alternately raised and incised red and black lines, centred by a large blue circle like a bell-push, around which the skin was flaky like puff pastry. Each scar had its own sad, interminable tale. She said they still throbbed and pained her: sometimes I'd kiss them while she talked.

She'd been on the game locally before, with most of the youngest and prettiest girls, fleeing south from the Sutcliffe murders. She'd done the Bayswater hotels, with a mainly Arab clientele. 'I don't think it did me any harm,' she said. 'You just get used to it.' When things got rough Our Terry was always there to help out. A pimp-lover had once punched her in the stomach for leaving creases in his shirt cuffs: before he got in a second shot Terry had appeared out of nowhere and, having pinned him to the board, first spray-starched his face and then ironed it smooth. 'Cosmetic surgery,' chortled Chris. Then she'd got a job as a croupier — Punto Banco and American Roulette — but hated it. All the men had settled like vultures on her table, their doomed bets buying them the right to ogle and insult her until the money ran out. Contrary to what the pit boss had promised, watching them flap away penniless gave her no consolation.

Sometimes as she talked her head vibrated between my hands like an egg about to hatch: I felt as if I was preventing it from splitting into pieces. My hands seemed to have been created solely for holding her head, which had been created to fit perfectly between them. Chris didn't share my conviction that this congruence extended to the rest of our bodies – to every organ, every atom, every particle of whatever substance composes the soul. 'You can't half talk,' she'd say. She cuddled up to me but only in a way that reminded me that her mum had apparently, as a lesson in thriftiness, never replaced the beloved teddy bear she'd left on a train.

Some evenings she'd get out her Ideal Home scrapbook: features cut from the magazines I'd seen her reading in The Bollocks about the homes of movie stars, rock dinosaurs and supermodels. She'd always turn to the mansion of some actress I'd never heard of, with eyes set far apart and no apparent nose. One of her windows had a panoramic view of the Rockies, another seemingly overlooked Central Park. Small trees and shrubs were growing naturally out of the Persian carpets; chairs and sofas were covered with the skin of some weird hybrid of leopard, zebra and tiger; there were no mirrors but plenty of reflecting surfaces. The bathroom ceiling was a mass of shaggy white fur like the underbelly of a mammoth, and the bath-taps and shower fittings were of gleaming gold. It was hideous. I told her the story of a reporter who, having been shown round Tina Turner's house, commented: 'I didn't realize it was possible to spend five million dollars in Woolworth's.' 'What's wrong with Woolworth's?' Chris asked.

She told me her nights were hell because she kept imagining spiders in the darkness: but she didn't dare to leave the lights on in case she saw the ones that were really there. Once, when the half past two alarm went I offered to stay and protect her.

She gave me a terrible look of fear and hatred: 'There's worse things than spiders,' she said. That night, when I got home, the phone was ringing: it was Chris – until dawn she gave me a running commentary on the TV programmes she was watching with the sound turned down. Although my common sense told me that, if we'd started out with no chance we now had even less, I still had the unshakeable belief that one day I'd put my arms around her and we'd ascend into the sky, like Chagall lovers.

It was quite a while before Chris disclosed to me her main source of income – although from the costumes in the wardrobe and some elliptical comments by Ken, I'd already guessed. She was a stripper. Our council had long since revoked all local licences, so she was working a circuit of a dozen or so pubs and clubs between Halifax and Manchester. She was an old-fashioned classical stripper, regarding lap-dancers like Louis Armstrong had be-bop, with contempt. Lunchtimes and evenings she'd be nun, cowgirl, French maid or schoolgirl, though always with incongruous elbow-length fingerless black lace gloves. For the private functions or lock-ins, however, she had a speciality act for which she styled herself Miss Marshmallow.

The first time I saw her routine I spent more time watching the audience. I'd expected an atmosphere of fear and loathing, furtiveness and shame, violence only just kept in check but they stared into her thick russet merkin with the mild intensity of meditating saddhus or detectives pondering a locked room mystery. Whatever was going on, it seemed to have little to do with sex.

I soon realized that Chris had a loyal following. There were a couple of Sikhs who beamed throughout, tapping their feet in time to her music and always presenting her with little sprays of orchids or alpine flowers with telephone numbers written on their paper twists – ringing one, I got an unobtainable blare; Glittery Gus who for some reason wore a pearly king jacket although he was as Yorkshire as they come – he never missed, unless Halifax Town were at home; a man in Rochdale who looked exactly like William Burroughs (sometimes he turned up with Allen Ginsberg – it seemed no more unlikely than anything else).

One lunchtime Gus lumbered up to me: 'Can I ask you a question?' He was pointing at Chris as she failed to get a bullwhip to crack: I steeled myself. 'Will she be making you a nice tea?' I lied and told him she would: it was what he wanted to hear. His deepest fantasies weren't of leather-capped dominatrices but of trays bearing pyramids of triangular fish-paste sandwiches.

There was plenty of anger and aggression but it all came from Chris. It wasn't just the merkin, she was different. Her breasts swung menacingly like well-filled slingshots, when she shook her head her hair crackled. If her eyes met mine it was without recognition, except perhaps for a slight narrowing. Her nostrils flared, zones of her body seemed to be moving independently and she panted heavily, as if breathing with more than one pair of lungs. When she sweated it didn't drip, just lay on her skin as if it had instantly frozen there. She appeared much larger, raging and flailing as if throwing out a challenge to someone or something: I half-expected Godzilla to appear – my money would have been on Chris. Her big stacky heels crashed down on the boards like an invading army: one place had a tiny round stage of sea-green Plexiglas that gave a strange, sharp echo as if, from a cell below, a prisoner was tapping back.

I had the uncomfortable suspicion that for thousands of years we men – me, Gus, Burroughs, our dads, their dads and so on – had been taking out our soul-sickness on women until at long last we'd voided ourselves of it . . . but now as we approached, finally able to love, we found that we'd infected them with our former disease . . . and far from falling into our arms they began to revenge themselves on us . . . and there would be no happy ending, not even any respite . . . For the next few thousands of years the same old shit would still be flying – only in the opposite direction.

For her speciality act Chris walked on naked, without even the gloves, balancing a box of marshmallows on top of her head, as if in some debutante's deportment exercise. She proceeded to squash and smear the chocolates on her body, then enlisted the punters to lick them off her arched back, flat stomach or mounds of buttocks and breasts. She had a trick of seeming to masticate them with her labia, from which issued, by some ventriloquism, a deep growling sound. At the finish she'd squat facing the audience and with her free hand let the marshmallows fall behind her to simulate shitting. As she stalked off, nasty scuffles would break out over who would get to gobble them up. Afterwards, her face looked much older: her skin had greyed and there were twin striations at the sides of her mouth. Her body seemed to sag: her tits were no longer unbelievable but soft, pulpy and slippery wet – as if melting along with the marshmallows.

A lone woman sometimes figured in Chris' audience. Chubby,

eyes swimming behind thick lenses, she nursed an untouched half of lager and beamed like a mother watching a child taking its first faltering steps. When I mentioned this Chris revealed that it was her younger sister: she seemed slightly disconcerted, as if surprised that I could see her too. They'd been fostered together for a while: she was still with that family. I named her Sister Sister: she worked in a hospice, organized car boot sales for the Cat Protection League and never stopped smiling. She was one of those people who from sixteen to eighty always look forty-two: her skin had a faint dusting of talc or icing sugar. She had Chris' mouth and eyes – she too couldn't blink – and many of the same mannerisms. When she turned her head towards me her pupils also refocused with agonizing slowness, as if the two mechanisms had slipped out of alignment: it repelled me although I loved it – thinking of the tragic doll Olympia in *Hoffmann* – in Chris . . . but then Chris was beautiful. 'We're all so proud of her,' Sister Sister told me. I imagined her regaling some eager domestic gathering: 'Then after she'd rubbed the boa through her legs she put this old man's head between her breasts and squeezed and he started making these chicken noises . . . it was lovely.' She gave me the creeps: I had no inkling about what it might be like to be her. I guessed that she must be one of those normal people my mother used to tell me about.

Folk took me to be Chris' minder, though if there'd ever been any trouble I suspect she'd have ended up minding me. Some were plainly terrified: I was rather flattered at being taken for the most dangerous man in West Yorkshire. I was really her roadie, borrowing the band van. I loved to drive her round the narrow, twisty empty lanes of Calderdale: a perpetual mist descended from the fells, as if the world was slowly condensing. Chris never wore a seat belt: she bounced next to me, singing and laughing and waving enticing scraps of clothing out of the window at the sheep. It felt like we were MacGraw and McQueen in *The Getaway*, heading from a daring crime towards some dark and even more dangerous destination – but when we did arrive it was always just another dingy pub, with Glittery Gus' bald head gleaming under the lime and pink spots. One thing bothered me: the way I drove, how did he and the Sikhs always make it there before us?

I also became her musical director, replacing David Rose and Donna Summer with Beefheart, Black Flag, The Fall: the punters didn't care so long as all Chris' bits and pieces remained in their usual alignment. I became increasingly ambitious, even persuading her to dance to Ellington's 'Asfahan', but she jibbed at the ländler of Mahler's Ninth and at Tallis' 'Spem In Alium' – or 'Spam In Aluminium', as she retitled it. She accused me of blasphemy – which I thought a bit rich coming from a nun with unusual uses for confectionery. Her reaction was even more violent when I suggested The Carpenters: I received that evil arm punch again.

Things between Chris and I gradually became even weirder. When we were alone a terrible feeling of panic always rose in my throat, as if something awful was about to happen. Then she turned up at one of our gigs and sat at the front, heavy petting with a smirking bullet-headed DS copper: it didn't faze me though – I'm a pro: I was as bad as usual. Later, though, in The Bollocks, she pressed herself against my bruised arm and, nipping gently at my ear lobe, whispered, 'Wait for me tonight.' So I stayed on as the pub emptied: Chris appeared to have gone to clear the back bar. At last there was only me and a large man dressed all in black, except for the pink flash on his knitted Cardin tie. I knew his name was Marcus: he'd been in love with Chris for years – he dropped in once or twice a month to see if she'd changed her mind. He kept raising his empty glass to his lips: he looked to be shrinking away inside his best suit. Our eyes met: we both knew that we were there on the same false promise. I felt even sorrier for him than I did for myself. 'Everyone's gone, lads,' said Ken, with subtle, kindly emphasis. We left by separate doors, without speaking.

'You're just like all the others.' I got no apologies from Chris. We were splitting apart: it was as if we were no longer the same age – as if she was getting younger as I got older. Now as I watched her I felt like some senile granddad trying to bestir himself to rape a toddler. I wanted to fuck her, hurt her: my hands itched to crush the head they were cradling. I blamed her, of course: she deliberately turned her face to expedite my sudden urge to slap her, crooked an arm in a way that begged me to stub out a roach on it, twined her hair round my fingers to dare me to clean-jerk her off the floor . . . 'You're just like all the others,' she kept on saying, although I was still managing to act as if I was different, special: maybe she was reading my mind? I was having recurrent nightmares. In one I was inside her body, burrowing my way out like a plucky foetus. In another I seemed to have turned into a lumbering but dangerous animal – something like a bear, although I felt to be wearing a tight-banded hat – and was vainly ripping with long blue-steel claws at her unconcerned, laughing face. I awoke to the sound of my own laughter replacing hers. This reassured me: although I was obviously going insane, some abiding sense of the ridiculous might just pull me through.

Her stage act became ever more disturbing: she moved through the audience like a stoat among hypnotized rabbits. Even the regulars who used to cluster at her feet were edging away, giving themselves a fighting chance of reaching the exits if she came for them. One evening she was stamping on the little Plexiglas stage as if the spiders she feared were crawling over it. For the great final chord of J. Geils' 'Love-itis' she jumped halfway to the ceiling, landing full force on both wooden heels, shattering the stage like a car windscreen. People were screaming, bleeding: some poor oblivious soul playing the bandit had taken most of the shards in the back of the neck: Sister Sister was giving first aid with bar towels. It was like a Robert Crumb cartoon — I didn't stop laughing until hours afterwards. Chris was infuriated by my reaction, as if she'd been under the misapprehension that it had been my stage she'd destroyed.

Next Sunday lunchtime in The Bollocks Gabe and I did our Jim Hall/Bill Evans tribute, 'My Funny Valentine': he cut me to pieces — it was like simultaneously drowning and falling down an elevator shaft — but at least we started and finished together. As I came off the stand, Chris — still in her Karen Carpenter rig — grabbed me and kissed me. It was the best kiss she'd ever given me: gentle, tender but passionate beyond any definable passion. Her hand slid between my shirt buttons: it felt as if there was a pulse in the centre of her palm that beat in time with my heart. My instincts had been right all along: we'd gone beyond different and special, beyond sickness and madness — I saw stars, we were becoming constellations . . . At this point her other hand pushed my head away in a rugby-style hand-off. 'That was Wayne just went out,' she said. 'Another of my ex-es. Didn't hang about, did he?'

I think I was still in shock half an hour later in the car park when she kissed me again, lapping at my mouth as if slaking some desperate thirst. 'It was Marcus in that white Nissan,' she said, when we disengaged. In the taxi I felt I had to speak out: suppose, heartbroken, they did something silly? Suppose Wayne was to throw himself under the wheels of Marcus' speeding car? She found the idea hilarious: 'I'm a demon, aren't I?' It didn't seem to occur to her that I might feel like doing something silly myself. She described the many times they'd proposed to her: 'Maybe they should marry each other? You wouldn't think that big lads would snivel so much, would you?' I wasn't a big lad but I'd done my share of snivelling too. 'Let me out here,' I said to the driver, halfway down a street of semi-derelict mills. I tossed a fiver into his lap. Of all possible valedictory lines — Rhett Butler's, John Donne's, Othello's — Wayne County's seemed the most appropriate: 'Fuck off,' I said and slammed the door. When the taxi passed, twenty yards on, Chris' head didn't turn to look at me. My only regret was that I hadn't at least slapped her: not even Terry could have blamed me for that. I walked on: every rusty gate bore a NO ADMISSION notice over a crude design of a prick-eared Alsatian but I couldn't hear any dogs barking.

Chris didn't call round or ring to apologize or demand an explanation. I stopped drinking in The Bollocks. Fearing that she'd appear and smooch in front of me with Wayne or Marcus, I started to play with my back to the audience, Miles Davis style, but there were no reported sightings. I threw away her address and phone number although I knew I would never forget them. I didn't miss her much: sometimes a whole hour passed without my thinking of her. Rage and pity, love and disgust contended, clashing until they ignited, melted and merged into a slow dripping heaviness that gathered like lead at the pit of my stomach: Guilt – but what did I have to feel guilty about? Alternate nights I slept too heavily or not at all. I thought I'd got constipated but then realized I wasn't eating. My palms itched: either they were missing holding her head or I was going to come into some money to compensate.

While I'd known Chris I'd regularly run into her by chance but now it was as if she'd vanished off the face of the earth. I've always tended towards solipsism: 'esse est percepi', like Bishop Berkeley's God – if I'm not there to look at people I fear they'll fade away. I realized it was crazy but I half-believed I'd killed Chris until Dave told me he'd seen her. She was driving by in a flash new car: he blew her a kiss but she just stared straight through him. At least she hadn't been cast into an eternal limbo of non-being: I wasn't so sure about myself. One desperate night I picked up the phone to ring her but I couldn't remember the number: I then wrote her a seventeen-page letter but discovered that I'd forgotten her address too. Next morning I walked down into the valley but I couldn't find her flat: someone seemed to have realigned the blocks. I knocked on a few random doors but nobody answered. I cursed my own ruthless recuperative powers: my palms didn't itch anymore, I shat and ate, I slept well.

After a time Chris only came into my mind when nothing else occupied it. Standing at a bus stop, lying in the bath or waiting for a kettle to boil I'd suddenly see a hazy silhouette, grey like smoke, against a midnight blue backdrop: it could have been anyone but I knew it must be her. The bus passed, the water boiled away or froze. I started carrying a book everywhere, plugging these gaps with great tales of exploration: *The White Nile*, *The Voyage of the Beagle*, *The Worst Journey in the World* — I found them soothing, for some reason. The bus still passed and the water boiled away or froze. I never thought of Chris when I was with other women but I realized that now I'd started keeping my eyes tight shut while making love.

The band's reputation — that we usually turned up — was spreading: we started to get out-of-town gigs. One night we arrived at a pub in Sowerby Bridge that I recognized from roadying for Chris. Its walls were lined with cases of mounted fish and religious images of pietàs and martyrdoms: the landlord looked like a cod undergoing an acute spiritual crisis. He remembered me too and asked after Chris. 'She cost me my stripping licence,' he told me. Apparently they'd argued after she'd demanded wooden clothes-hangers for her tiny dressing room: 'I told her wire ones had been good enough for Sinatra and Dietrich but she took it the wrong way, somehow.' That lunchtime Chris had done the full triple-X Miss Marshmallow act to a horrified office crowd, including half the council, watching furtively via the tilted mirrors above the bar optics. 'I should have stopped her but it were like I were spellbound.' She'd climaxed it with a new refinement: bending over, she'd slowly, one by one, with a dainty index finger, inserted four marshmallows into her anus. Then she walked out, stark naked, got into her taxi and drove away. 'No one moved for two or three minutes, then all hell broke loose. That were the licence gone: the last stripping pub in this valley.' He grinned and shook his head admiringly: 'She never even came back for her clothes' — he made an elegant corkscrewing gesture with his left hand — 'Crazy cow.' He didn't seem to bear a grudge: at least it had been a big finish — the Götterdämmerung of Calderdale burlesque. 'That's why your lot are here: we've got to have summat to put on yon stage.' I considered sending out for a few boxes of marshmallows.

Six months later I still hadn't forgotten Chris but she figured only as the tragic heroine or butt of some of my routines: hilarity was unconfined as I described the circles into which I had followed her. Then one day we were down in London for another of our periodic doomed assaults on Tin Pan Alley. Leaving the band to lower the tone of The Morpeth Arms I went next door to The Tate's exhibition around Seurat's Bathers. I'd never liked the painting — nor any of the others Chris had on her walls. There were dozens of preliminary small oil studies and pencil and conté crayon sketches: Asnières teemed with people, boats and flora and fauna that never made it into the final version. It looked like he'd over-prepared and finally settled on his last, tired conception. It was a masterpiece only because of its size, the date of its execution and the way the paint went on: those blockish figures, the oh-so-neat composition . . . for me, he should have kept the boot-tabs and straw hat bands and thrown the rest away. As I stared at it the sour smell of Chris' flat once again filled my nostrils and despair hit me — a physical blow, like a gust of wind, so that I literally staggered. I slumped on to a bench and shook. I didn't want to look at any more pictures: all I could think of were those terrible empty ovals and rectangles where her mirrors had once hung. I'd lost her: I tried to recall to mind her lovely face but couldn't.

Back in The Morpeth a chubby Aussie girl – radiating a rude health and simplicity that had never attracted me – inscribed on my Guinness a clumsy shamrock that vanished even as I bore the glass to my lips ... but with the first sip I suddenly saw Chris again. I saw her snaky neck, her silly tan, those unbelievable tits, the wrist scars that now struck me as a treasure map I hadn't been able to read, the wrinkling fold that had appeared across her upper lip when she'd sucked my cock, betraying the depth of her disgust at me, herself, everything ... But above all I remembered one particular expression. After some of her crying bouts she'd turn her head, face dead white, eyes bugging impossibly as if she'd seen a ghost: the first time, I'd spun to see what horror she was looking at with such entreaty and fear before I'd realized that it was myself. After a couple of minutes she'd snap out of it – go all brisk, make more coffee or retrieve the day's fetish object for another bout of worship – but during those times – as I felt and shared her suffering, a desolation beyond even Karen Carpenter's – I'd known that we were true and predestined lovers. I drank my pint straight down and got another round in for the band. I understood that it was necessary for the rest of my life never to forget Chris.

Perhaps I should have guessed that this hard-won serenity would immediately be shattered by her reappearance. The next evening I was back up North – sans contracts, sans session dates – shopping in Sainsbury's. I was among the beers when my scalp started to prickle and my hair felt to rise, even through the gel. I stared wildly down the empty aisle: it must have been a good twenty seconds before Chris appeared, pushing a trolley full of lemons, tinned cashews and industrial-sized bottles of gin. She was wearing her old outfit of cream blouse and blue jeans but now it was real silk and Ralph Lauren. She was tanned berry-brown but by foreign suns not eighteen tubes. There was gold at her wrists and neck and a new short haircut that set its twin blades scything across her cheekbones. My heart didn't pound, I didn't sweat or faint: I didn't feel anything in particular except the realization that I hadn't been alive for the last two years. She showed no surprise, as if she'd been expecting me. 'I'm giving a party,' she said. 'Right now. A housewarming party. And you're invited.' I upended my basket of vegetables and Staropramen into her trolley and pushed it towards the exit. She picked out the head of broccoli and contemplated it: 'Still green, I see.' As she leaned forward I saw on her newly-revealed golden nape a faint pattern of white downy hairs: I knew that I was going to let myself believe once again that everything was going to be all right ... At the checkout all the women stared at Christine and all the men stared at me: I couldn't read their expressions. Christine was radiant, like a goddess: I hoped I might be looking just a little like a god.

'I'm still in showbiz,' she told me as she drove, 'but I've retired from dancing.' I said I'd heard about her farewell performance. 'I'm a demon, aren't I? I just wanted to give them something to remember me by. I started getting a bit scratchy with everybody after you'd gone.' She stopped at a red light and I ran my finger along her jaw: the line had always reminded me of something but I could never quite identify it – probably nothing in this sad, piss-poor world. 'You're special,' she reminded me in a flinty, warning tone and turned the driving mirror as if to check herself for damage. There was something different about her: although more made up than ever before her face looked natural, softer, less mask-like, with more play of feature. 'You don't know how miserable I was in that bloody place,' she said. 'It was driving me mad. Now it's like starting a whole new life, like being born again' – she giggled – 'Don't worry, I haven't gone religious. Satan got me long ago.'

She drove back into the city: I wondered what mansion, what magic castle she was carrying me off to. The shops and banks looted in the summer riots were still boarded up – they would never reopen. We passed The Bollocks – neither of us suggested a drink for old times' sake – then the mill district: the streets were still littered with old broken bobbins and wool cards. The same old turnings: she was obviously still living somewhere down in the valley. Knots of Asian youths were hanging about, talking into mobile phones, trying to strut like Prince Naz but only looking hurt and fearful – though none the less dangerous for that. Then we turned down her old street. 'A sentimental journey, is it?' I asked. She laughed again: 'You wait.' We stopped fifty yards on, in front of the blocks. Chris put a finger to my lips: 'Just you wait.'

With her leading I remembered the way. The paving flags had started to rear like gravestones but there was the same trench-mud – although it hadn't rained for weeks – and I glimpsed the pale shape of the eternally skulking, pissing shaggy dog. As before, she ran on ahead: the stairwell seemed to have been carbonized, with cinders crunching beneath my feet. I could hear her heels clattering far above. At the top she was standing waiting with key in lock. She threw open the door

with a conjuror's flourish: 'Welcome to The Penthouse Suite!'
The same sour smell hit me: either it pervaded the building or
it was Chris' own – a smell of disillusionment and fear beneath
the Anaïs Anaïs.

She'd obviously just moved in: the hall was full of stacked
cardboard boxes. The rooms were in the same alignment as
two floors below with the kitchen seeming if anything to be
rather smaller. There was a new addition to the pictures on
the living room wall: my favourite late Bonnard floating nude
filled one of the empty mirror positions. I saw without regret
that Moby and Wanda appeared to be no longer with us. There
was a new three-piece suite – or maybe the old one recovered
with Strawberry Thief chintz. The chairs were filled by two
enormous men. Square-headed, with big veins throbbing in
their necks, they sat silently, hands on knees, staring at each
other. Chris made no introductions but I knew that neither of
them was Terry: they were working too hard at it – the most
damage they'd do would be by toppling over on you like
wardrobes. I took them to be her current admirers, ready like
rutting stags to contend for the right to stay until 2.30 a.m. –
the alarm clock on the mantelpiece was still set for its old
familiar time.

The sofa's design clashed with a repro Persian carpet. The
bear-rug remained but, freshly-cleaned, was now white, not
yellow. Sister Sister – still beaming and even chubbier – was
sitting on it, cross-legged, looking from one man to the other,
as if following an invisible tennis rally. She was presumably
there for her emergency medical skills, although from the looks
on their faces a priest or an undertaker might have been more
useful. Chris put some music on her new Minidisc player and

tried to get them to dance, but they just mumbled incomprehensibly into their gins, so I lamely copied her gyrations to the plastic funk to which she had inevitably reverted. She came in close and tried to chew my lips but I escaped into a clinch: she worked inside, suckling my ear lobe, bucking her groin into my upper thigh. I didn't dare to look at the others: I could feel their glares beginning to melt my spine. 'Who are those guys?' I whispered to Chris. She looked genuinely puzzled. 'They're my friends,' she said, far too loudly. 'Like you.' Were they too disqualified by excessive sensibility and sympathetic insight, different and special?

The doorbell rang: Sister Sister scuttled out on all fours to answer it. I prayed for deliverance but a third man entered, even bigger and squarer than the others. When he saw them his smirk faded and he sagged momentarily but then retumesced into ultra-aggressive mode: they went even stiffer and a couple of shades redder. The silence deepened: they seemed to have left off breathing. In desperation I put on a Krautrock tape I'd once compiled for Chris. Kraftwerk's 'Calculator', Kriedler's 'Traffic Way': robotic songs about machines and gadgets seemed to have a beneficent effect on the atmosphere – music hath charms. They started up a guarded conversation about cars, then discovered that they all supported Leeds United. I had some good bush which nicely scumbled the gin's sharp edge: its blue haze began to dispel the testosterone fug . . . But then its seeds started to explode. They jumped every time as if it had been gunfire, while the tiny red cannonballs burnt holes in their Top Man sweatshirts. They started to get mad again . . . I gave up and went to help Chris slice the lemons: she clicked her tongue and gave me a dazzling smile but pulled away when I tried to kiss her. So I asked her why she was not only in the same hated area but the same hated block. I asked her what – apart from thirty feet of elevation – this great big difference was supposed to be. She became very serious. 'Go and look in the bathroom,' she replied.

I made my way down the darkened hall, tripping over the boxes, and groped for the light cord. The first thing I noticed was the absence of that huge dark wardrobe, although the room itself was even more ridiculously large than the previous one. The ledge-army of cosmetics seemed to have been considerably reinforced and there were still, of course, no mirrors. The bath was sky blue, round and deep with three little steps leading up to it like some Greek oracle. It was half-full of murky, tepid water: sitting on the edge I agitated it with my hand, in case it was Moby and Wanda's temporary home. I was none the wiser. On the way back, I lifted the flaps of the topmost box: it contained twenty-four shrink-wrapped videos, all with the same title – ROSEBUD'S FIRST TIME in crimson on their flesh-pink spines. I decided not to enquire too closely about the source of Chris' new-found prosperity. I tried the bedroom door in passing: it was still locked.

When I re-entered the living-room everyone for some reason was on their feet, as if in a dramatic tableau like 'When Did You Last See Your Father?' Or 'The Oath Of The Horatii'. Chris put her hands on her hips and cocked her head: 'What do you think?' 'Nice,' I replied. She frowned and did a little boxing shuffle: 'And –?'

'Er . . . big? Bigger?' Her right hand reached out to me – 'You just don't get it, do you' – and once again her thumb hooked around my belt-buckle as she drew me back to the bathroom. Behind us I could hear – even over Can's 'Dizzy Dizzy' – a roaring sound like maddened bulls.

She bolted the door and pointed heavenwards. I'd never seen her looking so beautiful: I half-expected her to begin to ascend – if she did I was ready to grab her feet, to hold her there or be carried off with her. Then, after staring numbly at her finger-end, I followed its direction: the ceiling was covered with rolls of white fur like gravity-defying snow – the light shade was green and jagged like an inverted Christmas tree. She led me to the bath: 'The taps,' she said. They were shaped like strange creatures, swan-necked but eagle-beaked, of a dull yellow metal. 'Gold.' She leaned over to flick them with her thumbs, setting them resonating like Tibetan temple-bells. 'Golden bath-taps. But that's not all.' She rolled up her sleeves and reached into the water's depths: her old cuts and scars showed as lividly as ever through the tan. Outside, someone kicked hard at the door: once, twice, three times . . . Then, with a terrible death rattle, the water was sucked away and Chris' silver-nailed hand emerged to brandish triumphantly, gleaming at the end of its golden chain – like a miracle, a sign of God's good grace – the golden bath-plug.